DAYS OF MIDNIGHT

DAYS OF MIDNIGHT

LEO HUNT

CANDLEWICK PRESS

First U.S. paperback edition 2016

Library of Congress Catalog Card Number 2015934259
ISBN 978-0-7636-7865-4 (hardcover)
ISBN 978-0-7636-9243-8 (paperback)

16 17 18 19 20 21 BVG 10 9 8 7 6 5 4 3 2 1

Printed in Berryville, VA, U.S.A.

This book was typeset in Palatino.

Candlewick Press
99 Dover Street
Somerville, Massachusetts 02144

visit us at www.candlewick.com

For my grandparents

(the circle opens)

The first thing that happens is I unseal an envelope and Dad's death falls out onto the breakfast table. I always thought I'd learn about it from the papers first, or that maybe news like this would be delivered by an angel, holding out a gilded scroll, its perfect face scribbled with sorrow. Instead I'm sitting with bed head, wearing inside-out pajamas, reading a letter printed in ordinary black ink on white office paper. The letterhead reads *Berkley & Co.,* and they've sent a short message informing me of his death. I'm requested at a meeting with his solicitor this afternoon, "with regard to my inheritance."

There's no mention of Mum, which is strange. It's addressed only to me. I'm not really sure what to feel. I was halfway through a bowl of cereal when I opened the letter, and my wheat flakes have melted into something that looks like wet brown sand. I pick up the remains of my breakfast and move over to the sink. Outside, in the back garden, Ham whimpers and bats at the door. I put him outside and forgot; he must be soaked by now. Leaving my bowl in the sink, I cross the kitchen to let him in. I get the door open, and he shoots past me like a dog possessed, streaking wet prints across the tiles.

I haven't seen Dad, except on television, since I was six. He isn't—wasn't—exactly *famous* famous, but most people would probably recognize him. His face comes up a lot if you go rooting through the discount-books bins in supermarkets, or watch late-night reruns of his various paranormal shows. I'd get a card on my birthday up until a few years ago, and since then not even that. I think I could've spoken to him on the phone if I'd made a big effort to—maybe left lots of messages at his office—but I never tried. He made it clear that he didn't want much to do with us. I always assumed we'd have some awkward reunion when I was older, but I guess now I won't even get that. I look out at the garden, autumn apples hanging red on the tree. Past the trees there's a drystone wall, and then grass and sheep. The sky is gray, the clouds sagging and out of shape.

I hear Mum on the stairs, and before I really think about what I'm doing, I've rushed back across the kitchen and hidden the solicitor's letter in my pocket. Of course I should tell her. It should be the first thing out of my mouth: *Dad's dead.* Two small words, but I don't say it. I stand pretending to examine my orange juice as she comes in, dressed in the poncho-type thing she wears every morning, and starts clattering around looking for breakfast. Does she know already? It doesn't seem like it. She barely dealt with their separation; if she knew he was dead, I doubt she'd be standing upright. I'm worried about how she'll handle this. He was famous enough that it'll be in the news somewhere. She's going to find out. I really ought to tell her now.

"Morning," I say to Mum, as if nothing unusual were happening.

"Morning, love," she says, turning half around, giving me a sleepy grin.

Mum cracks an egg on the side of the pan. She's clearly no longer in a vegan phase. The time to speak seems to pass, as I stand doing nothing. Ham reappears, claws clicking on the tiles with every step he takes. He's a hunting dog, a compressed spring of gray fur and sinew. His snout is long and regal, but his head is topped by a crown of pale fluff, which reminds me of a newborn chicken. He presses his damp head against my hand. Despite all the crimes I've committed against him—the vet visits and worming tablets and forced walks in the rain—Ham believes I'm a good person. He grumbles as I knead his shoulders.

Mum's name is Persephone—though she's keen on

reinvention, so I think her actual birth certificate might say something different. She's not close with her parents. Mum is tall and wiry, with blond hair like fraying rope. I think the best way to explain her is to say that she doesn't *do* a lot, or more that she starts things and then doesn't finish them, whether that's a letter or a book or a meal or her long-running plan to set up a crystal shop. She's interested in the restorative power of crystals. She's also interested in tarot cards, numerology, past-life regression, ancient astronaut theories, Reiki, and books by people who've met angels or changed their lives through positive thinking — the perfect partner for a professional ghost expert like Dad. Or should've been, at least. Mum's less interested in getting a job or cleaning the house or going to parent-teacher conferences. I think Dad must have handled the money side of things, despite the split, so don't go thinking I've had it rough: power cut off or empty boxes at Christmas or anything like that. We're good customers at the organic food shops, and since the start of high school, I've always had the right sneakers, the proper haircut, clothes with brand names, which is important if I want to keep hanging around with Kirk and Mark and the rest of them. I don't know what's going to happen about money now that Dad's gone. I notice Mum's looking out the window with a glazed expression, which makes me think she's already had one of her pain pills.

See, Mum has these things called cluster headaches. I feel bad enough when I have a normal, standard-issue headache, like someone's wrapping a rope around my skull, but cluster headaches are the premier league of headaches. Worse than a migraine. They're so bad it's like someone is driving a red-hot spike into your face, according to the pamphlets they give family members to help us understand the condition. When Mum has an attack going on, she has to retreat to her bedroom with the curtains firmly drawn and stay in there for days and days with a blindfold over her eyes and ice on her forehead.

So that's how things are with Mum. She's not that bad, to be honest. We get along pretty well because she's really not that interested in how I do at school or who my friends are and how long I stay out with them, which is what my friends fight with their parents about. She's weird, but at least she doesn't drink on weeknights like Kirk's mother and doesn't have a rictus smile and flowchart of polite questions like Mark's, who I think is a maternal android that his dad constructed from a mail-order kit.

"Bit of a blue day," Mum says. There's nothing about the day that could remotely be described as blue, but the comment confirms she's not heard the news. I have no idea how to bring it up.

"Yeah," I say, pummeling Ham's shoulders and back. I've realized I'll have to skip school today. I'm already very late thanks to the letter, not that Mum's noticed. My meeting with Dad's solicitor is in the early afternoon, but the buses to the city take the long route, and it's easier to just not go to school rather than try to sneak out at lunch break. If they ask where I was, I've got a nuclear-grade trump card. The teachers'll be scrambling over themselves to accommodate me when they find out what happened. I'll have a couple of months of them jumping through any hoop I like.

"Hope we'll see some birds today," she says, gesturing at the feeder she's got hanging from one of the apple trees. This is a recent project.

"I bet they'll go nuts for it," I say.

She scrapes her egg onto a plate.

"You know . . . because it's full of nuts."

Mum's smile comes on slowly. She doesn't turn around, but I can see the ghost of it in her reflection. It only lasts a few moments.

I walk over to her. Ham follows me, snorting and butting at my legs. "I've got to get ready for school now," I say. "And I'll be home late. I've got rugby practice tonight."

I don't, but I'm not sure how long the meeting will take.

"Do good things today," she says. "You're a special person."

When I hug her, I can feel all the bones in her back.

∘ ∘ ∘

My name is Luke Manchett, and I'm sixteen years old. I live in a town called Dunbarrow, up in the hills of North East England. I was born in the Midlands, but Mum, once the separation was in the works, had a romantic idea of escaping to a house in the country, which turned out to be a lot less romantic after ten years of relentless downpour and small-town gossipmongering. Don't get me wrong: I'm sure this is a great place to visit on a tour bus if you're sixty years old. There are plenty of historic churches and burial mounds and Celtic sacrifice stones and whatever. When you're sixteen, Dunbarrow is a tacky main street, one pub that might not ID, wet fields of sheep, and a maze of redbrick council estates, where you don't want the kids to catch you unless they know your face. I live on Wormwood Drive with Mum, which is considered posh because we have a back garden and a front garden. We're on the outskirts of town, and the garden wall separates us from the sheep paddocks, which stretch from here to pretty much forever. Mum is enthusiastic about this because it's natural and organic, and the sheep are so *incredibly* organic—and rural—and totally don't make you want to commit suicide if you mistakenly meet their flat dead eyes.

We excuse the fact that Dunbarrow has nothing going on, because we're closer to the region's only city, Brackford, than Throgdown and Sheepwallow and all the other pathetic tiny towns farther out into the moors.

Brackford is a rusting iron giant, fallen, still getting up on its feet decades after they closed the mines and shut down the shipyards. The sky is always gray and the wind comes hard off the concrete-colored sea, running wild through the rows of terraced houses.

Anyway, what happens next is I walk down our hill like normal, with my schoolbag and everything, and then I go to the bus station and change out of my uniform in the restrooms there. I spend forty-five minutes being driven to Brackford. Once I'm there I get lunch (burger and fries), wander around some music shops, and look at fancy pairs of soccer cleats. Everywhere's all decked out, ready for Halloween: There are paper skeletons and plastic witches dangling in shop windows. Usually when we skip school it's because Kirk has a free house and we can crack some of his mum's beers and play Xbox. I'd prefer that to meeting with my dad's lawyers. I really should've told Mum about this. She ought to be with me. I know I should go back home and tell her and then arrange to come in another day, but at 1:45, I'm sitting in the reception area of Berkley & Co. At the desk opposite me is a blond secretary who scans her computer screen with the compulsive head movements of a trapped bird. After half an hour she gives me a harried nod and I make my way in.

Mr. Berkley's office is what I expected — sterile and businesslike. There's a heavy black desk, dull gray filing cabinets, a wall calendar covered in annotations. His desk is barren of everything but a fountain pen and an antique gold clock with a bright wagging pendulum. There are no family photos.

Mr. Berkley has plenty of lines on his face, but he's still pretty striking, one of those old people you can tell used to be good-looking, with ash-white hair that he slicks back like the leading man in a 1930s movie. He's got a neat beard, and large, even teeth that look like they cost more than some people's cars. He's dressed in a light gray suit and a pink shirt, no tie, and he's reading something from a little notebook, which he tucks into a desk drawer as I enter the room. He looks rich, more than rich—he looks like money came to life and sat down in front of me. He stands and nearly blinds me with his smile before reaching over his desk and firmly shaking my hand and guiding me down into the seat opposite him all at once. He smells of peppery aftershave. It's all a bit overwhelming.

"Luke," he says, grinning like we both just won the lottery. "Master Luke A. Manchett, I presume? Son and heir of the late Dr. Horatio Manchett?"

"Uh, hi," I say. His eyes are so blue that the irises look artificial, like they're made of plastic. He's friendly, but I feel like he's sizing me up for something. I shift in my seat.

"I do apologize for the wait," he continues. "I've had a lot to deal with today. Unexpected petitions, old friends asking to renegotiate agreements. . . . I've been over-whelmed. I do hope you'll forgive me."

"It's all right, really."

"Thank you, my boy. Forgiveness is a great virtue, wouldn't you say? The unburdened soul floats easily in the cold river."

"Is that, like, poetry?" I ask.

"No," he says, "not really. It's advice, I suppose. But I forget whom it is from. Anyway, I wanted to say, before we get down to the details, that I like to think I was rather close with your late father. Horatio was a great man. Your loss is all of our losses."

I'm not sure that hosting a cheesy paranormal-themed TV show qualifies you as "great," but it doesn't seem like the right time to argue this point.

"I didn't really know him that well," I say.

"He regretted your estrangement. I can assure you of that."

"I'd rather . . . I don't know you. Sir. I'd rather not talk about it. Sorry."

"Apologies, apologies. Well, Luke, as you know, we asked you to come in with some urgency regarding your inheritance. It was your father's express wish that you be contacted as soon as possible. I appreciate the short notice may have been somewhat inconvenient. I hope your tutors were understanding."

I shrug.

"Anyway. Let's get down to business. Luke, I've brought you here today to inform you that you are the only named beneficiary of Horatio's will. You stand to inherit his properties, both domestic and overseas, as well as future royalties from book and digital video sales. There is also the matter of a bank account intended for your personal use containing a sum in excess of six million dollars, which when converted into sterling is about four million pounds. . . ."

He keeps talking, but his voice has faded to a whisper compared with the thundering fireworks display that just lit up in my head. I feel like my chair just sent a thousand volts into my body. I assumed Dad did all right from his TV show, but I didn't know it was *this* good. I'm a millionaire. Not just that, a multimillionaire. A series of magazine-exposé photographs is flashing through my head: VIP tables, bottle service, penthouse suites. I can't believe just yesterday I was worried about my exams. Who cares? I won't need to beg Mum for my own car either, which is great because she's been completely deaf to my hints and hasn't noticed the car magazines I've been leaving around the living room for the past six months. I picture myself at the wheel of a bright-orange Ferrari, with Holiday Simmon in the passenger seat, her hair glowing in the light of a tropical sunset as we—

"Luke?"

"Yeah," I say, not having listened to a word Mr. Berkley was saying.

"So you understand what I'm telling you today?"

"Uh-huh. Dad's estate. Six million dollars. Domestic and overseas. DVD sales."

"That was the general outline, yes. Now, as sole beneficiary of the will, there are certain steps you're required to take in order to inherit—"

"He didn't leave any of it to anyone else?" I always thought there must at least be another woman: blond, thin, half his age.

"As I said, Luke. Sole beneficiary. He required that you alone be contacted about this matter, not your mother or anyone else. He was very clear about that. Now, the first thing you need to do is sign some documents, indicating that you understand what I'm telling you today and that you're willing to accept full responsibility for your father's estate."

Bring it on, I want to scream at him. Whatever it takes. Show me the money. I came in expecting to inherit some cuff links or a watch. Berkley roots around in a desk drawer for a few moments. I watch the clock pendulum swing.

"Here we are," he says, laying some sheets of paper on the desk. I leaf through them. The top few are normal legal documents, computer-typed, printed on legal paper. I sign them with Berkley's fountain pen. The bottom sheet is different, and I pause. It's a rough, yellowing sheet of parchment, and the text has been written by hand in weird brown ink. The script is tiny and ornate, a frantic mess of Gothic lettering. I squint, but I can't read any of it.

"What is this? Is this in English?" I ask Berkley.

"Latin, my boy. Is there a problem?"

I run my fingers over the parchment. It feels rough, fibrous.

"Vellum," says Mr. Berkley. "Made from goatskin. Difficult to source these days, as I'm sure you can imagine. We have a man in Cumbria."

I rest the pen on the blank space at the bottom of the page. Berkley leans forward in his chair. I withdraw the pen nib. The gold clock ticks, a steady brittle sound.

"What am I signing?" I ask.

"As I explained, Luke, your father—"

"What am I signing right now? Why is this written in Latin on goatskin?"

Berkley runs a hand over his slick hair. He blows air out of his nose.

"Luke, I know this probably seems . . . unusual, but Horatio was assuredly not a paint-by-numbers man. There are a number of stipulations before you can receive any of his money or property. The first of these is that this particular document be signed by you, today. This is a very specific request, made in a legally binding last will and testament. Unless you sign this document, here, now, I am under instructions to dissolve the late Dr. Manchett's estate and contribute the proceeds to various charitable organizations. You and your mother will not receive a single penny. All very noble, I think you'll agree, but probably not the outcome you'd like, and frankly not the outcome I'm looking for today either. If you want to read your father's instructions for me on this matter, I have the papers here."

Berkley reaches into another drawer and pushes some ring-bound documents at me. There are more paragraphs and subclauses than I could read if I sat here all day, but it's unmistakably Dad's signature on each one. I recognize it from the birthday cards he'd send.

I look down at my sneakers. The whole thing is just off. Dad leaves everything, every last thing, to a son he hasn't spoken to for a decade? Why not Mum? Did he not trust her with the money? Is that one of the reasons they broke up? He just decides to make me a multimillionaire? If I didn't know better, I'd almost expect there to be a hidden camera watching what I do, like this is a setup for a prank show. And Mr. Berkley is starting to creep me out, smiling far too much, asking me to write my name on some *goatskin* . . .

I decide there isn't much choice. The image of me and Holiday driving through the Alps is too strong. I'm being given more than I ever thought I would earn in my life, and that's just for starters. Freedom from exams, from having to get a job, freedom from Mum, even . . . who'd say no? I press Berkley's pen into the vellum and create a passable version of my signature. The nib gets stuck in the fibers and I need to use more force than normal. As I lift the pen the clock seems to hold its tick in for a moment longer than it should, golden pendulum frozen in space, like the room decided to skip a beat.

Mr. Berkley relaxes, leaning back in his chair. He smiles, and the expression reaches his eyes for the first time.

"I think you made the right decision," Berkley says. "I must note that there are some other conditions that must be met before the financial and property transfers can be made, which I'm not currently at liberty to disclose. But I'm confident that they will resolve themselves shortly. If not, I will contact you within the fortnight to furnish you with the full details. Oh, and there are some miscellaneous items you've inherited, which I'm under instruction to give you immediately." He reaches into another drawer and brings out a bundle of papers tied together with ribbon, a dull metal case that looks like something you'd keep a pair of glasses in, and a small green book.

"What's this?" I ask, picking up the book. It's small and thick, only a bit larger than the Bibles they leave in the drawers of hotels. It smells old, almost ripe, and what I can see of the paper looks as yellow as a smoker's teeth. It's bound in pale-green leather, with no visible title or author. There's an eight-pointed star embossed in gold on the front cover. The book is fastened shut with a pair of dull metal clasps. I try to open them, but they're stuck somehow, and they dig painfully into my fingers.

"An antique, I'm given to understand," Berkley is saying, "quite what it meant to your father I'm unclear, but he was insistent that you be given it immediately. It's — do be careful—it's rather valuable. I suggest you treat it gently."

I put the book down and pick up the metal case. It rattles when I move it, sounding like there are a lot of small loose objects inside. It opens at one end. I tilt it and a shower of rings fall out onto the dark wood of the desk: golden rings, rings set with red stones, blue stones, black stones. A ring in the shape of a lion, and another with a grinning skull set into it. I count nine in all. I pick up a few of the rings at random, turn them over in my hands. They feel cool, heavy. I've never seen Dad without them; they were sort of his trademark. Someone must've pulled them off his fingers after he died.

I put the rings back down.

"He didn't expect me to wear these, did he?" I ask.

"He intended for you to have them," Berkley replies. "What's done with them is entirely yours to decide."

"What about these?" I ask, pointing at the papers.

"Items from your father's desk, I believe. Correspondence and so forth. He wished for you to read them."

I look at the tattered stack of papers.

"I've got exams, you know?" I say.

"And I'm sure your father would be thrilled to hear how devoted you are to your studies," he says, smiling, without a detectable trace of sarcasm. "In their present state, they're somewhat inconvenient to transport. . . . Here, let me get you a document wallet." Mr. Berkley stands and moves over to a cabinet at the back of the room. He returns with a heavy brown file folder. "Don't want to be caught without one of these in my line of work. Never know when you'll need somewhere to keep a contract. . . . There. All safe."

The lawyer stuffs Dad's papers into the folder and then arranges the green book and ring case alongside it. He pushes them toward me.

"Is that everything?" I ask. My mind flashes again to the money, and then I wonder again if this is some kind of trick. I'm half hoping he'll pull out a briefcase full of fifties.

"For now. As I said, you won't receive the money right away. There are those lingering conditions that need to be met, tax to be negotiated, that sort of thing. Details, details. I'll be in touch once everything's settled."

"OK," I say, scooping Dad's ring collection back into the case. I stand up and put the book and rings into my coat pocket. The documents are tucked under my arm. Mr. Berkley springs to his feet, thrusts his arm at me. I shake his hand.

"May I say once more how sorry I am for your loss, Luke. Horatio was very dear to me. It's been extremely interesting to finally meet his heir. I hope very much that if there is ever anything you need, anything I can help you with, you won't hesitate to contact me."

"It's nice to meet you as well," I say, prising my hand from his grip. I immediately decide that, once I get Dad's money, I will never speak to this man again, for any reason. I've never been more sure of anything. I want to get as far away as possible from his clicking golden clock and his creepy stare. I step backward, away from him, waving good-bye with my free arm.

"A pleasure," Mr. Berkley says, "a pleasure, Luke. I feel certain we shall meet again."

I take some more time to wander around Brackford afterward so it looks like I've been to practice after school, and I get the bus back into Dunbarrow at six o'clock. As I sit on the top deck, watching the darkening sky unroll endlessly above the highway, bits of my day ricochet around my head like pinballs. Golden dreams of wealth, of shoes, new jeans, cars, houses, mixed with darker thoughts: the letter, Mum standing at the sink, saying today was *a blue day*. Berkley sizing me up, peering without any warmth through his vivid blue eyes. The parchment I put my name on, the green book that I've got tucked in the pocket of my raincoat. I feel like I got offered something I couldn't refuse, and in return I agreed to something I don't understand. Why did Dad name only me in his will? What about Mum? How did he die, and why does nobody but me and Berkley seem to know anything about it? What happened to Dad, exactly?

The last time I saw him—other than the day he left us, other than glimpses of his face on the cover of discount paperbacks—I was fifteen, home from school with the flu, slumped in front of our TV. My forehead was crying sweat, and my body felt inflated and sore, like someone had stuck me with a bicycle pump. I was channel surfing, and Dad's face came up on the screen.

He'd been eating well, you could see that, and his white suit looked a size small for him. His beard was like something you'd pull out of a drain, his fingers laden with rings.

Dad was talking intently with an old woman who was convinced her dead husband was still lingering in their house. She had seen him in his favorite chair, she said, or not seen him exactly but she had sensed him. She had smelled his scent, the aftershave he'd always worn since his days in the army. She mentioned this point several times, that he'd been in the army, giving it greater weight than the fact he was dead. A man of habit, Dad said, sympathetic, and she agreed. The woman said she'd seen cushions pressed back, as if by an invisible head. And every morning, she said, his shoes would be laid out beside the welcome mat—*no matter how many times she put them back in the attic.* She said this last part with the breathy intensity of the truly batshit insane.

My dad nodded and said he'd like to see the chair, if he might. The camera followed through to the living room. She solemnly indicated the chair her husband still favored, and Dad took off one of his rings and hung it on a chain, then dangled it over the chair saying, "Yes, yes, I can feel his spirit lingering here. He has not crossed over." He took the widow's hand in his and, looking into her eyes, told a grieving old woman that her husband needed help getting himself to the afterlife, and that he was the one to provide it.

Seeing the look of feigned love and concern on his face—because he looked at me like that before he left, whenever I fell down in the park or came to talk to him about the monsters in the closet—hurt an amazing amount, like being stabbed, and I changed the channel and was careful not to watch his show again.

It's fully dark, spotting with rain, as I walk down the drive and come in through the front door. I realize with a jolt of annoyance that I'm not muddy or carrying my sports bag, which calls my rugby story into question, but Mum doesn't come close to noticing. She's sitting on the sofa with a face mask packed with ice strapped to her head, which is never a good omen. She's ignoring a soap opera. Ham lies like a living rug at her feet.

"Hello, love."

"All right, Mum." I squeeze her hand.

"We had some sparrows in the garden today. I've always been so glad we came out here. Real birds, you know? Not just pigeons. How was your day?"

I discovered that my estranged father—your ex-husband—is dead. I met Dad's weird solicitor and signed for four million pounds, conditional upon who knows what. I don't know if I did the right thing.

"School was all right. Nothing happened."

Mum smiles in a half-focused way.

"Are you OK?" I ask.

"I've been getting some fireflies, just this past hour. Don't worry yourself."

The "fireflies" are sparks and flashes Mum gets in the corner of her eyes when a big headache is coming on. I should have said something to her this morning. She'll barely be able to stand up for the rest of the week. I won't get any help from her. I decide we can talk about Dad when she gets better. She looks strange in her neon-blue ice mask, like an extra on a cheap superhero show.

"Get some rest, Mum. I'll get myself dinner."

"Good lad. Glad to hear it. Be a darling and feed Ham, would you? He's been doing my head in all day, scratching and yelping."

"All right."

I feed Ham a tin of Mr. Paws' Doggy Deluxe before shoving him outside. I put some pasta on, and by the time it's done, Mum has dragged herself up to bed. She probably wanted to go hours ago, but I know she likes to wait until I'm back in the house so that I don't come home to empty rooms. There's a proper rainstorm starting, and when I let Ham back in, he's soaked to the skin, his downy gray fur plastered over his thin back and legs. He gives me a pained look when I laugh, and slinks off to lie under a radiator. I check my texts. Kirk sent one this afternoon, saying he and Mark set Nick Alsip's tie on fire with a Bunsen burner in chemistry today. Kirk says it was "legendary." I obviously missed a big day at Dunbarrow High. I wash up and then, on a whim, go into the hallway and take Dad's green book from my raincoat pocket. The wind rises outside. I look the book over in the dim light of the hall. Berkley said it was valuable. What's so special about it? I run a finger over the eight-pointed star on the cover. The leather is smooth and cold.

I go and sit on the sofa in the living room, with the TV still burbling in the background. I mute it and try to undo the clasps on the book. They're stuck, stiff as corpses. There's no give to them at all. I try to work out how to force them, but I don't want to damage the book. It looks so old. I definitely don't want to break it open—that'll ruin the sale value. I put it aside and watch soccer on TV. The white ball is a tiny speck against green grass.

I don't know what time it is. The windows are black eyes in the wall. The TV is on standby, projecting a hollow blue light. Ham lies asleep in front of it, furry chest inflating and contracting as he whines in his dream. The wind is a muted rushing noise outside, and I can hear something— a pipe, maybe—rattling in the walls. I'm lying on the sofa. Dad's green book is on my chest, clasps closed.

I sit up slowly, feeling like I'm still asleep. I move the book off my chest and onto the arm of the sofa. The boiler must have shorted out or something, because I can see my breath hanging in clouds. I stand and walk quietly across the living room into the kitchen. There's no light except the glow of the microwave control panel. Weren't the lights on when I sat down on the sofa? Did Mum come back and switch them off? As my eyes dilate the darkness seeps into me and I see more clearly, the way you do when there's no light, see the kitchen in soft shades of gray. Outside the window in the garden, the apple trees are thrashing. The noise of the wind is louder in here. The sky is a whirl of blacks, the horizon stained dirty orange by distant street lights.

The cold from the stone tiles is climbing my legs, heading for my insides. I want to turn the lights on, but something stops me, saying that if I turn on the lights then whatever is outside the house will be able to see me.

This is stupid. I'm scared because it's dark and cold and my deeply buried monkey brain has been programmed by millions of years of evolution to be freaked out in situations that are dark because my eyes are not as adept at seeing in the dark as our predators' eyes used to be. This is the reason I'm afraid. There's nothing outside the house. I listen for Mum coughing or moving, but there's no sound from upstairs.

Walking with deliberate care, I exit the kitchen and stand in the hallway. There aren't any windows in here, and even though that makes it darker than the kitchen, I feel calmer. This is ridiculous. I'm sixteen, not a six-year-old with a night-light.

Before I can think this over anymore, I stride back into the kitchen and flick on all the lights. For added defiance, I turn on the kettle. The house echoes with the sound of bubbling water and angry steam. Relaxing completely, I walk over to the fridge and pull out a packet of processed turkey. As I eat one of the delicious, if rubbery, slices, I congratulate myself. It's perfectly natural to feel uneasy when alone in a dark place, but giving in to such animal fears is shameful. I am a candle of reason in the demon-haunted world, etc.

I'm interrupted during these thoughts by a gigantic crash upstairs, like someone just dropped a bowling ball through the roof. Ham starts yowling. He rushes into the kitchen and presses himself against my leg.

I put the turkey back in the fridge—I should make it clear that my hands are definitely not shaking as I do this—and reach over into the fancy-cutlery drawer and take out the sharpest meat skewer that we own. Emboldened by the eight-inch spike, I force myself across the kitchen and into the dark hallway. Ham follows with his head bowed, moaning softly.

"Shut up," I tell him, and he obeys. I try to ignore the sick feeling in my stomach like I just stepped off the side of a bridge and am plummeting toward black frozen water. I focus on the skewer. I am an Alpha Male with testosterone leaking out of my sweat glands. Ham, my loyal and subservient pack member, is looking to me for guidance in this situation.

"Mum?" I ask, projecting my voice upstairs.

The trees creak.

"Mum!"

Ham pushes his head harder against my legs. It would be just like her to sleep through this, but the stillness upstairs is freaking me out. I need to know that she's all right.

I take a deep breath, straighten my spine, and quietly put one foot and then another on the stairs, and then the landing. It's hard to say exactly where the noise came from. Was it the bathroom? Ham pads past me and points his nose toward Mum's room.

"You're sure?" I whisper. He whines.

I stare at the white wood, breathing hard.

There's nothing inside the house . . .

I put my hand on the door.

Ham shifts his weight and whimpers.

I close my eyes and imagine that Holiday Simmon, blond and gorgeous, is watching me somehow, on TV maybe. She wants to see me win. This is where I prove I'm worthy.

I grip the skewer tightly, and then, before I can think twice, I burst into Mum's room, ready to stab as many burglars with my meat skewer as I can before they take me down.

There's nobody except Mum in the room.

I whirl around in case they hid behind the door, but there's simply nobody else here.

I also can't help but notice that Ham didn't actually follow me into battle. He's still standing out on the landing, with just his shaggy head peering around the door frame.

"Judas." I spit the word at him, waving my skewer. "You furry little Judas."

He pads into the bedroom and licks my hand.

Cowardice aside, it seems Ham was right about coming in here. The windows are completely open, and wind is ranting into Mum's bedroom. This must've been the source of the noise. Mum's green-and-orange curtains are flapping about, but apart from that, nothing seems out of place. Her tribal masks are still hanging on the wall, her map of the stars is still in prime position. She's lying in bed, hair tangled over her pillow.

"Mum?"

She raises her head like a swimmer, takes a breath.

"Yes, love?"

"Mum, your window just flew right open. You didn't hear anything?"

"No, no. Oh, gosh . . ."

"You didn't—"

"Luke, love . . . please. I need to rest."

"OK," I say, unable to believe she didn't notice her window blowing open in the middle of a storm. Her doctors aren't shy with the prescriptions.

She's already sinking back down onto the pillow.

I close her window, making sure to latch the bolt properly. I stare into the backyard, which is lit by the lights still burning in the kitchen. Mum's breathing becomes deeper and slower. There's nobody out there, or rather no evidence of anyone that I can see. I don't know what I was looking for, whether I expected to see Mr. Berkley out on the lawn or what. It starts to rain again, and the droplets are like little diamonds on the glass. Soon there are too many of them for me to see anything.

"It was probably just the—" I start to say to Ham, and then stop myself. Whenever someone in a film says *it's just the wind*, they're immediately murdered.

"Let's not let our guard down."

Ham rubs his head on my thigh. Outside, the storm roars. Mum sighs and turns over. Two of her pills and she's out of it. No help.

"Look," I say to Ham as we leave, "this will be a one-time-only event, but how do you feel about sleeping in my bedroom tonight? On the floor, obviously."

(sunny-side up)

I wake with a woozy headache and a mouthful of sticky gray fluff. There's a warm weight on my back, which turns out to be Ham, who decided at some point during the night that the floor was the raw end of the deal. He whines bitterly when I push him off the bed.

In the sunlight, last night seems like a strange dream. Dad's green book is sitting on my bedside table. I remember trying to get it open, and then sleeping, waking up, Mum's window. . . . I lie still, looking at the ceiling, and think about Dad. I decide that I'm going to be fine about it. What was I expecting, that he'd come back and apologize to me? Beg my forgiveness? Whatever final grovel I've missed out on, it's probably for the best. He's gone and he left me his money and that's all I need to think about. Me and Mum are going to be fine.

I spend a little bit longer in the shower than usual to wash every trace of Ham from my hair, then wrap myself in a towel and take a good look at my face — the face of a millionaire, I remind myself with a sugary thrill. I'm not looking like a millionaire, it has to be said. My midnight adventure took a toll. My eyelids are dark and baggy, and my teeth are kind of furry because I forgot to brush them. I do two swirls of mouthwash rather than one, and then spend ten minutes taming my hair with gel. I'm working on a new style of bangs where they kind of swirl to the right rather than the left, but I'm not sure about it yet.

When I feel my face is in order I stroll back into my bedroom and put on my uniform — black trousers, gray sweater, and my newest sneakers. They're Lacoste, green accenting on white leather. You can't wear sneakers to lessons, obviously, but it's not done to turn up at school wearing school shoes. You come in your sneakers, have a kickabout, let everyone see them. I keep my school shoes in my locker. Since I woke up in good time I have a little look at the sneakers from various angles in my full-length mirror before heading downstairs to feed and reassure Ham. I have yet another thought about the money Dad left for me. I can have new shoes every day of my life if I want.

I walk into the kitchen, and my good mood vanishes like there's a bucket of fear balanced above the door. The kitchen is empty. The sun is starting to highlight the storm clouds nearest the horizon. Everything is perfectly still.

The reason I'm so unnerved is there's a full English breakfast sitting on the kitchen table at my spot. There shouldn't be a full English breakfast sitting on the table. There shouldn't be a full English breakfast anywhere in this house, because I've only just woken up, and Ham, to my knowledge, is unable to operate the stove or can opener. Mum'll barely stand up today, and besides, she won't ever cook meat for me, so there's no way she's responsible. I move tentatively over to the breakfast, like it's attached to the trip wire of a bomb. I examine the eggs, the bacon, the mug of tea. There's even a side plate of toast, a napkin folded into a triangle, a small glass of orange juice.

Hypothesis: I've started sleep-cooking.

I walk past the impossible breakfast and try to locate Ham, who is the other piece of this puzzle. Why hasn't he eaten the breakfast? Unless food is carefully guarded, Ham will devour it, with extreme prejudice. He's been downstairs more than half an hour now.

I find him in his crate in the laundry room. He rolls his eyes at me when I walk in but won't get up to greet me. He's shivering with cold.

"Ham?"

He still won't move. I run upstairs and get my meat skewer again. I do a swift check of the upstairs and downstairs rooms, but nothing is out of place or missing. I don't understand. Who would break into my house and lay out a cooked breakfast for me? Some sort of consentless butler service?

Hypothesis: There is no breakfast. I'm going nuts.

I stride back into the kitchen. It's still there, steaming away, tea the exact shade of brown that I like.

I want to call someone, but I'm unsure what to say. Can I report an unauthorized breakfast? I take my phone out of my pocket. I'm not going to be a victim even if I'm not sure what I'm a victim of. I dial nine three times and then stand there with my finger on the call button. I imagine various conversations with the police, none of them especially productive. Maybe I could just say someone broke into my house? But then they're going to ask what they took and I'll have to explain what happened, and then they're going to laugh at me.

The mystery meal is starting to cool. I don't know what to do. I walk upstairs and push the door to Mum's room open. She's still asleep, lying twisted up inside her duvet. I lean down and take hold of her pale wrist.

"Did you make breakfast for me today? Hello?"

She opens her eyes but doesn't move her head.

"Luke," she says, "it's not such a good time for me today . . ."

"Mum, I know, but—"

"It's very difficult to listen to you talking, love," she says, putting her hands over her face.

"Seriously," I begin.

"If you could get me some water," she says, and closes her eyes again.

That's all I'm going to get. I shut my mouth.

She's supposed to help me, not the other way around.

In the end I decide not to call the police. Like, what are they going to do? They'll ask some questions, and my name gets put on a computer somewhere, and they save the file and mark it LUNATIC and forget about me.

Instead I scrape the breakfast into the bin, and then put all the dishes in the dishwasher on extra hot in case the food genuinely was laced with cyanide. I eat some more cold turkey from the fridge and wash it down with mango juice straight from the carton. After I've done this, there is a brief moment of panic when I think that maybe the invader has poisoned everything in the fridge as well, but I don't get stomach cramps, so I'm probably all right. I head upstairs and bring Mum water. I get my bag, and then I'm out the door into the gray morning.

Forty years since they built it, Dunbarrow High School is crumbling like an ancient slab of shortbread. The once-zestful green doors have faded to a sickly pea color. There are five times the number of students the school was originally built for, and it's staffed by the obligatory crew of dictators and divorcées.

My friends are in the schoolyard, like every morning, hoofing a ball around. The center of the yard is dominated by the upper classman, and the maggots that populate the lower years have to play their games at the edge, near the trash cans. Kirk Danknott deftly flips the ball off one toe and it arcs through the air, landing just at Mark Ellsmith's feet. Mark subdues the ball under his heel and sends it skidding over to me.

"Manchett," says Mark.

"All right, lads," I say.

Kirk grunts.

Mark is tall and broad, with eyes the color of a swimming pool. He's the rugby team captain, which means I have to laugh at his jokes.

I flick the ball over to Kirk.

"You see the match?" he asks.

"Nah, I was busy. Saw the highlights last night."

Kirk and me have been playing soccer together since we were eight years old. Kirk's heavyset, with hair shorn to a dusting of fuzz on his skull. He's wearing dirty orange sneakers with the laces trailing.

"Where were you yesterday?" Mark asks.

"I had family stuff," I say, knowing this will shut down any further questions on the subject. The less Mark and Kirk and the rest of the guys know about the situation with Mum and my dad, the better, has always been my strategy. One thing about Dad being so separate from us is no one ever suspects that I'm related to the guy on TV with a bunch of rings and a white suit. He doesn't even look like me, thanks to the weight he carries—and that's fine by me. To survive Dunbarrow High you want to be as normal as possible, and that means no ill Mum, no ghost-hunter Dad, just ordinary Luke Manchett who likes soccer and rugby and doesn't like schoolwork.

Mark nods at my excuse and turns away.

"Here, you're coming to the park tonight?" Kirk asks. Tuesday's the only time none of us have any kind of practice, so it's normally a night to hang out.

I think about the solicitors, and my dad's will, and Mum lying in her bed like she's drowned. I think about strangers preparing a traditional breakfast in my kitchen and somehow leaving before I wake up.

"I dunno, man," I say.

"Are you joking? I've barely seen you. Besides, Holiday's definitely going."

Holiday Simmon is the most eligible girl in our year, bar none. She has honey-blond hair and the kind of face and body you normally have to buy a magazine to look at. She recently came back on the market after breaking up with her boyfriend, who was purportedly at college in Brackford. Since then I've seen her several times at our rugby games, standing at the edge of the field in various flawless outfits. Kirk immediately noticed that I had noticed and hasn't let up about it.

"So what?" I say to Kirk, keeping watch on Mark's face. He betrays no interest.

"I just don't want you missing out, mate."

"I've got . . . homework," I say, instantly regretting my terrible excuse. Mark and Kirk give me identical grimaces of contempt, as if to say, *Who are you, and what did you do with Luke?*

"You sure you're all right?" Mark asks. "The Head didn't actually get you with all that stuff about the 'most important year of our lives,' did she?"

"School's a joke," Kirk adds. "They don't teach you anything you need to know to get a real job. When are we ever gonna use any of this stuff once we leave?"

"Kirk," I say, trying to take the heat off, "is it true Mr. Richmont drew a vomiting face on your last history essay?"

"Look," he says, "I can make a thousand quid a week selling broadband door-to-door, all right? They do it on commission. I'm a natural sales personality. You don't need to go to uni to get a job. Pass the ball."

I skim the ball over to Kirk. He intercepts the pass and then in one smooth motion draws his leg back and sends the ball cannoning across the yard, toward the glass-fronted school office. The ball hits Elza Moss, Public Weirdo Number One, in the back with a thud I almost feel. She whirls around, hair flaring out.

Elza Moss is the kind of girl who would've been burned at the stake a few hundred years ago. I know it sounds cruel, but it's true. You only have to look at her to see she doesn't fit: tall and pale, with a dusting of freckles under her eyes. She's got a redhead's complexion but dyes her hair midnight-black, the contrast making her face white as a waxwork. Her hair is sprayed and back-combed until it towers over her, enormous, like a captive storm cloud.

I don't exactly hate Elza, but there are very strict rules at Dunbarrow High School, among the students at least. Girls are supposed to have neat, glossy hair, not foot-high thunderheads. Jewelry may be worn, but not too much. Your clothes can't be bought from charity shops or handed down by relatives or discovered in the attic of some stately home somewhere, which are the vibes I get from Elza's non-uniform wardrobe. Girls are permitted — encouraged — to have eye makeup, but trying to look like Cleopatra is not part of the brief.

She could get a pass if she made any effort to fit in, but she refuses to meet even the loosest of guidelines. She wears army boots to school and reads too many books and uses too many words and smokes cigarettes outside the gates on her own. I would bet money that her room contains a bale of poetry and that none of it rhymes.

"He shoots, he scores," announces Kirk. All the lower years are sniggering, but I'm not laughing, since Elza's known to have something of a sharp tongue on her. Just as she's about to start yelling, she makes eye contact with me, and her face changes. She turns calm and almost curious-looking, searching me with her gaze. This is all I need, on top of everything else, some outcast developing a psycho-crush on me. I scowl at her, and she shrugs before nudging our ball into the thick October mud that passes for a flower bed and pressing the full weight of her boot on it, pushing it down until it's almost completely submerged. She raises an eyebrow at me and walks away.

"Aw, whatever," says Mark.

"Kirk, you're getting that out, mate."

"What a freak."

The morning is so overcast that every classroom has the lights on. I'm sitting in math, slouched forward on my desk, watching as the teacher draws rows of numbers on the whiteboard. I'm normally all right at this, but I can't follow any of it today. Every column of figures makes me think of my inheritance, the four million, Mr. Berkley. Not to mention that there's something about last night that I can't seem to get my head around. I know that I left Dad's book on the sofa, downstairs. I went upstairs with Ham, burst into Mum's room, and then went to sleep. The book was on my bedside table this morning. Normally I'd just assume that I brought the book upstairs myself and forgot about it, but the appearance of the mystery breakfast this morning suggests that someone is moving things around in my house.

I shudder. It seems such a bizarre thing for a stranger

to break in and do, that I'm tempted to think either Mum or me has started sleepwalking. You hear about people doing all kinds of mad stuff while they're asleep. Some of them even commit murders.

I try to refocus my attention on the morning's algebra problems, but thoughts keep blaring: the money, the mystery breakfast—and from there I start thinking about Dad.

I don't know much about his early life. He met Mum at a psychic fair back in the days when she lived in a van and never wore shoes. Dad's mother died when he was really young, and his dad, Grandpa Archie, started drinking a lot. Grandpa died about a year after I was born, so I don't remember him at all. Dad worked as a builder from when he was pretty young before deciding he'd become a psychic and exorcist for reasons Mum's never really explained. He got a TV show, which became pretty successful for a show like that, married Mum, had me, and then left us when I was six.

If Dad had never been around at all, it'd all be a lot easier to stomach. Just me and Mum, doing our thing. But my memories of him are good ones. I really liked him. We lived in the Midlands back then, only moved way up north to Dunbarrow after the separation, and our house was nice, fancier than the one me and Mum have now. Dad's show (I wasn't allowed to watch: "too frightening") had been going only a couple of years at that point, but he was getting decent money out of it, and Mum was working, too. Dad'd be in his office a lot with the door shut, doing stuff for his show, but he always had time for me: In winter he'd come build a snowman with me, and in summer we'd fill up the wading pool and play with this plastic crocodile I liked. All that wholesome stuff. I remember being at the beach one evening, and Dad and me charged the seagulls, scattered them up into the air like a snowstorm in reverse.

I don't know when things started to go wrong. I remember Mum got badly sick, the first time she ever had one of her headaches, so bad she was in hospital for a few days, and she was lying in their bed for weeks afterward. She told me much later that she was so sick they thought, for a few hours, that she might die. Anyway, Dad really went to pieces while this was going on. Up in his study all night, talking on the phone all day, saying things I couldn't understand, languages I'd never heard anyone speak before. He was drinking a lot, too. I have this vivid memory of waking up one night and hearing someone shouting in the garden. I looked out my window and saw Dad pacing around, next to the pond. There was a full moon, I remember that, and Dad's face and hands were really vivid and pale in the dimness. I couldn't work out what he was doing, because I remember he sounded like he was having an argument, but with someone who wasn't there. He'd pace and wait and seem to be listening to the dark garden, and then he'd turn and start waving his arms and shouting again. I didn't know what to do. I definitely didn't want him to know I'd seen him talking to himself. I went back to bed and closed my eyes.

As soon as Mum could walk again, they started arguing. Not loudly, but in hisses late at night. I remember them both being on the phone a lot. Around this time, there was a weekend when we were supposed to be going somewhere, and Mum was getting all ready and taking forever, and then as she was walking down the stairs, she started crying and sat down, and nothing Dad said could move her, and then she went back into their room and locked the door. It was at that point that he sat down on the stairs himself and told me that he and Mum weren't going to live in the same house anymore.

He didn't stick around much longer after that day, and we moved up to Dunbarrow. Mum looked for jobs but never quite seemed to get one, and she got really into Positive Thinking and reading books like *Changing Your Life in Just Ten Days!*, but that didn't happen for her either. Everything just stayed the same. I thought Dad might come back, but he never did, and things went on like that until he died.

I'm on edge when I walk back up our driveway from school, sky darkening already, but the house is a normal temperature and nothing has moved around since I left in the morning. Ham is happy to see me, prancing around in the hallway, and I can hear Mum playing one of her whale song CDs upstairs. I make myself some tea, and when it's done I walk Ham down to the bottom of the nearest field and back. I decide that I really do want to go hang out, do some normal stuff with Mark and Kirk, maybe get to know Holiday a little better, forget all about breakfasts and books and Dad, so in the end I decide to get the bus down to the park.

I sit right at the front, on the top deck, so I can enjoy what little view there is in the darkness. The interior of the bus is lit up and the windows are black, and I get a decent look at the other passengers in the reflection without having to turn around. There are only two other people sitting up here, already on the bus when I climbed the stairs, and both are weird enough for me to take an interest. They're men, older than me. They're sitting at the very back. I think they're talking to each other, but I can't hear over the mumbling of the engine.

The guy sitting on the left side is tall and bulky, with a shaved head and flattened features. There are three gold earrings glinting in his ear, and he has plenty of tattoos on his arms and neck, though I can't make them out in detail. He slouches in his seat, with his feet up on the headrest in front. He's wearing a red-checked shirt, buttoned to the throat, with stonewashed jeans and cherry-red Dr. Martens. He has bright-white suspenders cutting over his chest. I didn't know you saw skinheads anymore, not in the wild.

His friend is even stranger, sitting poised and upright, as if about to begin a piano recital. His hair is black and greasy, and he's got a pointed black mustache. He would probably be handsome if it weren't for the angry red blotches on his forehead and jawline. He's wearing a navy-blue suit, a white shirt, and a rumpled purple cravat. This is an inadvisable look when going out drinking in Dunbarrow, unless you really like having pint glasses smashed in your face.

I don't know how, but they must have realized I'm staring at them in the reflection. They stop talking and look at me. The skinhead gets to his feet. He must be six seven at least; his chest is overloaded with muscle. His shirtsleeves strain against his arms. He takes three strides down the central aisle, red boots clomping.

Should I turn around and say something? The guy is standing halfway down the aisle, holding the seats, staring at me. Kirk says if you have to fight someone bigger than you, then you should just try to hit them in the balls and run. If this skinhead gets any closer, I'm going to aim a foot directly into the crotch of his bleached Levi's. I refuse to be antagonized by people who can't move on from the youth culture of thirty years ago.

The guy takes another step forward.

I turn around and look at him properly. My face is

unsmiling, jaw set. I'm trying to show I won't be a push-over. We make eye contact, and I realize I've made a mistake.

In the flesh he's even uglier, with an unshaved face the color of cheese. There's a cross tattooed on his forehead, and a long white scar on his left cheek. His eyes are gray pools. Whatever it is that normal people have, that makes you feel like they're decent and sane and still able to think — there is not one spark of it inside this man.

I hold his gaze, unable to look away.

In a few seconds' time he's going to leap at me and twist my head off like a champagne cork. I can already hear them making the announcement in assembly at school. *I'm saddened to say that one of our best-liked students was decapitated on the top deck of the X45 on Tuesday night . . .*

The skinhead grins at me, showing a mouthful of crooked yellow teeth, and then he winks and walks back to his friend.

Before he turns around I think I hear him say something like this:

"Sorry, boss."

I must have picked a, like, seven-leaf clover this morning and not realized it.

My legs are still shaking from adrenaline when I get off the bus in the center of Dunbarrow. The square's not busy, but even though it's a weeknight, there are a few groups smoking outside the pubs. I walk past, avoiding eye contact, and cross the bridge over the river, heading into the park.

It's dark and still here, lit only with a couple of street lamps, but I know where to find my friends. It's the normal crowd—Mark and the rest of the team, someone throwing a ball, Kirk and a couple of guys from his neighborhood, shaved heads and cigarette burns in their tracksuit bottoms. They're all sitting around on the children's play equipment: There are people up on the climbing frame, some girls laughing as one of Kirk's friends pushes them on the merry-go-round. It rained earlier in the evening, and as I walk toward the park I see that each blade of grass is shining in the light from a nearby street lamp, like someone varnished the whole bank. Kirk spots me, lurches over, drunk already, holding out a big plastic bottle of cider.

"Luke, mate."

"Hey Kirk," I say. He topples into me, hugs me too hard.

"Luke, you're all right, mate."

"Yeah, I'm fine."

"No, you're all right, you're all right."

"I'm all right," I echo. I don't feel it. I'm keeping too many secrets. I've got more money now than Kirk's parents probably make in a lifetime, and I don't know how to go about mentioning it. What would he think of that? What if I told him who my Dad was? I've known Kirk eight years, and I barely know how to hint at what's happened to me since Monday morning. He's offering me the bottle of cider. I take it, swig as much as I can, hand the bottle back.

"Holiday's here," he says, then swills the cider himself. It's cheap, nasty, tastes a bit like felt-tip pens smell.

"Really?" I say. Honestly, when Kirk claimed she was coming down, I took it with a big dose of salt. I'd assumed Holiday Simmon would have something better to do on a Tuesday night than drinking white cider in the park, but it looks like I was wrong about that. I can see the back of her blond head. She's sitting at the bottom of the slide in the playground, next to some other girl.

"Go for it," Kirk says, "get in there."

"You think?"

"Don't . . . don't think too much. Just do it."

"All right," I say, and take another drink of cider. I don't know why Kirk drinks this stuff. He pays a homeless guy to buy us booze, so I guess he probably can't be too picky. I make my way over to Holiday. I've seen her on the sidelines of our games and had a few classes with her and stuff. I know her to say hello to, but I've never really spoken to her past that. She has her own circle of mates who aren't quite the same as mine, and she had her boyfriend in Brackford—not to mention I've basically always been scared of her. I'm nervous right now, watching her blond head drawing nearer as I cross the park. I'm not exactly sure what I'm going to say. I remind myself that I'm a millionaire. Millionaires don't have trouble with girls, ever. I try to get myself into the millionaire mind-set, cross the last few steps with a millionaire walk. There's a queue of underwear models and French actresses waiting to take her place if she doesn't want me. I mean, that's if whoever left a breakfast for me this morning doesn't gut me before Berkley can transfer the money . . . come to think of it, those guys on the bus were definitely looking at me . . . they know something . . . no, stop thinking about this . . . you're talking to Holiday right now . . . she's literally saying something right now. I need to reply. I need to stop thinking about hypothetical French women and hypothetical murders that might happen to me and reply to Holiday.

"Hello!" I say, sounding more shocked than glad to see her.

"Well, I was asking how your day went," Holiday says, "but hello will do." She smiles. I was already essentially struck dumb, but her smile completes the process.

She's not exactly dressed up, wearing jeans and a North Face jacket, but she looks incredible, radiating the kind of casual beauty that's a gift and can't be earned. Her hair's done up in a bun, and she's wearing heavy-framed glasses, which I've never seen her in before. She's still smiling, expectantly.

"Luke Manchett," I say finally. "I'm on the team? The rugby team."

Someone kill me. Strike me dead.

"We know who you are," says the girl next to Holiday—named Anna or something?—thin and sour-faced. You can just tell by looking at her that everyone knows her as "Holiday's friend."

"*Alice*," Holiday says. "Luke, do you know Alice Waltham?"

"Nah," I say. "Hello."

"Hi." Alice glances up at me with industrial-strength disinterest, and then gets a cigarette pack out of her coat and starts fiddling with that instead.

"Do you smoke, Luke?" Holiday asks me brightly.

"No," I say. "Training. I mean, I can't because of training."

"I don't smoke either," she says. "Mum's got a nose like a bloodhound. I'd never get away with it, even if I wanted to. But, like, I think my *little brother* is smoking, and he's twelve. Do you think that's weird? To smoke when you're twelve? I mean I can't prove it, but I'm pretty sure he does. And Mum doesn't say a *thing*."

"Even twelve-year-olds don't know what twelve-year-olds should be doing," I say, which I don't think really makes sense, but Holiday laughs anyway. I can't believe we're actually having a conversation. It was this easy the whole time. I just had to walk over and talk to her.

"Do you have any brothers?" Holiday asks.

"No, just me."

"I ought to know that," Holiday says. "My mum actually knows yours. They were on a Reiki retreat together or something. My mum's into some weird stuff like that."

"Oh," I say, "I didn't know that." I'm really surprised to hear about Mum talking to anyone else in Dunbarrow. She's never really been that interested in getting involved in the town. She's happy to live in the countryside, and that's as far as it goes. I don't think she knows the names of the couple who live on our right-hand side. I have a sudden chill when I wonder if Mum told Holiday's mum about Dad and the separation. Whether Holiday knows I'm Dr. Horatio Manchett's son. If she does, she hasn't shown it.

We talk a bit more, about school and exams and mutual friends, and somewhere along the line Alice snorts extra hard with contempt and gets up and leaves us alone, and I sit down on the slide beside Holiday. Things are going smoothly and our knees are just starting to touch when I look up and see something at the tree line, up the bank, that nearly makes my heart stop.

The two guys from the bus, the skinhead and Blotch-Face, are standing under the farthest street lamp. The skinhead is leaning on a tree, mostly in shadow. I can see the glim of a cigarette at his face. Blotch-Face stands ramrod straight, right under the lamp, and he's looking directly over at me, like he wants me to see him watching.

"Luke?" Holiday says.

"Yeah?"

"Are you all right? You're shaking."

She's right. My hand is fluttering on my knee. I grab at it with my other hand, to try to keep them both under control.

"I think . . ." I try to find a way of putting this. "I think there's someone following me."

She raises an eyebrow.

"These two guys . . . two weirdos. They're right over there, at the top of the bank. Don't look yet. Look slow. Over by the street lamp. They were watching me on the bus, and now they're here. I'm serious."

"What guys?" Holiday says, smiling.

"*Those* guys," I say. "I can't point at them. They're by the lamp."

"There's nobody there!" Holiday punches me in the leg. "I know it's nearly Halloween, but stop trying to scare me! My dad pulls this all the time. I'm not falling for it."

"Holiday," I say, looking her dead in the eye, "I'm really serious. There's two of them watching us. Right up on the bank."

"There's nobody there," Holiday says. "I know you're messing with me!"

She just looked right at them. Do her glasses need a new prescription? Blotch-Face is exactly where he was before, staring at both of us. He's probably six feet tall and right under the street lamp—you can't possibly miss him. As I watch, the skinhead leans out of the shadows, says something only Blotch-Face can hear.

"Are you messing with *me*?" I ask. "How can you not see them?"

"See who?" comes Mark's voice from behind. He claps me on the shoulder, making me start like someone fired a gun next to my ear. Holiday gasps, too, then giggles.

"Luke's being a jerk," she says. "He's trying to freak me out."

Her tone is light, jokey, but there's a little hint of something else in her eyes. Like she's starting to see that I'm genuinely scared.

"Am I nuts?" I ask Mark. "There's two guys watching us up on that bank. Look."

"Huh," he says. "Well, if they were there, they're gone now."

He's right. There's nobody up on the bank anymore. Just a lone orange street lamp and an enormous dark oak tree, branches rippling in the wind that's rising.

∘ ∘ ∘

The night doesn't really get back on track after that. Whatever moment me and Holiday were having is lost, and Mark stands behind us while he's talking, so I have to crick my neck to look him in the eye. I keep waiting for him to leave, but he doesn't. I can't relax. I keep thinking about the two men and the breakfast, wondering if they put it there, wondering if they knew Dad somehow. After a while it starts raining again, and I take it as an excuse to leave. Holiday says something about a Halloween party at her house, and I nod without taking it in. The buses don't run this late and I walk up to Wormwood Drive the long way, drizzle fizzing on the shoulders and hood of my raincoat, the gutter running with a shimmering flush of water. Every step I take I'm thinking of Blotch-Face and the skinhead, trying to work it out. Maybe they know about the money, are trying to get hold of it somehow? What exactly were the complications Mr. Berkley was talking about? Kirk's been robbed for twenty quid—don't want to think about what people would do to me for several million. I need a bodyguard or something. By the time I reach the crest of our hill, I'm convinced that the skinhead'll be lunging out of every shadow, and when a car drives past, I flatten myself against a fence, wondering if it's going to stop and unload a pack of ski-masked kidnappers. As I reach my road, I imagine that they're already in my house. Mum's alone, and Ham's a coward: He'll hide in the laundry room.

The wind's dropped, and the trees along Wormwood Drive are still, but this only adds to my unease. It seems like the whole road is holding its breath. I make my way down to our house, ears alert for any unusual sound, wishing I had my skewer. The dark windows remind me of empty eye sockets. I'm holding my breath, expecting movement at every moment. The fear intensifies as I open our front door, and I'm cringing away from the darkness inside our house, absolutely certain a man's shape will appear in the hall.

I hear a gentle movement in the kitchen and nearly jolt out of my body, and then Ham's gray form appears from the blackness, and he calmly thrusts his warm head into my legs and waits to be petted. I burst into laughter and push him off me.

The house itself is fine. There's no mystery meal waiting on the table. Television remote, sneakers, schoolbag, Mum's house keys, frying pans, the fruit bowl in the living room, Dad's papers on my desk. Each object sits in its proper place. Mum is asleep in bed. Seemingly hasn't moved all day. If anyone came in here, Blotch-Face or the skinhead or anyone else, there's no sign of it. I check every room and make sure every window is locked. I walk to the bathroom, fill a glass, and drink. Walk to my bedroom. Close my eyes.

(the host)

Slate-gray Wednesday morning. When I open my door Ham is lying outside it like a draft stopper. I shouldn't have let him sleep up here the other night. It set a dangerous precedent.

"Get downstairs," I tell him, but he refuses to budge.

The chill I noticed yesterday is back, creeping into my toes. The relief I felt when I got home last night has vanished completely, replaced by a queasy sense of doom. I know I haven't seen the last of those men. I need to check the kitchen. I take the stairs as quietly as I can and push the door open softly, using the finger of one hand.

Someone made me breakfast again. I stare at it, stomach churning. The mystery chef is back. The spread is less fancy this time: slices of processed turkey and a glass of mango juice. The meat has been arranged in a dainty fan across the blue plate. The air inside the kitchen is nearly subzero. I swear there's frost on the glass of juice and the kitchen windows. I refuse to believe this is happening. I grab the plate of turkey strips and fling it as hard as I can into the wall. It smashes in a cascade of blue shards and flopping slices of meat. I feel calmer. I stride into the hallway, grab the cordless phone, and dial nine three times.

"Hello? Police, please. I want to report a break-in. Number seven Wormwood Drive."

"Is this an emergency?" asks the operator.

"I think there might still be someone in the house."

"You think the burglar may still be on the property?"

"Please just send someone over," I say. "I'm afraid."

I hang up the phone and then walk back into the kitchen, scanning every corner twice over. I go over to the cutlery drawer and pull out my trusty skewer. I climb the stairs as quietly as I can, check the bathroom, my bedroom, Mum's room, where she's sleeping, curtains drawn, body knotted up in her duvet. As I'm closing the door to her bedroom, I hear a small, sly movement, definitely coming from the kitchen. Ham is still lying outside my room. I know he heard the noise as well. I motion for him to follow me, but he doesn't move. My skin is crawling with fear, my arms and legs itching and prickling like I'm covered in invisible insects. Every step of the stairs seems to take an age, every tiny creak of wood under my tread sounds as loud as a cannon blast.

I cross the hallway before I can think better of it, and throw the kitchen door open.

Blotch-Face is kneeling down, doing something on the floor. I realize, with a growing sense of unreality, that he's cleaning up the fragments of the plate I smashed, sweeping with a brush and dustpan. He turns to look at me. His face is long and greasy. The blotches are more like pustules; he's got worse skin than anyone at Dunbarrow High. We look at each other, him holding a brush, me clutching a skewer.

There's a cough to my left.

The skinhead is sitting at the kitchen table, staring at me. I nearly choke with horror. He must be able to move without making a sound. I grip the skewer so hard my knuckles glow white. He's smoking a roll-up, leaning his thick arms on the table.

"If you move one muscle, I'm going to stab you," I tell him, voice steady. "I mean it. The police are on their way."

He just shrugs, says nothing. Takes another drag on his cigarette.

"I've called *the police*," I tell him, voice starting to waver.

"I must confess," Blotch-Face begins, standing up, "I am confused."

"What are you doing in here?" I ask. "This is my house!"

"A thousand apologies, sir," Blotch-Face replies, bowing slightly. He's got the clear voice of a news anchor. "Have we caused some sort of offense? You appear to be . . . aggravated."

"Who are you?"

"Bloody hell," says the skinhead.

"I am the Vassal," says Blotch-Face, "a guide when the way is dark."

"What?"

"This is my colleague, the Judge," continues Blotch-Face, waving his hand at the skinhead.

"All right, boss," the skinhead says.

"Who are you?" I ask again. The skinhead looks nothing like any judge I've ever seen.

"Was my explanation inadequate? We can delve into detailed biographies if need be, but I thought it best to give a brief outline. The others should arrive in the next few days, I would imagine."

"The others?"

"The rest of your Host, sir," says Blotch-Face, the Vassal.

"You're mental. 'Host'?"

"Is this about last night?" asks the skinhead — the Judge — uneasily. If I didn't know better, I'd say he seems afraid of me. "'Cause if it is, then we're properly sorry and humble, honest. Well out of line, manifesting like we did."

"'Manifesting'?"

"We would never ordinarily presume to attend to you when you had not specifically requested us," says the Vassal. "My colleague and I were simply anxious due to a lack of instructions following the transfer."

"You ain't seem that keen on my cooking," says the Judge. "Felt like I should ask what you wanted to eat."

"'Transfer'? Please, in as few words as possible, explain who you are and what you're doing in my house."

"I think," says the Vassal, "we have presumed too much."

"Can say that again." The Judge shorts.

"You are Master Luke A. Manchett, correct?" the Vassal asks.

"Yes," I say, still gripping the skewer in case they rush me. "That's my name."

"Your father is Dr. Horatio Manchett," he continues.

"Was," I say. "He's dead. Is this about the money? Because I don't have it. The lawyers didn't give me it yet. I'm still waiting. I don't have the money."

The men exchange a puzzled look.

"We have precious little use for money these days," the Vassal says slowly. "We are part of your father's Host. I take it you don't understand the term?"

"Clearly I don't."

"We're his Host," says the Judge. "His crew, his boys, his power."

"We are—were—your father's servants," says the Vassal. "And in the event of his death, dominion over his Host transfers to the eldest living heir. Which, so far as we are aware, means you, Luke. Didn't he explain this to you?"

"He left me some papers. I haven't read them yet."

"I'm sure they will illuminate these affairs better than we," says the Vassal. "I am not an expert on matters of succession."

"I still have no idea what you're talking about," I say. "You're his servants?"

"Slaves, more like," remarks the Judge. The Vassal shoots him a look.

"My colleague and I have differing opinions on this subject," he explains, "but, yes, we are servants. We have been signed for and are now indebted to you until the event of your own death."

"So I . . . own you?"

"Yes," he says, bowing again. The Judge tips his stubbly head down, too. "We are your Host, your property to do with as you see fit."

"You're my property? There's laws against that. Dad kept *slaves*? How many?"

"The Manchett Host numbers eight souls," says the Vassal. "They are not all as . . . reasonable as the Judge and myself. However, they will present themselves when called."

"But . . . you can't have slaves! It's illegal! What am I supposed to tell Mum? Oh, yeah, we've got an extra eight people living in our house now? Don't worry about it? Dad left them to me?"

"It is illegal to keep living bodies as slaves, yes," says

the Vassal. "Unfortunately, no such laws govern the soul. Since—well, this is a delicate matter for both of us—since the Judge and I are no longer alive, there are no laws about keeping us in bonded service."

"You . . . what?"

"He really don't know?" asks the Judge. "Or is he just out to trip us?"

"You're dead," I say. "You're telling me that you're both dead. I'm talking to dead people right now."

"Well, all right," says the Judge. "Touchy subject. No need to rub it in."

"You're ghosts," I say.

"We are spirits," says the Vassal. "Your late father was a necromancer, one of those who use ancient rites to raise and bind the dead into their service."

For a moment we all stare at one another, and then I burst out laughing. It's too much. The Vassal and the Judge grin at each other in an unamused way.

"You're priceless," I say. "This is ridiculous."

There's a heavy knock on the front door. Thank you, Dunbarrow Constabulary, your timing is perfect.

"All right," I say, "you stay here. That's the police now. I'm just going to let them in, and then you can tell them about 'ancient rites' and how you're ghosts left to me by my father in his will, and then when you've told them that, the men with white coats and nets are going to come and take you both away."

"Let them in, by all means," says the Vassal. "Neither of us would presume to tell you what you may or may not do. But I do not expect they will be able to provide the aid you imagine yourself to need."

I don't bother to reply. The second these maniacs are out of my kitchen and sitting in handcuffs in the back of a van, the happier I'll be. I realize that opening the door to the police while holding a weapon tends to create a bad impression, so I hide my skewer in the umbrella stand and open the door. The policemen are sensible-looking, red cheeked and broad shouldered.

"Morning, sir. So what's the problem exactly?" the taller one asks, stepping into the hallway.

"There are two men in my kitchen," I say. "They claim they're friends of my father. They came into my house without being asked and now they won't leave."

"I see," he says. "I see."

"Please, can you ask them to leave?" I ask, "I'm on my own here."

"Let's see what's going on," he says. "I'm sure we can work this out."

He walks past me, turning awkwardly in the narrow hallway, and enters the kitchen. I breathe out with relief. His partner stays in the hall with me. Everything's going to be OK.

"The kitchen, you said?" comes his voice.

"Yes, that's right," I say.

"Nobody here, son."

"They were just there," I say. "Maybe they've gone to another room." I follow him into the kitchen and freeze up all over again. No. No. This is not happening.

The policeman is wandering vaguely toward the fridge. He looks at the rows of silver pans, at the toaster, at the shards of the blue plate sitting in the dustpan. He doesn't look at the most important things in the room, which are the two maniacs.

"Are you all right, son?" the policeman asks. "You're a bit pale."

"Almost as if he can't see us. Funny how that works," the Judge remarks.

"They're right . . . they were right here."

"I'll have a look around the other rooms," he says. "My partner will check upstairs. You just stay here and yell if you need me. Is there anyone else here?"

"My dog," I say. "My dog's upstairs. And my mum. She's . . . she's sick, though."

"Right you are," he says, and wanders into the living room.

"This isn't happening," I say.

"We tried to explain, sir," says the Vassal. "I am so sorry. I hope this is not too distressing for you."

"You . . ." I struggle for a word. "You're real ghosts. You're dead."

"In one sense," says the Vassal, "yes. In others, no."

"So you're—what?" I ask. "I'm not very—this isn't scientific at all. It's rubbish. This is nonsense."

"Science got nothing to do with it," says the Judge. "We ain't crossed over, we lingered. That's all there is to it."

"So you . . . you're a human consciousness? Something that survived death, some part of a human that isn't physical. Some kind of energy or—"

"If I may, sir," says the Vassal, "I would advise against thinking about it too much. It's never done me any good, I know that much. Better minds than yours or mine have chased their own tails for lifetimes regarding such questions."

"I'm going to need to sit down," I say.

"Sorry, lad?" says the policeman behind me.

"Oh, nothing," I reply.

"Nice dog you've got," he says. "What's his name?"

"Ham."

"Very nice dog. Anyway, son, we had a look around, and there's nobody here. Your mum's asleep, seems like. Perhaps these blokes left when they heard us come in."

There's something in his tone that makes me think he doesn't believe there was anyone in the house and is on the verge of delivering a lecture about false emergency calls, but I think he can also see I'm genuinely upset about something.

"Must have," I agree.

"Anyway," says the policeman, "I know it must have been a scare, two strangers in your house. You said they were friends of you dad?"

"They said they were," I say. "They were a bit . . . odd."

"Well, you give me their descriptions and we'll keep an eye out for them. And make sure to call if they come round again. Have they threatened you at all?"

"No," I say. "They're just really weird."

I give the policeman a fairly accurate description of the Judge and the Vassal, which to his credit he records without raising an eyebrow, and then he closes his notebook and tells me to stay safe and leaves me alone with the dead.

"Bit of a rat, ain't you?" says the Judge. "Getting all talkative with the coppers."

"Aren't you supposed to be my servant?"

"Speak me mind," he says and shrugs. One of the policemen shuts the door with a bang. Their car growls in the driveway. The ghosts look at me expectantly. I put my hands over my eyes for a few moments, but when I take them away, the ghosts are still there. The trees outside nod in the wind.

"I've got a lot of questions," I tell them after a moment. "Seems like I'll be missing school again today."

"Understandable," says the Vassal.

"Could . . . could one of you make me a cup of tea?"

o o o

Unfortunately, my burning question—what it's actually like to die—goes unanswered by the ghosts. They don't remember the actual dying bit, and apparently once you're dead, it's difficult to even realize what's happened to you. Some ghosts never work it out. Not all dead people, as the Vassal explains, are equally cognizant. Souls are as varied in death as they were in life.

"The Judge and I," he tells me, "have retained the majority of the soul, our animus. We still have a strong sense of time, self, and place. We know that we exist only in spirit. Not all of our colleagues were so lucky."

"You said there were how many in the Host?"

"Eight. A full Host of eight."

"So do they all have names like you? Are they all 'the Something'? Do you have real names?"

"Lost my proper name when I died," the Judge tells me. "Can't remember it."

"As I say, I am not an expert," the Vassal says. "From what I understand of the process, when a spirit is bound, it must be titled, given a bond name, so that the commands that are given to it cannot be resisted. There are certain positions within a Host that must always be filled. I and the Judge fill two of those roles."

"So there's always a Vassal and a Judge? Why?"

"The purpose behind our titles is explicated in the Book."

"The book?"

"The Book of Eight. An infernal tome. The Book contains the rituals of binding, and much else besides."

I keep my expression calm. I have a good idea what might be inside the little green book Dad left me.

"What are the others like?" I ask. "Why aren't they here?"

"They're shirkers," says the Judge. He's making my tea, leaning against the counter, waiting for our kettle to boil. I get a sudden rush in my head when I look at the steam condensing on the window near the kettle. The kettle really is on; it's really boiling. If this is a hallucination, it's a very good one.

"I mean, they're around and all that," the Judge continues. "They're in L.A., most of 'em."

"Los Angeles? Why?"

"Discussions was being held with your dad."

"A motion picture," says the Vassal.

"Really? I thought he died in England."

"Foreign soil, I'm afraid," says the Vassal, bowing his head.

The kettle boils, and the Judge picks it up and pours the water into my mug. If I look out of the corner of my eye, I can see the kettle floating in midair. When I look straight at him, the Judge comes slowly into focus, blurry at first before adjusting into a bright, sharp figure.

"So you were all in Los Angeles, and Dad died. Have the others just stayed there? Are they going to come back?"

"If you call them," says the Vassal, "they must come. All of them."

"How long would that take?"

"Call them right now? A day, maybe," says the Judge.

"But . . . you're ghosts. How can it take you time to go anywhere?"

"I didn't realize you was now an expert on being dead, boss. How does it take us time to go anywhere? Same as it takes you bloody time."

"Well, I'm sorry," I say.

"We enjoy certain advantages due to our incorporeal state," says the Vassal. "We can travel as the crow flies, so to speak. There are limits on where and when we may voyage, but they are not the same as those that limit the living. Walls and flames, mountains and oceans: such things pose no boundary. We are restricted by the movements of the stars, the music of the spheres. When the planets are in the wrong configuration, there is very little we can do."

"So you can't just go back to say, America, right now?"

"There is only one who can be in all places at all times, and we are not he."

"Like God?" I ask. "Are you saying there's a God?"

"That all right for you, boss?" asks the Judge, thumping the tea down at my right elbow.

"I know that there is," says the Vassal, "although this heathen may tell you otherwise."

"It don't seem very likely," says the Judge. "I been

dead near thirty years now, and I ain't got one sniff of a pearly gate."

"And by whose judgment is that counted as evidence?" asks the Vassal. "You have not been to the other side, colleague. None of us has."

"The Shepherd's been," says the Judge. "Went to the other place and came back, too. Told me about it."

The Vassal stares at the ceiling.

"The Shepherd?" I ask.

"Another of the Host," replies the Vassal finally.

"We ain't speaking ill of the dead," says the Judge.

My head is starting to hurt.

"Listen," I say, "can you all, like, take another order or whatever?"

"Of course," says the Vassal.

"Take a day off. I'm sure normal service, whatever that was, will resume . . . soon. I would think. But for now, you can all take the day off. Look around the town, or something."

"Our gratitude is boundless," the Vassal says.

The Judge gives me a crooked grin, then nods.

"You want supper made?" he asks.

"I'll get a pizza. Just, like . . . enjoy yourselves, I suppose?"

For the first time the ghosts are genuinely smiling. They bow to me and then walk out through the wall and into the garden. The Vassal keeps walking, toward the town center. The Judge lingers, as if deciding what to do. When he sees that I'm still watching, he grins before vanishing, like someone switched him off.

I take a deep breath and walk upstairs with my cup of tea. Ham is in my room, wrapped up in my duvet. He grunts anxiously.

"It's all right, boy," I say. "They've gone."

I sit and rub his head, running my fingers through his tangled fur. I don't know what to think. When the dead were here, in my kitchen, it was easier. I couldn't doubt myself, because it was happening to me. Now that they've gone, the doubts come flooding in. This is just stupid. There is no such thing as ghosts, because—well, there just isn't, no matter what the ghosts themselves might tell you.

But this has been too orderly for a hallucination. I think when you go insane, it tends to be things like hearing voices from the TV telling you to assassinate the president. I don't know how convincingly my mind could create different people, but the ghosts seemed unique and distinctive, and they were lucid, making a twisted kind of sense. Neither of them was anything like people I've met before. The Vassal doesn't seem like someone from this century, even. He's dressed like someone who really is from the past, rather than an actor playing someone from the past.

Assuming this is real, I don't know what to make of

Dad anymore. He had ghosts bound into his service? It makes sense, I suppose, of the time I saw him talking to himself: There was someone else there, someone I couldn't see. What kind of person gets himself into this? Why? Were all the ghosts on his TV show real? Does this tie in with his surprisingly large fortune? All this time, I realize I've been wondering why he left, why it was so sudden, what happened between him and Mum. Now I'm starting to wonder if there wasn't something else, something neither of us had any idea about, pulling him away.

I open the door to Mum's room and shuffle in, bowl of soup in hand. Her room is dark: moss-colored carpet, wooden tribal masks glowering from each wall. She's lying in bed, hand over her face, duvet rising and falling. I put the bowl on her bedside table.

"Mum?"

"Yes, love."

"How are you today?"

"I'll be fine . . ." She waves one hand at the soup. "Is this for me?"

"No. I just felt like carrying it up here. It's for the dog."

Mum doesn't even attempt to laugh. I wondered if she'd ask why I wasn't at school, but I don't think she even knows what time it is.

"That's very kind of you," she says. She hasn't sat up,

and I know that she wants me to go away, but I have to ask something first.

"Mum, does Dad believe in ghosts?"

"Love, please speak quietly."

"Sorry . . . but, Dad's show was . . . I mean, is, about ghosts. He's a ghost expert. Does he actually believe in them?"

"Your father is very spiritual. He read my aura when we first met."

"Did he ever talk to you about ghosts?"

"Sometimes. He said they were like . . . light, is what he said. Energy. The ones that stay around on earth, they're lost. He helped them."

Or kept them captive. Somehow I'm thinking he didn't mention that part to Mum.

"Did you ever see any in our house?" I ask. "A skinhead? A guy with a blotchy face?"

I watch her face when I mention the Vassal and the Judge, but there's no flash of recognition, no surprise. She just frowns.

"It's not really about seeing them," Mum says. "It's more about believing, being open to experiences? Being attuned to the energy of the other world. I never *saw* anything, exactly, love. I never needed to. Why are you asking now?"

"I had a look at his TV show. I wondered if you believed in it or not."

"I think it's good to keep an open mind," Mum says.

"Your father is very much in tune with the universe. He sees further than some people. Scientists think they've got all the answers. But they don't."

A few hours ago I would have strongly disagreed with this, but now I just nod.

"You should call him if you're really interested," she's saying.

"What?"

"Call him. I know he'd like to hear from you."

"Maybe."

"I know you're . . . angry. But he's not as bad a man as you think."

"All right, sure."

"Now I'm really very tired, love," she says.

"Try and eat something," I say, and leave her room. I don't know what to make of that conversation. Mum believing in ghosts isn't a surprise; she believes in anything you can find written up in a spirituality paperback. She doesn't seem to have ever seen one, let alone had a conversation with one, so it seems like Dad was keeping her in the dark about a lot of stuff.

I decide to take Ham for a walk across the fields behind our house. The hedges shiver in the wind. Ham trots around, sniffing the damp earth. Other than seagulls squabbling above a newly sloughed field, we don't see anyone, alive or dead.

o o o

I spend the afternoon alone. My secrets are multiplying. The world as I understood it to exist last night is no longer relevant. There is an afterlife. I don't have to take it on faith: I know. Mark texts me, reminding me about practice. I ignore it. I'm going to work even harder on pretending to be normal, but I don't know how right now. I watch TV, play with Ham. Mum stays in bed. The Judge and the Vassal don't come back, and I make my own supper.

In the evening I'm doing my homework and hear someone screaming.

As I push the bedroom door open, meat skewer in hand, it occurs to me that this has something to do with the ghosts and there's probably nothing I can hit with a weapon anyway.

The screams are louder now. They're definitely male, so they're not coming from Mum. The screamer gasps, shouts indistinguishable words, screams some more. Standing in the corridor outside my room, looking at the landing, I see something strange. There's a source of very bright light at the bottom of the stairs. Deep yellows and oranges pouring up from the hallway, casting huge flickering shadows around the darkened landing.

"Hello?"

I'm answered by more shrieks. I'm poised to take the stairs two at a time, then stop.

Standing in my hallway is a blackened human skeleton cloaked in flame. Scraps of flesh and hair are still clinging to the bones. There are stringy globs of fat dripping down the skeleton's ribs and legs, pooling on the floor. The skeleton turns and looks at me, raising its arms up into the air. The blackened jaw falls open and fire streams around the thing's head.

"Pater noster, qui es in caelis, sanctificetur nomen tuum!"

"Who are you?"

"Adveniat regnum tuum!" shouts the thing. The jaw swings open and shut dramatically as it shouts, like a ventriloquist's dummy. The thing is grotesque but not exactly frightening. There's something dismayed-looking about its posture, like it's as confused as I am.

"Are you always on fire?" I ask.

The skeleton bellows with pain, the noise reverberates throughout the house. Ham starts to bark in the kitchen.

"Fiat voluntas tua, sicut in caelo et in terra! Panem nostrum quotidianum da nobis hodie, et dimitte nobis debita nostra sicut et nos dimittimus debitoribus nostris!" the ghost shouts, jaw flapping madly.

"I'm six feet away from you. I can hear you fine."

"Et ne nos inducas in tentationem, sed libera nos a malo!"

"What do you want?"

"Pater noster, qui es in caelis! Sanctificetur nomen tuum! Adveniat regnum tuum!"

Ham is still barking, throwing himself against the kitchen door. I have double chemistry tomorrow morning. This isn't what I want to be dealing with. The ghost starts to walk up the stairs toward me, hobbling on charred stubs.

"Sometimes one needs a classic ghost in the retinue," says a voice from the landing behind me. "For old times' sake. It's tradition. You need a screaming skeleton in your collection if you wish to hold your head up in the company of accomplished necromancers."

"Thanks for warning me about this," I say, waving my hand at the skeleton. The Vassal raises one thin eyebrow, tugs at his cravat.

"The Heretic is . . . tiresome, I must admit. He's the eldest of all the Host. He's forgotten everything, even their reason for burning him."

"So all he does is scream?"

"He can recite several prayers in Latin. It seems to be all he managed to retain."

"Awesome."

"His animus is badly corroded. He was bound by several necromancers before your father. There is power in old spirits, but a long binding dissolves their reason."

I can see the scraps of melting skin up close now, blackened fat bubbling on his bones. I try to work out where the fire is coming from exactly, but it seems to flow out of the Heretic's bones. There is no heat cast by the ghost, but I can still smell the burning flesh. The ghost takes another halting step toward me.

"Fiat voluntas tua, sicut in caelo et in terra! Panem nostrum

quotidianum da nobis hodie, et dimitte nobis debita nostra sicut et nos dimittimus debitoribus nostris!"

"What's he talking about?"

"The Lord's Prayer," says the Vassal. "First section. He could recite it in its entirety when your father first acquired him, but even that seems beyond his abilities these days. It is a sorry sight."

The Heretic is right in front of me, empty eye sockets bubbling. He takes another step and suddenly his flesh-less face is right inside mine, and then through, the spirit lurching into my body and out the other side. I feel cold and greasy. The ghost continues to stumble onward, across the landing and through an outside wall. I can still hear him screaming.

"Can you make him shut up?" I ask. "I've got home-work to finish."

"I do not have great influence over the Heretic," says the Vassal. "Nobody does. There is not enough of his animus left to communicate with."

"So I just *wait* until he shuts up?"

"If I may, sir, a quiet word . . . I hope you will not feel me outside my bounds to say that you seem very lax on the Host."

"You're all dead. I'm still sort of getting my head around the whole 'ghosts exist' thing. How am I supposed to act, exactly?"

"Your father, sir, he understood the needs of the Host.

We need discipline, structure. There must be rules and boundaries. There used to be control, sir. You have shown no control of the Host at all. We are not usually given days off."

"I tell you all what to do, don't I? Isn't that enough?"

"For me, sir, it is. I am a loyal servant. I believe that if I must be bound, then I will bear it with the dignity befitting a gentleman. You will never need to use any discipline on me, sir. However . . . my colleagues are not all willing servants, sir. Some of them see themselves as slaves. Some, like the Heretic, have no conception of their position in the world at all."

"What are you saying?" I ask.

"The Host needs proper discipline. You need to learn the protocols, the rituals. You need to issue a general summons to every member and clearly lay out boundaries."

"I thought you were bound to me? I thought you all had to do as I said?"

"We are, sir. We are your Host, your property. However, words of command mean nothing to us if they are not backed up by spiritual power. You are a necromancer now, sir, by inheritance, if not by choice. You must fulfill your role."

"Well, Dad left me his book."

"It might be wise," says the Vassal, "to read everything that he left to you. Ordinarily I would never advise anyone to delve into the Book of Eight. I am a God-fearing man, but I fear the works of the Devil even more. However . . .

some of the Host . . . some of them are dangerous, sir. I won't speak ill —"

"—of the dead. I know."

"Quite, sir. Nevertheless. Your father's collection was the envy of many who moved in his circles. We are not some flea-market amassment of second-rate chain rattlers. We must be managed, as one would manage anything that one knew to be powerful and dangerous."

"Well, that's nice to know."

"My pleasure, sir. I would advise that you look at your father's correspondence, at the Book itself. He left them to you for a good reason."

"I will."

The Vassal nods and fades away into the darkness. He's got a point. I don't know the first thing about the Host, except for what the Vassal and the Judge have told me. If I'm going to be the boss, I need to know what I'm doing, especially if the ghosts are dangerous.

The Heretic keeps it up most of the night, bellowing out the Lord's Prayer at foghorn volume. He walks a loop around the outside of the house before marching into the kitchen, setting Ham barking again. Mum, unbelievably, sleeps soundly. I'm very tempted to pop some of her pills. I'm sitting at my desk, homework forgotten, trying to make sense of the documents Mr. Berkley gave me. You'd think if he knew he was leaving his Host to me, if this was all planned, Dad could've left me a simple sheet of paper. Bullet points, typed up on a computer.

Instead I'm faced with a kaleidoscope of bullshit. Dad's papers are a mess. They're in no particular order and don't seem designed to be read by anybody who isn't him. Some were composed on a typewriter, some written by hand. Some of the papers are yellowing and crinkled; a few are caked with something thick and dark that I can only hope is spilled chocolate milk. Most of the hand-written pages are done with an old-style dip pen and ink, with script packed into dense little rows, hundreds to each sheet, both front and back. They're completely covered in tiny columns of numbers, like the math homework from Hell. Some of the numbers, I realize, squinting closer, seem to be written backward. They're unreadable. The pages are gibberish. I sift through the pile until I come across something that isn't.

Thursday:
Ice in sink again. Poss some manifestation of guilt/loss?
Stars out last night. Equinox approaching—feel it in my bones. They're starting to strain at the bonds again, like they always do.
S & J are right, I fear. Ahlgren has to go—I'm exposed. Only way. He can turn against me at any time. But knowing I must betray him makes the taste no sweeter.

It seems like a diary entry, but without context or date there's not much I can learn. He sounds depressed. Who is Ahlgren? Why betray him? Did Dad have enemies that I don't know about? How did he die, exactly? I look for other pieces of clear prose like this, something that might follow on from here, but I can't find anything.

I put the papers to one side and pick up Dad's green book. The Book of Eight. I hold it in one hand, turning it in the glow of my desk lamp, the golden star on the cover reflecting the light. The Vassal called it an infernal tome, I remember, but it's the key to necromancy. I run one finger down the book's spine. The leather is supple and smooth to the touch. I remember that the last two times I tried to open it, the clasps were stuck, but I have a feeling that if I try them now that I've actually spoken to ghosts, something different will happen.

I pull at the clasps, expecting them to snap open, but they're stuck as fast as ever. I really ought to tear the clasps off the book. Who cares about damaging it? I need to know what's inside. I get a pair of scissors and prepare to cut the front cover away from the book's binding. The scissors are poised to cut through the green leather when I start to feel really strange.

(gray skies)

I wake up at my desk with a headache. Somehow I managed to fall asleep in my chair, at the desk. I remember reading some of Dad's notes, and then trying to open the Book of Eight, and then — this doesn't feel right. The Book sits in front of me, looking as innocent as it can. There's a pair of scissors next to it. Something happened, I'm sure of that. I just don't understand what. I try to open the Book's clasps, but they're fastened shut. I can't feel the cold of the ghosts anywhere in the house, and I decide that I'll try to pretend to be normal today.

I catch my usual bus.

The road to the school gates is dark from the night's rain. The gutters are tiny rivers, frothing downhill into greedy sewer grates. I brush past a wall that's coated in ivy, and the leaves stroke my shoulder like cold fingers.

My head feels heavy, as if at any second it'll snap off my neck and roll back down the hill. There are other kids walking the same route as me, younger students from Dunbarrow High. I swear I was never that short or high-pitched. They're scuffling about, a mass of hair gel and sports bags, pushing one another and screaming.

I can see the school gates now, aging pillars of concrete set against dark fir trees. Kids are crowding through them, pointedly avoiding Elza Moss, who's leaning against a wall, smoking. Her head is tilted upward, and she's staring at me over the heads of the crowd. I meet her gaze.

I don't know what this girl's deal is. I've known her by sight since we were twelve, and she's never shown the slightest bit of interest in me before this Tuesday. I'm tempted to keep the she's-in-love-with-me hypothesis, but it isn't ringing true. Like, what, I'm going to spend time with her and start seeing her inner beauty and then I'll slow-dance with Elza at the prom and everyone will start to clap and cry and see how empty their judgmental lives are? I don't know her, I don't want to know her, but I'm already having the strangest week of my life, and I'm not stupid. Whatever's happening to me, a freak like Elza suddenly showing an interest in my life can't be a coincidence.

"Morning," I say, smiling as best I can when confronted by her stupid haircut.

Elza blows a wall of smoke in front of her face.

"Hi," she says.

"So," I say, "hello. Hi."

"Can I help you?" she asks.

"I was just wondering why you keep staring at me. You know, like a massive weirdo?"

"I wouldn't dream of acting like a weirdo. Nor would I dream of staring at anyone. Least of all you, Luke."

"Well, if you weren't staring, what were you doing?"

"Observing."

"Observing who? Because it really looked like you were staring at me."

"I was observing interesting things." She taps her cigarette with one long nail. The ash floats to the ground, leaving an apple-red ember.

"Like what?" I ask. This conversation is pissing me off even more than I thought it would. Elza takes another draw on her cigarette. She plays with her hair, a bracelet jangling on her wrist.

"Look back down the road."

There's a group of girls walking up the hill. They wear expert mascara and lipstick, and their legs are so tan and sleek they look digitally enhanced. One of them, I realize, is Holiday Simmon. The girls walk in smooth strides, laughing about something.

Beside them lopes a monster, stumbling on long brown legs, wispy hair like white mold, wiry arms swinging as it walks. The thing is naked apart from grubby boxer shorts.

His torso and arms are crisscrossed with long scars. He walks from one girl to the next, passing through their bodies like mist. A pair of shears glint in his hand.

"What are you talking about?" I ask, hearing my voice catch.

"Yeah," she says, smirking. "No idea what I'm talking about. That's why you've gone as white as . . . well, as white as a *ghost*."

"I was up late," I say, still looking at the horrible thing.

"You know exactly what I'm talking about. I know you can see it. A man looking like that, holding a pair of shears? Out in the street? There should be panic. But instead . . ."

I look at the girls again, at the ghost.

"So you really see it?"

"I'm as surprised as you are. I'd gotten used to being the only one. No fun, is it?"

"There's just no way."

"It's happening," she says.

"You've always seen these things?"

"Look, second sight isn't even that big a deal. It can be pretty useful."

"Your whole life?"

"Let's put it this way," Elza says. "Would you rather be blind? Rather be in a wheelchair? Sure, we're different, but plenty of people are worse off than us. Some people think it's a gift, actually."

Holiday walks on, smiling, oblivious. This new ghost is the most horrible by far. What the hell was my dad getting himself into? What has he gotten me into? The ghost's skin is dark, wrinkled, and stretched over his bones. Close up, I can see that almost every inch of his skin is cut with scars, some trailing all down his body, others small dashes only an inch long. His face is like something left in a bathtub on a warm summer day. His eyes are milky, like he's got cataracts. His mouth is wide and wet, lips barely covering small white teeth. Holiday grins at her friends, and the withered face leers over her shoulder.

It occurs to me that Holiday is about to notice me and Elza, and I try to arrange my face into a normal expression, rather than a slack mask of all-consuming horror.

"I haven't seen him around before," says Elza. "He's one of yours, I assume."

"Oh, man."

Holiday has definitely seen me, and she's heading our way. I never thought there would be a situation where I didn't want to be looking at her perfect face, yet here it is. She's followed by Alice — and the ghost.

"Luke!"

"Holiday, Alice. Do you know —"

"We've met," says Elza.

"Elza," says Holiday, "great to see you!"

"Pleasure's all mine," Elza replies, and exhales another wall of smoke.

I keep flicking my gaze from the ghost to Holiday and back again. She's smiling expectantly.

"How are you?" I ask.

"Great," Holiday says. "Another exciting day at school, right?"

"Big fun," I say.

"Where were you yesterday?" she asks as I will her with all my heart to leave.

"Are those shoes, like, vintage?" Alice asks Elza.

"I suppose," Elza replies.

"Oh, you know. I had some stuff to do," I say. The ghost stands behind Holiday, opening and closing the shears. He radiates cold, like the open door of a freezer.

"They're really, like, dorky, but in a cool way," says Alice.

"Well, thanks," says Elza. "Your fake tan looks good. Really thick."

"You're so mysterious, Luke! So listen: Are you coming to my party tomorrow? I told you about that, right? I mean, I know it's like a whole week before Halloween, but this Friday was, like, the only time my parents would let me do it, with exams and stuff, oh, and yeah, I decided it's going to be full costumes." Holiday finally takes a breath. "You . . . should come too, Elza."

"Sure thing," I say. I feel queasy.

"Wouldn't be seen anywhere else," says Elza.

"How do you know Luke?" Holiday asks Elza.

"I don't, really," Elza says. "He was asking for a cigarette."

"I didn't think you smoked," Holiday says to me with a frown.

"Er . . . not usually," I say. "Only on special occasions."

"What's the occasion?" Holiday asks.

"It's Thursday?"

Nobody says anything in response to this. Alice is giving me and Elza the kind of look you'd usually reserve for someone you saw eating a slug in the street.

"Well . . . we're going to be late," says Holiday with slightly forced casualness. She's right: The flow of students around us has dwindled to a trickle of stragglers. "Let me give you my number? I'll let you know about the party tomorrow?"

"I'd . . . like that. Yeah. Thanks," I say.

So I exchange numbers with my dream girl, while Elza and Alice face each other down like panthers about to lunge, and the scarred ghost opens and closes his mouth, breathing wetly. I notice his tongue is missing. Holiday and Alice take their leave and stride away. The ghost stays with me and Elza, picking at its teeth with the shears.

"Who are you?" I ask it when they're out of earshot.

It says nothing. Gulps. Looks at me with milky eyes.

"Where's the Vassal?"

The ghost grins and then fades away, becoming

thinner and fainter, until only the shears are left, like a rusting Cheshire smile.

"Gosh," says Elza. "Are your ghosts always that charming?"

"I've never met that one before. I don't know how you manage to make jokes—"

"I got used to it early on. I've always been this way; I never changed like you did. Listen, you need to get better at acting, fast. You spent the entire time looking like you'd just pissed yourself."

"This is all a bit of a shock, you know?"

"Oh, I feel the same. You've got yourself some ugly spirits, Luke. That was not a sight I wanted to see at eight fifty-five on a Thursday morning."

"I'm really sorry."

"I'm sorry, too," she says. "I'm guessing your dad just died, right?"

"How do you . . . yeah. Don't worry. We weren't close."

Elza flicks her cigarette butt into the gutter. The water carries it away from us. I watch as it rushes down the street and vanishes into a sewer grate.

"I think we've got a lot to talk about," she says.

"I agree."

"No time like the present," Elza says. She looks up at the clouded sky. "It probably won't rain in the next hour or so. Let's skip homeroom and take a walk."

○ ○ ○

To my surprise Elza leads me through the school gates, but instead of heading up the hill to the front yard, she turns right, staying close to the wall, pushes her way through a close copse of pine trees, and ducks under a half-collapsed wire fence. Neither of us says anything. This feels like a condensed version of everything that's happened to me this week. I thought my life would be taking the obvious path, to a place I knew, and instead I've been pulled off into the dark undergrowth. I follow Elza into an overgrown garden of some sort that doesn't look much different from the school grounds we just left: thigh-high grass, enormous dripping fir trees. Elza moves past the trees, and I follow her into an open space, a flat lawn studded with crumbling stone blocks. A stone angel looks down at us with a dismayed expression, its head half hooded by a froth of yellow lichen.

"I thought this would be appropriate," Elza says. "Do you like it?"

"I'm hanging out with a goth in a graveyard."

If Kirk and Mark get wind of this . . .

"It's the far end of Saint Jude's," she says. "Most people don't know about that route out of school. I've been coming down here at lunch for years. And I'm not a goth. I'm a free thinker."

"If the combat boot fits . . ."

"I don't have to help you," she says mildly.

"How are you going to help me, exactly? I mean, what are you? Are you a necromancer, too, or something?"

"A necromancer? Not at all. I think there might be witch blood somewhere in my family, but that's not unusual. I was born with second sight. That's it, really. So when did you sign for the Manchett Host?"

She sits at the base of the angel statue and starts rolling another cigarette. Some pigeons take off from the tree above us, slapping their wings through the branches and vanishing into the sky. I haven't been able to talk with Mum about what's been happening, or with my mates, or Holiday . . . And the idea of speaking to a teacher about Dad and the ghosts is so ludicrous, it never even crossed my mind until now. And here I am, laying out my deepest secrets with a girl I've barely said three words to before today.

"Monday afternoon. His solicitor . . . he said I'd inherit everything. There's money, too, he told me. That's what I wanted. He didn't mention the part about the Host. How do you know about that?"

"It should be apparent," she says, lighting up, "that I'm not stupid. I've had my eye on you for a while, because really, how common a name is Manchett? So I heard your father had died and then when I saw you in the schoolyard, I felt this really strong spike of power coming from you. Plus, then the town ghosts started going to ground—"

"Town ghosts?"

"People die all the time, Luke. Try to keep up. There are ghosts everywhere. Dunbarrow's an old town. It was here before the Romans came. We've got suicides, murder victims, plague victims, crib deaths, sweet old granny ghosts, headless horsemen . . . They're all part of Dunbarrow. They'll always be here. In general they're harmless. Worst they do is knock on your windows at night. Poltergeist stuff. Make a chair float of its own accord."

"All totally normal and harmless."

"Well. It's a matter of perspective. But bound ghosts, spirits like the ones that make up your Host, they're different. Your dad never explained any of this?"

She's looking at me the same way she looks at people when they mispronounce words in English class.

"I haven't seen him for ten years. I haven't even had a birthday card for the past three. So no, he never explained any of this."

"OK. Sorry. But the Host, those spirits are bound to you. The bond gives you, their necromancer, power, but it also — this is very important — it also gives them power. It works both ways, and half a necromancer's job is making sure his ghosts are under tight enough control that power is no use to them."

"Being enslaved makes them stronger?"

"It's not a concrete science. None of this is remotely a science. But yes, usually. For the Host, your life force, it's a kind of anchor to Liveside. They can influence the living world to a greater degree than free spirits ever could."

"Liveside?"

"Here." Elza waves her hand, cigarette leaving a sketch of smoke. "This is Liveside. Sorry, I post a lot on Second Sight Support forums, so I know the terms. It's good to talk to other people who know what you go through every day. Liveside and Deadside are forums jargon. I don't know what real necromancers call it. Deadside is . . . not easy to describe from what I can gather. It's formless mist, a labyrinth, a void, a chaos. It's not surprising so many spirits choose to stay here."

"OK. Spirits in a Host are more powerful than normal ghosts. They said that themselves."

"They were right. But you shouldn't trust anything they tell you. Dead people are like living people: They lie a lot, they're selfish. And then in other important ways they're nothing like us at all."

I think of the Heretic, stumbling through my hallway as everlasting fire boiled out of his bones. I think of the Judge and the Vassal and whoever the hell that scarred, tongueless guy with the shears was. I shudder.

"Yeah. You could say that."

"I don't know how to put this, Luke, but you're in a lot of trouble."

"I know."

"No, I mean *really*. A lot of trouble. You, me, the entire

town. You've had these things for three days, and you've just been letting them do as they please, haven't you? Don't frown at me. You have."

"All right, yeah," I say, "but—"

"It's not all right. It's very dangerous. They're not on your side. As soon as they realize you're not in control, that there's nothing to be afraid of, they'll turn on you. You need to be a ruler. You've been the heir to the throne your whole life and not known it, and I know you never asked for this, but you have to rule them."

"How?"

"I don't know."

Elza blows smoke out of both nostrils.

"You don't know?"

"I don't know!" she says, making a face like the words taste sour. "I'm not an expert on Hosts. I know they're dangerous. I know your dad had a full set of eight, which is extra powerful and bad. Second sight isn't very common, and some of us are oddballs, but we're not . . . I mean, your dad was deep into something not many people are into. Necromancy, Luke, I mean, raising spirits from the dead, binding them to your own soul. It's the blackest of black magic, I'm talking deals with the Devil here."

"Er—"

"Sorry to be so blunt. Do you know what demons are?"

"Oh, man . . . was that what the guy with the shears was?"

"They're spirits that were never alive at all. They come from the deepest parts of Deadside. Unfortunately, I think the man with the shears was human once. Who knows what he did in life to look like that in spirit? But demons don't even look *that* human, I'm told."

"Dad owned demons?"

"There are rumors to that effect, yes. I've never wanted to see one. But if we're unlucky, we'll both get the chance."

"So what do we do?" I ask.

"Well. I've heard that there's a book. It's old — supposedly the first copies were written in Babylon thousands of years ago. It tells you all about the dark arts, how to raise the dead —"

"Yeah, the Book of Eight. I've got it on my desk at home."

There's no small pleasure in telling Elza something she doesn't know. She looks like she's about to choke.

"You've got the Book of Eight and you didn't mention it?"

"I can't read it," I say.

"Is it in another language, then, or —?"

"No, I mean I literally can't open the book to read it. It's clasped shut. I've tried a few times and there's just no way. It's locked."

"All right," Elza says. "Is there anything else you haven't mentioned?"

"Dad left me a big bunch of his papers. I can't read most of those either. They're in code."

"He didn't make this easy on you, did he? All right, that's a start. A much better start than I expected, actually. The actual Book of Eight . . ."

"So why are you even helping me? What do you get from this?"

"Well. I hate to heap disaster upon disaster, Luke, but this is just about the worst time of year you could've inherited these things. Hosts are always powerful, but bound spirits become exponentially more dangerous during certain days of the year. Of which Halloween is a major one. If they're planning to break free of your control—and I'm certain they are—they'll do it then. It's Thursday today, and next Friday is Halloween. If they break free, there's no telling what they might do to Dunbarrow. Some of the things I've read . . . These spirits can develop *appetites*. I want to do everything I can to stop them from getting loose."

"Right. Great."

The Vassal never mentioned that particular detail to me.

"What?"

"Luckily we've only got a half day of school tomorrow, so you're going to bring everything—the Book, everything—up to my house as soon as possible. And then we're going to work on this thing until we find a way of banishing your Host, bringing it to heel, whatever we find. We've got next week off for half-term so we've got time."

"Why your house?"

"I've got hazel charms around my street, and around my house especially. Keeps the uninvited dead away. I mean, we can go to your place if you want them to hear every word we say."

"Point taken."

"In fact, forget about school today. Go and get your stuff right now and come to my house. Number 19, Towen Crescent. This is more important than school."

"All right," I say. "One thing, though."

"What?"

"We should probably be careful about being seen in Dunbarrow together. You know, if the Host is dangerous. You could be in danger."

"I already am. Your starved spirit saw us talking. Don't worry about me. I've got some tricks up my sleeve." Elza gestures at the small stone hanging from her necklace but doesn't explain further.

"Still, though. We should just be careful."

"Wait," Elza says. "Is this in case Holiday Simmon or Mark Ellsmith sees us together?"

"No, I just think —"

"Oh, whatever, just say it. I know nobody likes me. I don't like any of you either."

"It's not that," I say, though it is, a bit. I worked hard to get where I am.

"I've got a reputation to uphold as well, you know. What'll people say if they see me with a boy from the rugby team? They'll revoke my platinum library card. Look, we've got just over a week to find a way of rescuing you from what might possibly be a fate worse than death. I would not want to be in your shoes when your Host breaks its bonds and turns on you. So let's worry about that, no? Once we're safely past Halloween, you and I never have to speak again, and you can go back to pretending 'who's in and who's out' actually matters."

I can't really think of anything to say to that, so I just nod. Elza finishes her cigarette and stamps it out in the long grass. A fresh drizzle has started to fall from the darkening sky, drops arriving in furtive gangs, darkening the shoulders of Elza's jacket. I pull my own coat tighter. Elza seems like she's about to say something else, then doesn't. I look around us, at the wide still trees, the old graves.

When I get home, I discover every light in my house is on, blazing out against the dim morning. The windows on each side of the front door are like orange eyes. When

I touch the doorknob, I feel the chill of the dead. I move into the house. Downstairs is empty: no ghosts, only Ham, hiding in his crate in the laundry room. Standing in the kitchen, shivering even in a coat, I hear a snatch of conversation coming from the room above me.

"Mum? Mum!"

I'm up the stairs, across the landing, into Mum's room. I come to a halt, heart thumping. Mum is asleep, and there are two men sitting at each side of her bed. On the left-hand side sits the scarred man I saw outside school, nearly naked, wearing boxer shorts. He rolls his white eyes at me. The shears lie on the floor by his chair. The second man is leaning over Mum, looking into her face. Neither is reflected in the mirror attached to the wardrobe.

"What are you doing in here?" I ask, braver than I feel.

The second man, the ghost I don't recognize, stands.

He's taller than the others, older-looking, too, dressed in a black three-piece suit. His shoes are beetle-shell shiny, and he wears a white shirt that's fastened at the throat with a strange silver pin. His face looks like a waxwork, with a drooping nose and overripe lips. His hair and beard are full and bushy, granite-gray with hints of white. His hair hangs over his shoulders in a thick mane. He's wearing round, dark-tinted glasses and a black hat. He looks like an acid casualty dressed up as an undertaker.

"Who are you?"

"I am bonded as the Shepherd." The ghost dips his

gray-haired head in the shallowest bow I've ever seen. "This is my colleague, the Prisoner." He indicates the scarred ghost with a wave. "You are presumably Luke Archibald Manchett, and we find ourselves in your service."

"Did I say you could be in here?"

"We were merely keeping vigil over your mother." The Shepherd's mouth twists into a small sour smile. "She appears to be infirm. I'm curious as to the nature of her affliction."

"Get away from her. Now."

"As you wish."

The ghosts stand and move closer to me. I look into their eyes and try not to flinch. The Prisoner opens his mouth and closes it with a chewing-gum noise.

"Where *is* your tongue?" I ask.

"It was cut out," says the Shepherd, "by his father, I believe."

"Sorry to hear that."

"I understand he's grown used to it."

The Prisoner shrugs and then fades into nothingness. The Shepherd remains in the room, hands clasped behind his back, like he's waiting for something to happen. Rain taps at the window. Mum is sitting up, looking at me, I realize with a sudden jolt. She's awake. Did she hear me talking to the ghosts?

"Luke?"

"I was just . . ." I struggle to find a coherent excuse.

"I'm really very tired, love," she says. "This head of mine. It's not letting up."

"Sorry, I just . . . wondered if you wanted—"

"That's nice of you," Mum says, in a tone that suggests she'd like me to leave now. She's lying back down. The Shepherd is looking at her with an expression that's impossible to read. I'm thinking of what Elza said. *Blackest of black magic . . . Who knows what he did in life to look like that in spirit?* Whoever these new ghosts are, whoever they were, they're dangerous. Even seeing them here like this, with Mum asleep, it's a threat. I have to be in control, I have to rule. They know I've got the Book of Eight. They don't know I can't read it and don't have a clue what it says. I can't let them know.

"I'll go downstairs," I say to Mum, but I look at the Shepherd as I say it so he knows I'm talking to him as well. I say it big and brave, like I'm talking to an underling, some underclassman nobody trying out for the rugby team. The Shepherd meets my gaze for a moment—at least I think he does; it's hard to tell where he's looking through the dark glasses—and then inclines his bearded head and nods.

Ham's in the kitchen, drinking from his water bowl, but when he sees me come in with the ghost, he backs off into the laundry room, ears flattened against his head. The Shepherd watches Ham leave and says nothing. I ignore both of them, move around the kitchen, put some pasta on to boil. My hands tremble as I cut vegetables. The rain is coming down outside, heavy and relentless, a steady dull wash that tells me the storm clouds aren't going anywhere. The Shepherd sits at the kitchen table, hands resting on the wood in front of him. They're big hands, with long fingers and a cobwebby wisp of white hair sprouting from each knuckle. He waits as I make my food. He has the air of someone who knows how to wait.

"So you're sixteen," the ghost says as I sit down with my lunch.

"Yeah," I say.

"Strange, how time moves. It seems not so long ago that you were a raw little scrap of a thing, held in a crib. Yes," he says, in response to my obvious surprise, "I knew you when you were young. We've met on several occasions, although you weren't aware of it at the time."

"You were with Dad awhile then," I say.

"I am his oldest servant. His left hand."

"Why are you called the Shepherd?"

"It is customary for a Host to be headed by a Shepherd. An ancient title. It seems odd that you would not be aware of this."

"Just making conversation," I say.

I fork down some food, not really tasting it.

"I saw that you were in possession of your father's copy of the Book," the Shepherd says.

"It's upstairs," I say. "Why?"

"Horatio naturally entrusted me with certain information and kept other aspects of his life and work from me. The education and training of his heir was one of the aspects I had little influence over. However, I presume you were educated in the rudiments of the art of necromancy? The Book of Eight is not, after all, something to be trifled with."

"Yeah, of course. I've got necromancy up to my eyeballs. Live and breathe it. Know the Book back to front. Definitely wouldn't want to step out of line if I was a ghost bound to Luke Manchett. I'd come down hard on anything like that."

"You know, of course, that the Book of Eight is considered to be infinite in length. It would not be possible for someone to 'know it back to front.' Even the most experienced necromancers will find pages they have never seen before."

"Figure of speech," I say, waving my hand.

"As you say."

"I am a necromancer. I'm legit. Are you trying to say I don't look like a necromancer?"

"Of course not, Luke. You carry yourself with all the dignity befitting a man of such ancient knowledge and arcane discipline. I and my colleagues have merely noted that you have been rather lax in terms of the bindings and restrictions you have placed on us."

"It's a new era, you know? I don't see why necromancy has to be all, like, black robes and blood sacrifices. Forget what you think you know. I'm hoping we're all going to be friends."

What am I even saying? I'm so scared of this ghost that my mouth is just moving and words are coming out. The Shepherd snorts and sits up straighter in his chair.

"We are not your friends. We are bound to you. It is a rather different proposition."

"All right, if you insist. I just wanted us to get along."

"Interesting that such a thing interests you at all."

"I'm not Dad."

"Issue a general summons to your Host," the Shepherd says.

"Why?"

"I want to see you do it."

"I don't want to. And to be honest, I don't appreciate being told what to do."

"Issue a general summons. You don't even know what position your hands should be in, do you? Horatio . . . that old devil. He didn't teach you a thing, did he?"

The Shepherd has his sly smile back.

"He taught me enough."

"Luke." The Shepherd holds his hands out, as if to beg from me. There are weird spiky stars tattooed on the palms. I think he wants me to see them, as if they're supposed to mean something to me. "In life I was a great necromancer. My Host was the terror of the world. I have forgotten more pages of the Book than most men have ever seen. If you hoped to bluff me, you could not have picked a worse approach. You have no mastery of the dark arts."

"No," I say, fumbling for something, "I—"

"There is no shame in it. You're a young man, not without wit or drive, and I appreciate the attempt at cunning you have shown in our dealings today. But you are no necromancer. You cannot manage a Host. You do not even want to manage a Host."

"So what are you suggesting?"

"Free us. Let us go. Do not live your life burdened by your father's sins."

I don't know what to say. This has to be a trick. Elza said they'd try and break free. I know this ghost is dangerous, I can feel it in my marrow, like he's radioactive. Maybe he's still afraid of me, a little? He's right, I don't want a Host. All I wanted was four million pounds, properties, DVD sales . . . I didn't want this at all. I want them gone. What's the harm in that, if I can just let them go? Surely everyone gets what they want?

"It's that easy?"

"Oh, certainly Luke. It's very easy. As easy as signing for us in the first place. We could do it right now. You don't want a Host, Luke. You want a normal, happy life. You don't want to follow in your father's footsteps, believe me. Let us go, and this can end here."

It can't be this easy. I need to be careful.

"Well—"

"All that's required," the Shepherd continues, flashing a gray rank of teeth, "is a suitable mark of relinquishment in the Book of Eight. Fortunately your copy is right here."

His tattooed hands move over the surface of the table, and there's a flicker, like someone changed the reel in a film I'm watching. The green book is on the table, just in front of the Shepherd. The cover's eight-pointed star gleams in the glare from the light fixture overhead.

"A simple spot of blood," he's saying, "and we leave your life, your home, forever."

He strokes the Book, and the clasps spring off the cover without being touched. The yellow pages move as if blown in a gale, and the Book falls open right in the middle. He pushes it toward me. I put my hand on it, spin it around to have a look.

There are no words on these pages. The double spread is covered in a psychedelic pattern of concentric circles and spirals, all of which look hand drawn, and they seem to be moving as I look at them. I feel like every time I focus on one part of the design, another part of the page will change. I'm getting a headache.

"This will free you?" I'm saying.

"Indeed, Luke. A general declaration of freedom from bond, for all eight spirits."

"Really. Wow."

The circles seem to have . . . depth, somehow, like there's more to this page than just the page. If I keep looking at it, I'll be able to see what it is. There are pages beyond the page. There are hundreds of them. Millions of circles.

"Quite something, isn't it?" the Shepherd asks.

"It's amazing."

My ears are ringing, roaring. I can feel my blood flowing.

All I can really look at now is the circles.

My hand is moving toward something, I realize it's my fork.

"A single drop is all we need," the Shepherd says. He sounds like he's talking to me from down a long tunnel. His voice echoes.

I push the fork into the ball of my thumb. There's a nice flush of red. It doesn't remotely hurt. When I look up at the Shepherd, I can still see the circles and spirals, weaving over his suit and face.

They're everywhere.

My hand is moving toward the book.

"You're doing the right thing," the ghost says.

My thumb is poised over the center of the design.

I'm about to press down.

There's an explosion of noise, and I'm thrown side-ways, landing hard on the floor. The rushing in my ears is gone. My thumb is fizzing with pain, blood running down onto the palm of my hand. Ham stands over me, barking and barking. The Shepherd looms above us.

"Restrain this beast, and seal the declaration of release," he says.

"Sir."

"Stay out of this!" the Shepherd yells, turning his head to look at someone else.

The Vassal is standing in the doorway of the kitchen.

"I can't recommend you do this," he says over Ham's barks.

"I was going to release you," I tell the Vassal, though I'm not sure anymore why it seemed like such a good idea.

"It's for the best," the Shepherd says.

"For you, perhaps," replies the Vassal. "He has not wronged you. He is guilty of no crime."

"You livestock," spits the Shepherd, "you servile, mewling animal!"

"A Host is unable to harm its master," the Vassal tells me. "It is at the heart of our bond. He may not kill you, but if you release him, you remove that deepest taboo, and he will stop your heart with a word."

"Why?" I ask the Shepherd. "Don't you want to be free?"

"Revenge," the Vassal says. "He is consumed by it."

The Shepherd kneels beside me and Ham. His glasses catch the light, two silver moons. Ham shrinks back but doesn't run. I can see blue veins under the ghost's skin. The wrinkles by his mouth shift as he speaks.

"You father defiled my tomb. In life I was the greatest necromancer the world has known. He bound me— bound me—and used me as *his Shepherd*. I do not forget. I do not forgive. I swore to rend his body and torment his soul, and, denied that small pleasure, I must turn to his heir."

"I've done nothing to you."

"Listen," the Shepherd says. He removes his glasses. His eyes are black and wet, with no whites to them at all, black like the eyes of a goat or raven. "Listen to me, child. I have voyaged to the dark lands of the dead. I have seen things there that our words cannot describe. There can still be some small mercy for you, if you release me this very day."

"I'm not scared of you."

"You are a poor liar. Worse even than your father."

The bottomless black eyes are a finger's length from mine.

"This isn't over," he says. "This is the beginning."

The Shepherd is gone.

"You could have warned me," I say to the Vassal.

"I was afraid."

"Of him?"

"He was the most terrible man in the world while he breathed, and he became worse for every day he spent beyond the veil. I fear him very much, sir."

"Thanks for saving me," I say. "You and Ham."

"I know you did not ask for such a burden as we. The father is not the son."

"So he can't kill me?"

"He may not. Without explicit instruction, however, we may allow harm to come to you, and many of the Host would do so."

"What will he do on Halloween?"

"I do not know, sir. The Shepherd has some stratagem, I am certain. He always does. Look to the Book of Eight."

"I don't know how! I can't even open it."

"And yet you must, sir. And yet you must."

I look at the Book, now closed, sitting on our dining table as if it were any old book, nothing to take notice of. My stomach is churning. The Vassal has his head turned away from me, frowning, as if he's listening to something happening in another room.

"I must go," he says suddenly. "They will not forgive me for this."

"I'm glad you helped me."

"I hope I have cause to be glad of it as well, sir."

The Vassal gives a small bow and vanishes.

I don't go to Elza's house. I don't know what to do. The Book of Eight sits on the table, and I'm afraid to go anywhere near it. I'm afraid to even try to open it. I keep thinking about the circles flowing out of the pages, the way they covered the walls and the Shepherd's face. The Book is a monster, and the Host wants me dead. I can't leave Mum and Ham here without me. The afternoon darkens into evening. The trees that surround the house take on the shape of whispering giants. Ham won't settle and paces the kitchen all night. I think of waking Mum, telling her we need to leave, but I don't know how I'd get her to believe me, and I don't know where we could go that they wouldn't follow. By one in the morning I can't keep myself awake any longer. I climb into bed with my clothes on and lie still, listening for any hint of the Host returning. The wind whispers at the cracks in my window frame. Outside, the fields are cold and dark. Animals shiver in their burrows, dreaming bleak dreams of running and dying.

(echoes and relics)

When I wake up on Friday morning, I hear a man's voice coming from Mum's room. I run in to her and find there's a crude star drawn in black paint above her headboard: a slashed, spiky rune that takes up half the wall — the same symbol the Shepherd had tattooed on his palms. She's lying still and straight, bedsheets covering her body up to her neck. Her hair is tucked behind her ears. She looks peaceful. I can't tell if she's breathing or not. The voice I could hear was her CD player, a man's cheerful voice reciting some self-esteem exercise.

"Only you have to power to effect lasting personal change," the CD player says to itself.

"Mum!" I yell.

I cross the room in what feels like one step.

"Look at yourself in the mirror. What do you see?"

I shake her by the shoulders. She doesn't wake. I can't find her pulse, but her arm feels warm. I hold a hand mirror to her face, and she breathes the faintest film of fog over it. She's alive, then, whatever they did to her. I sit on the floor beside her bed. I should've said something to her, but I don't know what I could have told her. She believes in the spirit world as an abstract place full of energy and good vibes rather than as a malicious storm of darkness. How would I have explained the Prisoner or the Shepherd to her? I should call an ambulance . . . and then what? They'll give her a CAT scan? Put her on a drip and wait for her to wake up? I'll get put in foster care. I can't think of people who'll be less responsive to my stories about evil spirits than a gang of paramedics and social workers. I'm on my own. Whatever the Host has done to her, I have to deal with it.

"Do you see someone who's confident and powerful? Most of us don't."

I turn the CD player off so hard that the power button breaks. I leave her room, shut the door, and walk out onto the landing. I feel like the ghosts must be watching me, watching Mum, waiting to see what I'll do.

"Show yourselves!" I'm shouting. "Come out! What have you done to her? Don't hide from me! Show yourselves!"

Nothing. What I'll do if the ghosts do appear I have no clue.

"Don't make me wait!"

There's a sharp rapping at the front door. My spine fizzes, like it's been filled with electrified ice. My throat tightens. Ham starts to yelp in the kitchen.

"Who is that?"

Whatever's at the front door doesn't answer. Peering down the stairway into the hall, I can see a dark human shape, silhouetted beyond the door's pane of rippled glass. I've met five of the eight ghosts.

What's waiting beyond the door?

Did Dad really summon a demon?

There's another flurry of knocks. I make my way down the stairs, one step at a time. The figure outside grows closer but no clearer. The morning is overcast, the dim light coming into the hallway almost feels like dusk. Ham yowls behind the kitchen door. I realize I left my meat skewer up in my bedroom, although what good it would do I don't know.

My hand closes around the doorknob.

I take a breath.

I swing the front door open.

"Elza?"

"Are you all right?" she asks. "You look terrified."

"What are you—"

"I waited for you all of yesterday. You were supposed to come to my place? What's going on? Is your Host here?"

There's a light drizzle falling. She's wearing muddy

combat boots and a black wool peacoat that looks like it was cut for someone twice her size. She gives me an impatient look.

"Am I talking to myself? Look, my hair's getting wet. I'm coming inside."

Elza pushes past me into the hallway.

"I'm sorry," I say. "There have been, like, developments. . . . I haven't been able to come by. I didn't get your . . . how do you even know where I live?"

"Internet," she snaps. "Your house feels haunted. Incredibly haunted. I don't even like standing in the hallway. What happened?"

"Elza, I don't know how safe it is for you to be here."

"Nor do I. I thought this would keep me straight, it usually does"—she holds up the stone that she wears around her neck—"but feeling what it's like in your house, I don't know."

"What is that?"

"Wyrdstone. Has a naturally occurring hole. They're very rare. Druids used them to ward off evil spirits. Is that your dog I can hear in the kitchen?"

"Yeah . . ."

"Well, are you going to let it out?"

I lead her down the hallway and open the kitchen door. Ham leaps up at me, dragging his paws down the front of my pants.

"Big dog," Elza says, taking a step back.

"He's a deerhound. Down, boy. Calm down."

"Hmm. I was expecting a terrier or something. Hello," she says to Ham. She grabs his head and starts rubbing the skin behind his ears. He grumbles with joy. I walk into the kitchen, not sure what I'm going to do. What does Elza want? Can she actually help me? What am I going to do about Mum? She's lying above us right now, trapped in sleep.

"So this is it," Elza says behind me. I turn around. She's still petting Ham, but she's looking at the kitchen table, at the Book of Eight.

"Dad's legacy," I say.

"Now, your dog is bigger than I was imagining. And yet the fabled book is smaller. It's practically pocket-size."

She pushes Ham away and picks up the Book. Her fingers start to work at the clasps.

"Elza, I'm not sure if—"

"What's wrong?" she says.

"It's just the book is delicate and—"

"No, what happened? You look completely hollowed out. You look like someone died."

"It's Mum. The Host tried to take over yesterday afternoon. This ghost, the Shepherd, he tried to trick me and kill me. Then they did something to her. . . . She won't wake up."

"Oh, Luke . . . is she—?"

"No. She's alive. Look, I'll show you."

I take Elza upstairs, with Ham trotting along behind us. I let us all into Mum's room. It's exactly as I left it: Mum's tribal masks still hanging on the walls, her books about ley lines and communication with angels still on her bookshelf. There's a single slipper on the floor, halfway between the bed and the doorway. It looks lost.

Elza steps past me and moves toward the bed, looking at the enormous spiky star on the far wall. She's still wearing her boots, and they leave small dabs of mud on the carpet. She looks up at the ceiling, then kneels down and lifts the sheets on Mum's bed, looking into the space beneath it.

"What are you doing?" I ask.

"Looking to see where the spell is coming from. I imagine it's produced by the obvious mark on the wall, but you never know. There's nothing under here, anyway."

"Can we remove the mark?"

"I don't think so. I mean, we could try, but you won't be able to wash it off. A mark like that, it's more than paint. Maybe if we took the wall out with a crowbar. But even then . . . I'd be worried about your mum if we did. It might make things worse."

"Do you know how to break the spell?" I think it's a measure of how much my life has changed that it doesn't even sound like a stupid question anymore.

"No," Elza says, "not really. When it comes to

magic, I'm like someone who can turn a TV on but doesn't know how to build one. I have a wyrdstone and I can make hazel charms, but I don't know why they work. I just know they do."

"So you can't—"

"I can't wake your mum up, Luke. I'm sorry. I wouldn't know how to start."

Ham is standing beside Mum's bed, sniffing eagerly. He starts to nuzzle at her pillows and whine. I look away. My eyes feel hot and swollen.

Elza looks at my face, frowning. I don't want her to see any of this.

"Are you all right?"

"I'm fine."

"You're not. You're about to cry."

To my surprise Elza steps forward and wraps me in a tight hug. She smells of cigarettes. I rest my chin on the rough, damp wool of her coat. I barely knew her two days ago, and here we are, embracing. Even with my eyes blurred by tears I start to smile. I don't know what Holiday would make of this. After a few moments, Elza slaps me hard on the back and lets me go.

"I think that's how you rugby boys handle emotions, right? Lots of backslaps? Someone downs a beer? I didn't bring any cans with me, unfortunately."

"That's more or less it," I say, dabbing at my eyes.

"I don't want to spend any longer here than we have

to," she's saying. "This house isn't secure, and I don't think I can make it safe for us to work in. I still think you should come across to my house in Towen Crescent. Bring your beast as well."

"Wait, what? I'm not leaving."

"Luke, I get that you're very worried about your mum. I'm worried, too. But realistically, the best chance you have of doing anything for her is not calling a doctor, and it's not sitting up every night next to her bed until Halloween. The best thing we can do is try to get the Book of Eight open and find out what's inside. Find something that'll help us."

"I don't even know if I want to open that book. The Shepherd, when he opened it up, the stuff I saw inside was —"

"Well, I don't think we have another choice. And I'm not staying here — they're probably listening to every word I'm saying. My house is warded with hazel charms, so uninvited spirits can't enter. The best thing you can do now is get everything your dad left you and bring it to my house immediately."

"I can't just leave Mum here."

"Then she'll die," Elza says. Her eyes are muddy green, the irises wide and dark. Her gaze doesn't leave mine. "She'll die. You'll die once they find a way to break their bonds. We all might. But today she's alive, which suggests to me that if they were going to kill her, they already would've done it. She's your blood, your mother, and that can be important for some types of magic. I think your ghosts have some plan for her, and the sooner we find a way to stop them, the safer she'll be. I can keep your book at my house without raising suspicion, but even if we put your mum in a wheelbarrow or something and take her over there, the first thing my parents are going to ask is 'Why is there a woman in a coma lying in our spare room?' and I won't have an answer for them. She'll be off to the hospital before you know it, and hospitals aren't good places. Lots of people die there, they'll be full of spirits. The walls between here and Deadside will be thin. Bad place to be come Halloween. The best thing you can do for her is leave her. Come with me. Now."

I look at Mum, at her bronze hair, her lined, worried-looking forehead, the sheets dipping and raising ever so gently as she breathes in her sleep. Ham butts at her pillows. They could come back and kill her right now and I wouldn't be able to stop them. I have to learn to use the Book. Just because I'm leaving doesn't mean I won't come back.

I drag my gaze away from Mum and look at Elza, thin-lipped, arms folded, a wet strand of hair trailing over her face.

"Well?" she asks.

"All right. We'll try this your way."

"Good," she says. "Because, honestly, I need to get out of this house right now. I feel like I've got a nosebleed in a shark tank."

I go into my bedroom, grab all of Dad's papers, and shove them back into the document wallet Mr. Berkley gave me. Elza is in the hallway with the door open, holding the Book of Eight in one hand and Ham's leash in the other. I don't know how long this is going to take, and I can't leave him here with nobody to feed him.

I notice the raincoat I wore to Berkley's office hanging in the hallway, and it nudges at my memory. So many things have happened since Monday afternoon, and I'd forgotten some details. I dip into the inside pocket and bring out the metal case full of Dad's rings.

"What do you make of this?" I ask Elza.

"We've got company," she says, ignoring me. She gestures out through the open door.

I put the rings in my backpack, alongside my keys. I look out through the door, to where she's pointing. My stomach lurches. A woman, dressed all in white, stands at the end of our driveway with her back to us. She's still as a stone, despite the rain, and I notice her dress doesn't move as the wind blows.

"You know that ghost?" Elza asks.

"New to me," I say. Hopefully she's come to apologize for the behavior of her colleagues. Which, admittedly, seems unlikely.

"We don't have to go past her," Elza says. "Fastest way to my house is out back, through the fields."

"I want to know what she has to say. She can't hurt me. Can she hurt you?"

"Not if the wyrdstone holds."

I lock the front door behind us, and we make our way down the driveway. The gravel crunches under my feet, and rain hisses at the hood of my coat. The bare trees by our gate move in the wind. Their branches are black webs against the sky. Ham flattens his ears against his head as we approach the ghost. Hearing our footsteps, she turns.

It's two spirits, I realize: a woman and a baby. The woman is wearing what looks like a wedding dress, white and ornate, with a full veil that obscures her face completely. Her feet are bare, but her arms are swathed in extravagant silk gloves. The second ghost, the baby, is wrapped in a well-washed blue blanket. Not one inch of its body is visible, but I see the blanket shifting as something moves inside. I'm amazed, as always, by how utterly real the ghosts are: every bobble and nub of fabric on the baby's old blanket is clear and sharp to my eyes.

"What do you want?" I ask the woman.

"I am the Oracle," she says. Her voice is soft and low, calming. "I bear the Innocent."

I glance at Elza. Her eyes are fixed on the ghosts, taking in every detail.

"What have you done to Mum?" I ask.

"I bring omens, Master," the Oracle replies. "I have tasted the wind. I have observed portents in the flight of birds."

"I don't want anything to do with you," I say.

"You will shake hands with an ageless man. There will be no lines on his palm."

"How do we open the Book of Eight?" Elza asks.

"You will walk the shores of an ocean of tears."

"I've got the Book and Dad's notes, and the Shepherd's going to be sorry he even looked at my mum," I say. "Tell the Host that."

The Oracle doesn't respond. The baby, the Innocent, makes a small sighing noise from within its blanket. I suddenly don't want to be anywhere near the ghosts.

"We should go," I say. Elza nods.

The Oracle steps aside. We make our way through the front gate. Ham flattens himself against me, shying as far away from the ghosts as he can. The woman's veiled head tracks me as we leave.

"These omens I have received bode ill," the Oracle says.

"Yeah, well," I reply, "I could have told you that."

o   o   o

Towen Crescent, Elza's neighborhood, is a part of Dunbarrow I've never had a reason to visit before. It's a fairly recent development, stuck right out on the northwest edge of the town, and Elza shows me a shortcut across some of the sheep fields behind my house. The houses were built between the smoke-spewing industrial estates and the highway, so the Crescent doesn't have much in the way of central Dunbarrow's tourist appeal. It's a border-land, somewhere you go if you don't fit in with the rest of our town. It makes sense to find Elza living out here.

"What did you make of that?" I ask as we walk.

"Of the Oracle? Never seen anything like it. Ghosts are never that keen to talk to living people. Your Host isn't shy."

"Do you think that was her baby?"

"I hope not."

"What about her prophecy? Do you buy any of that?" I ask.

"What, that she can see the future? I doubt it."

"So you believe in ghosts, but not psychic predictions?"

"I don't 'believe' in ghosts, Luke, and neither do you. I can see them. When I see someone's prophecy come true, I'll accept that as fact as well. Until then, I'll have my doubts."

The roads are deserted, the pavement dark with rain-water. The houses are pebble-dashed with steep orange roofs, the gardens cluttered with evergreens and the anemic stalks of telephone poles. Elza's house, number 19, is at the end of a cul-de-sac, right on the edge of the Crescent. The front of the house boasts a small unkempt lawn, a stone birdbath, a few shrubs.

The house's hallway is cramped and dark; most of the floor space is occupied with various plastic boxes, stacks of bathroom tiles, and planks of wood. The wallpaper is dark brown, the carpet is scuffed earthy red.

"Excuse the mess," says Elza without a trace of shame. "We're still in the process of unpacking."

"How long have you lived here?" I ask, unleashing Ham, who follows her into the kitchen.

"About twelve years. Mum and Dad both blame each other for how it looks around here. I think for either of them to start unboxing things now would mean they were admitting defeat. You might meet them later, I don't know. Mum's working, Dad is off for a fortnight, bird-watching."

"Really?"

"Oh, yeah. He was laid off last month, so now it's away to the lakes whenever he can. He loves it; he's in heaven. Every day is the weekend for him. Practically springs out of bed. It's quite sickening." Elza shakes her head with mock disgust. She's set the kettle to boil.

"No kidding."

"Sorry, am I boring you?"

"Not at all," I say. "It's just . . . you know. Bird-watching."

"My father happens to be extremely passionate about observing British birds. I hope you're not trying to cast aspersions on his interest, about the lameness or pointlessness of such an activity, because I would be offended on his behalf."

"It's totally a cover story. Your dad's a crack dealer. He goes off to London to resupply."

"That would delight me. Anything but the truth. He used to take me with him when I was younger. Hours of sitting in a hide, almost motionless. No music. No sweets, because if you rustle too much, birds won't settle. Plus there's always some Roman legionary who died out there and you have to watch him wandering around with a Pict's ax stuck in his head. It was torment."

"Huh. Mum's gotten keen on birds recently. They'd probably get along. Do your parents have second sight?"

"No," says Elza, pouring water into her teapot, "they don't. They got pretty worried about me, how I just wouldn't grow out of having imaginary friends. I took my pills for a few years, but the dead people didn't go away, and I realized there was nothing wrong with me. It was everyone else who couldn't see things right."

"That's rough."

I sit down.

"It's life," she says. "I don't blame them for it. What would you have done? Second sight is hardly a recognized medical condition."

"What I still don't understand is how you were born with it, and I've only just developed it. It doesn't make any sense to me."

"Which part?" she asks. "Your story makes more sense than mine. Dominion over a Host of spirits binds your soul to theirs. You're closer to Deadside than other people are; they're pulling you into it, as if you were tied to enormous helium balloons. As soon as you signed that contract, you started to get pulled upward, or deathward, whatever you want to call it. I'd be more surprised if you *couldn't* see ghosts. Me, though, I've never known why. Best I can do is maybe there was a witch or necromancer somewhere in my family, centuries ago. My parents are totally normal."

"It might be genetic, like a recessive trait. Is there any research into this stuff?"

"What do you think?" she asks.

"Why not? You could win a Nobel prize for this, easily."

"I mean, how do you even go about proving your premise that second sight exists? Ghosts are harder to prove than you think. And necromancers are usually a secretive bunch. Your dad was a bit of an anomaly on that front."

"I've been thinking about that, too. The TV show and all. Why do it?"

"A question for another day, maybe. Let's look at this book of yours."

"Right here," I say, tapping my bag. "The Host definitely can't get in here, can it?"

"I've got hazel charms on the front and back doors, and around my bedroom walls especially. Spirits can't enter this house, except perhaps on Halloween. All bets are sort of notoriously off on Halloween, as I have already mentioned."

"Yeah, I know. So we need to—hey! Get out of there! Bad dog!"

Ham has taken advantage of our distraction to rear up at Elza's sink, and is busy extracting a Bolognese-encrusted wooden spoon from the sink. He drops it with a start and slinks back down to floor level.

"I can't get over how huge he is. What's his name again?" she asks.

"Ham."

"Is it short for anything? Hamlet?"

"Uh, no, I named him myself when we got him. I wasn't that old. He's named after my favorite sandwich filling."

"Of course. I suppose it was a bit much to expect any literary allusions from you."

"I'm here for a ghost hunt, not so you can criticize my dog's name."

"Yes, yes. All right, bring your tea upstairs and we'll get started. Do you mind if we shut Hamlet out in the garden? I can't say I trust him in the house, sadly."

"His name's not—yeah. Fine. Come on, son."

I grab Ham's collar and lead him out through the glass door into Elza's back garden. Ham drags his feet on the tiles, scrabbling in protest. I apply extra pressure to his neck, and he stomps outside in a huff. The backyard is long and thin, with a tumbledown shed and a scrawny apple tree. The hedges loom above head height, so he shouldn't be able to escape. I turn back into Elza's cramped kitchen. She's standing in the doorway that leads into the hall, watching me.

"What?" I ask.

"Nothing. I just would never have had you pegged as a dog person."

She gives me one of her infuriating grins and walks out into the hallway, then up the stairs. I follow her across a landing cluttered with cardboard crates and half-assembled furniture and into her bedroom.

Elza's room is exactly what I expected. It's tiny, and there's stuff covering every available surface. There are old mugs and dirty plates in a greasy heap by her bed. There are posters for the Smiths and the Cure, David Bowie and Nick Cave. The wall above her unmade bed is covered in black-and-white photos of dead leaves, broken mirrors, abandoned buildings. Another wall is taken up by a bookshelf, which is collapsing under the weight of secondhand paperbacks and glossy art books. I can't see any poetry, but I figure she'd probably hide it.

Elza slumps onto her bed and pats the space beside

her. The sheets smell of cigarettes. She unzips my back-pack and pulls out the Book of Eight and the bundle of Dad's papers, scattering them all over the purple duvet. She frowns at his nonsense writing.

"Some kind of code, then."

"Like I said."

"And we can't get this open"—she gestures at the Book—"because the clasps won't come away. But you've seen one of your Host open it, so we know it's possible."

Elza looks at the Book of Eight for a few more moments, then leaves the room and comes back with a hammer and a chisel.

"You sure?" I ask.

"I mean, opening it is a matter of urgency. If you don't mind me damaging it a bit, I think this is the best way to go. Those clasps look ancient. If you don't mind," she repeats, giving me a look that suggests she's going to smash the Book open whether I mind or not.

I shrug. Elza puts the Book on the floor, kneels beside it, and arranges the chisel so it's pointed directly into the hinge of one clasp. She raises the hammer in her right hand, then stops. For a moment I think she's just trying to find the right angle to strike at, or is having second thoughts about breaking the Book, but she holds this posi-tion, kneeling, hammer raised to head height, for far lon-ger than looks comfortable. Her arm is starting to shiver with tension.

"Elza?"

She's frowning. Her jaw is clenched. Just as I'm starting to get properly worried, she sighs loudly and brings the hammer back down to the floor. She lets go of the chisel and sits back, looking at the Book with confusion and anger.

"Stupid thing's strong," she says.

"What?"

"Stronger than it looks. Must've hit it five times."

"Elza, what are you talking about? You didn't even try to break it open. You just sat there looking at it with the hammer raised."

"I did?"

"I was here. Seriously."

"My head feels weird."

"I don't think you should try to break into the Book again. I don't think it appreciates people doing that."

Elza picks up the chisel and examines the tip for damage. Finding none, she frowns and puts it down. She runs her hands through her storm cloud of black hair.

"Well," she says. "This just got even more interesting."

However irritating I find Elza's air of being Someone Who Knows About Things, she proves far more enlightened about the mechanics of Dad's code than me. After a few moments of intense concentration on the pages spread out around her, she goes over to her desk, picks up a small makeup mirror, and holds it to the side of one of the coded pages.

"OK," Elza says after a moment of peering at the mirror, "it's like I thought. Some of this is mirror writing. Not the most difficult encryption method in the world to break. I wonder why he even bothered."

I bend down and hold my head at a weird angle so I can see the reflected page. What was reversed is now the right way around.

"Why on earth would you write some of this backward? It's coded anyway, right?"

"Very cryptic," Elza replies. "So: What are these numbers? Are they dates?"

"Could be . . . No, I'm wrong, they make no sense that way. Look at the spacing."

Elza sits back against the wall. She winds a strand of black hair around her fingers.

"Maybe it's a spell in itself? Numerology? There's meant to be power in some numbers. Maybe you say them out loud?"

"The Shepherd didn't say anything when he used the Book."

"Oh, look, just try it? I'll read you the numbers."

I slide down onto the floor, spin the Book of Eight around to face me. I try the clasps, but they're locked tight. I put one hand on the cover.

"Seven," Elza says, "a one, but it's reversed, four, three, but the three's also reversed . . . OK, seven, five—"

I repeat the numbers, feeling like a malfunctioning robot.

"four, nine, three reversed, one, one," she continues.

"I don't think this is working," I say.

"How do you know?"

"I just don't think there's a combination lock to the Book that takes more than a few seconds to use. I mean, how many sheets of this stuff are there?"

Elza sits back upright, lays the hand mirror flat on her duvet. She riffles through the pages of notes Dad left me.

"A few hundred, I think."

"I mean, am I going to just repeat all of them? I don't think it works like that."

"Good point. So the numbers mean something, but we don't know what. Some are reversed, but we don't know why. We have a book we can't open, that resists any effort to break inside. So what else do we—OK, this sheet isn't just numbers. What's this?"

She's holding a sheet of yellowing letter paper with Dad's handwriting scrawled over it. It's less densely packed than some of the other pages.

I—the Shepherd. Leadership—vision—speaks for the dead.
II—the Vassal. Loyalty—honor—thankless service.
III—the Heretic. Dissent—naysayer—unloved by God.

IV—the Judge. Reason—closed-minded—pragmatism.

V—the Oracle. Intuition—wide-minded—prophecy.

VI—the Prisoner. Desire—ravenous—an insidious thief.

VII—the Innocent. Peace—purity—the kindling of being.

VIII—the Fury. Power—rage—enemy of life.

IX—the Necromancer. Mastery—sigil bearer—opener of the gate.

"Any of that mean anything to you?" she asks.

"Well, that's the Host, isn't it?"

"Obviously. But is this about your Host or every Host? Is there always a Shepherd and a Heretic, et cetera? There's so much I don't know . . ."

"The Vassal told me a bit but not much. And who knows if what he said was true? He acts helpful, but there's so much he never says a word about."

"This part here: 'The Necromancer—Mastery—sigil bearer.' What does that mean? That's talking about you, right? You're the ninth member of the Host. Their master. So what is the sigil?"

"Never heard that word before."

"Hmm." Elza gets up off her bed, walks to her over-stuffed bookshelf, and with cautious Jenga-playing movements eases a fat dictionary out from the bottom of a pile of hardbacks. Standing, she rests the dictionary on the edge of her desk and flips through the translucently thin pages. "OK: 'From the Latin *sigillum,* "seal." A magician's mark, through which his power is exercised.' So that's interesting. This note of your dad's says you're supposed to bear a sigil. Where's your sigil?"

I reach into my backpack and take out the metal case full of rings. I unscrew the lid and let all nine tumble out onto Elza's floor: golden rings, silver rings, a ring made from smooth green stone. A ring that's lion-headed, another a silvery skull, a ring set with red stones, another studded with sapphires. Elza raises an eyebrow.

"These are Dad's," I say. "He left them to me, with the Book. Do they fit the bill?"

"Quite probably," she replies. "A seal . . . Traditionally seal rings had designs engraved so they could be pressed into hot wax. Animal sigils . . . maybe this lion?"

She picks up the lion-head ring, turns it over in her hands. She holds it close to one eye, squinting, like she's trying to see through it, peek at whatever's hidden inside. She puts it back down.

"Not that one," she says.

"How do you know?"

"I just do. It's too obvious, anyway."

"What even makes you so sure only one of these is the sigil?" I ask. "Maybe I have to wear all of them. There's nine, right? One for each of the Host."

"Sure. And one for the necromancer. The note says 'the sigil'—singular. I don't think you'd want people know-ing exactly which ring was your sigil. If you wore only one, it'd be obvious. If you wear lots, it's not as clear. Best place to hide a leaf . . ." She trails off. She closes her eyes, and runs her hands over the pile of rings. She bites her lip and picks one up, eyes still shut. ". . . is a forest," she says, opening them. She's holding a dull silver ring with a black stone set into it. "It's this one," Elza continues. "I'm certain."

Elza hands the silver ring to me. I weigh it in my palm. It's no heavier or lighter than you'd expect, no hotter or colder either, but I notice the black stone is cut into an octagonal shape. The eight-sided black stone doesn't seem to reflect the light of Elza's room but instead swallows it, the stone appearing totally black and opaque. I slide it onto the ring finger of my right hand. Although I remember Dad's hands as far chunkier than mine, the ring is a perfect fit.

"So do you feel anything?" she asks.

"Not really. Are you totally sure this is it?"

I stand up, do a few mock karate moves, swiping at Elza with the ring hand.

"Abracadabra!" I yell.

She doesn't crack a smile. Tough crowd.

"Try the Book again," she says.

I sit back down, the Book in front of me. I pull at the clasps and to my delight and horror they spring open like the mechanism of a trap, with a small, sharp click. The cover is still shut. Elza kneels down on the floor beside me. Her eyes are wide, almost luminous. She's winding and unwinding a frond of hair in her fist.

"Do you realize how few people have seen inside this book?" she asks.

"Not many?"

"Not many at all. It's one of the biggest secrets in the world."

"Here goes."

I grip the underside of the front cover, about to turn it and read the first page, and the Book swings open by itself, yellowing hand-cut pages thinner than any dictionary's, thinner than new skin. The pages flow, moving by themselves in a blur, faster than my eye can follow, a torrent of pages that seems like it'll never end. I see flickers of writing, of drawings and diagrams, and then the Book of Eight comes to a rest, open at what looks like the very middle pages. They're both blank.

I reach out with my ring hand, my sigil hand, and turn one page to the right. This spread is blank as well. I turn again, and again, each time finding the pages blank and unlined, trackless, dumb.

"What?" Elza asks me.

"I don't know!"

I turn the pages faster and faster, leafing through ten at a time, grabbing at the Book in desperation, turning pages by the hundred, and each one is blank, blank, blank.

o o o

Friday doesn't get much better from there. the Book of Eight remains blank, no matter how we try to read it. Pleading with the Book, commanding it, threatening it, all result in empty yellowing pages. What's more, the pages seem to be inexhaustible. No matter how many blank pages I try to turn, we're always in the exact middle of the Book. Whether it's a hallucination or some kind of strange defense, we can't decide.

Instead we turn our attention to Dad's coded notes. Elza tries numerous code-breaking techniques she found online, without success. After a few hours of this, I'm gnawing at the walls. We need to try something else.

"I can't do this," I say to Elza, putting the stack of notes down.

"You're not giving up, are you?" she asks, glaring over the top of her reading glasses.

"There has to be another way. This isn't going any-where. We've been trying for three hours now. I can't just sit here copying numbers while my mum —"

"What do you suggest?" she asks. "We've got the sigil, the Book, your dad's notes. That's it. What else can we turn to?"

"There's got to be something else . . . like . . . Berkley and Company! My dad's solicitor. We could speak to him."

"Do you think he knows anything about the Book?"

I think of Berkley's electric-blue eyes, his predator's

grin. *Vellum. . . . We have a man in Cumbria.* He knew something, I'm certain. He knew what I was signing for.

"He definitely does," I say. "Let's go and ask him about it. And I don't think we should bother phoning ahead to make an appointment."

It's raining when we get into Brackford. Elza's face is tinted pink by her red umbrella. She clacks along in battered boots, pushing through the rolling horde of shoppers. Ham's nearly choking on his collar with excitement at how many new friends he can see. We pass a shop window with a display of orange plastic pumpkins, all cut with black leering smiles. I feel like they're mocking me. Halloween next Friday. We've got one week. The idea of Dad's solicitor offering any kind of advice seems remote, but I feel sure he must know something. I run my thumb over the stone set in Dad's ring.

"You come here much?" I ask Elza.

"My boyfriend lived in Brackford, so I'd be here most weekends."

"You've got a boyfriend?"

"Had. Past tense. And don't sound so surprised!"

Elza swats her free hand at my face.

"All right, all right! What happened?"

"Oh, he went to university in September. London. Two weeks in he tells me he's met someone else. So screw him, and screw Stephanie from Leeds, too. And no, I didn't stalk her online."

"I'm sorry, Elza."

"It's all right. I'm down to Mouthful of Lemon on the bitterness scale rather than Rubbing Salt into Both Eyes."

"It's hard for couples, long distance, apparently."

"There were signs, let's say that. So how are things with you and the princess?"

"Who?"

"Holiday."

"What has she ever done to you?"

"Well! We used to be friends, believe it or not. Back in lower school. And then we got to high school and suddenly she doesn't want to know me, going around with Alice, telling everyone I was a lesbian because I liked David Bowie. Or the time they took my woodcut of Edgar Allan Poe that I had made in art class and—"

"All right . . ."

"—plus the way she throws her hair about like there's a shampoo ad camera crew about to rush into school and start filming, and how she always smiles really wide like she's *reaaally* interested in what you're saying, she looks lobotomized—"

"She's not a bad person," I say, though I don't really know Holiday that well, and it seems like Elza might be better placed to judge her than I am. Elza makes a sour face. "Anyway," I continue, "we're here. This is the place."

Elza pushes through the double doors, which make a soft hooshing noise as they swing open, and we're in the lobby, all bright marble and frosted glass. Nothing's changed since Monday. A pair of plastic trees stand guard by the elevators. A group of old accountant guys pass us, trim gray hair and neat suits, glaring at Ham through rimless glasses.

"Do you think they allow dogs?" asks Elza.

"Act blind or something."

An elevator arrives. Ham looks at his reflection in the mirrored wall with bemusement, then turns his attention to nibbling Elza's hand.

"What floor was it?" she asks.

"Doesn't it say on the directory?"

"There's no Berkley and Company listed here."

"What?"

"Look at the signs. It's not listed here. There's Hodge and Ridgescombe, Moebius and Sons, Vostok Incorporated, Goodparley and Orfing, but no Berkley and Company anywhere."

"I know this is the right place. Floor seven. What does it say for seven? That was where they were."

"There's nothing listed for that floor," says Elza. "Blank space."

The elevator rushes upward. Ham grumbles, but I place a reassuring hand on his head and he settles. After a few moments the doors slide open.

The lobby of Berkley & Co. has vanished. The secretary's desk, the leather benches, the stack of rumpled magazines—gone. The room is bare concrete and brick. Someone is halfway through stripping the wooden paneling from the walls. There are big sheets of transparent plastic to catch the dust, and power tools lying on the floor.

"Looks like they're gone," Elza says.

"This isn't happening . . ."

I move into the lobby and pass through one of the doorless entrances toward Berkley's office. This hallway is stripped, too, with a pile of tiles lying under plastic at one end. The walls of his office have been hacked away with crowbars, revealing the insulation foam and wiring beneath. I cast one desperate look around the bare bricks and then come back through into the lobby. Elza is talking to a man in a fluorescent yellow jacket and work boots.

"You can't be here," he's saying. "No safety gear or nothing. Bringing your dog up and all. Dunno what you're playing at."

"What happened here?" Elza asks.

"Renovation," he says, rubbing his face. "This floor's been closed for months."

"I was here just this week! What happened to the old tenants?" I ask him. "They're my lawyers."

"I don't bloody know, do I? I'm a contractor, mate. Go ask downstairs if it's that much to you. Bye-bye."

"All right," Elza says. We retreat into the elevator.

"Well, that didn't work out."

"Indeed. *Merde.*"

"I can't believe it," I say. "Gone within a week."

"Are you sure he was a real lawyer?"

"He had a big office and an expensive suit. I didn't ask beyond that. That guy said this floor's been empty for months . . ."

"All right, so Berkley and Company are obviously involved with the Host somehow. Did you see them handle any other clients?" Elza asks.

"None."

"Further confirmation they knew what was going on. Do you think the Shepherd put them up to this?"

"It seems like his style."

"Weird that you had to sign for them at all," Elza remarks. "Who knew black magic involved so much paperwork?"

"Maybe it's like with vampires. You have to invite them in. But I don't see why the Shepherd would want me to sign for them. All they want is to be freed."

"Perhaps someone has to actually be their master before the bonds can be broken," says Elza. "Otherwise they'd just end up bound forever, without anyone they could even kill. That would give them plenty of motivation to set you up like that."

"Makes sense. So Mr. Berkley was working for the Shepherd."

"I think so."

We're wandering and talking. Elza is so aggravated, she's walking at double pace, elbowing past shoppers and businesspeople. It's nearly five o'clock, and the storm clouds are turning a plummy purple in the low sun. The street is gray, everything in Brackford is gray: the people, their coats, the flat shapes of the buildings, the gauze of rain. We make our way to the city center, a paved plaza with a tall monument to some war hero, looming over the crowds. Among the jumble of gray and black I catch a hint of something luminous and unearthly.

"Elza."

"What?"

"They're here."

"Are you sure?"

"Yes! Right in front of us. It's him."

The Shepherd seems less to stand up than to unfold like an awful black wing. I notice the small gold clasps on his boots as he adjusts his trouser legs. He tugs at his beard with a fungus-white hand and grimaces.

"Master Manchett, with hound in tow, and surely this is Ms. Moss?"

"What do you want?" I ask.

"I want nothing. I have everything I need."

The Shepherd grins. His teeth are as regular and gray as the buildings that press around the square. He seems larger today, fuller, somehow brighter than even the living people around us. The lenses of his eyeglasses, previously dark, shine with an internal light. Ham growls like a band saw and spools himself around Elza's legs, ears tucked back against his head.

"I told you, Luke, this witch child can't save you."

"What do you know about me?" Elza asks him.

"It speaks," the Shepherd says. "The witchlet speaks. Well, hear this: I lived for ten centuries and my life-in-death has lasted two more. Your hedge magic holds the bare scrapings of power. It is power's palest reflection. Stand with Luke and you too shall fall."

"If you're so strong," Elza says, "why am I still here? If you'd really won, we'd both be dead already, but here we are. I'm alive, and Luke is, too, because you can't kill either of us. And since you're so good at magic, I know you know what this is."

She holds up her wyrdstone for him to see.

"A trinket," the Shepherd says, "nothing more. On Halloween, with the dead's power at its height, I believe we shall come for you first, witch child. We shall see how your talisman helps you then."

They're standing almost face-to-face. Elza moves her hand with the wyrdstone until it's almost touching his waxy face. She stares into the glowing lenses of his glasses. Ham cringes back. The people walking through the plaza are moving to avoid us, although they don't seem aware they're even doing it. The Shepherd shakes his head.

"A brave show," he says, "but I feel her fear. Now, I came to say something to you, Luke. My colleague the Prisoner, although not exactly talkative, has ways of communicating when there's a need. He mentioned something to me about a party tonight? A girl. Holiday?"

I clench my fists in my pockets.

"If you dare . . ." I begin.

"We'll be there," the Shepherd tells me. "What is a Halloween celebration without its ghosts? We shall manifest at the Simmon girl's house. We shall see how brave—"

Elza thrusts the wyrdstone into the center of the Shepherd's face. He explodes soundlessly, ripping apart like a cloud of smoke in a sudden wind, and he's gone. Elza lets out a heavy breath.

"I'd heard just about enough from him," she says.

"What happened?" I ask. "Is he gone?"

"For now. Wyrdstones protect against evil spirits, like I said. The Shepherd, things like him, they can't touch me if I'm wearing it. But if it touches them, there's a reaction, and they find they have to be somewhere else."

"Where?"

"I don't know," Elza shrugs. "Somewhere that's not here. That's always seemed enough for me. So you can see, I'm safe. Now let's go home."

Back at Elza's house, we're having our first real argument. We sit in her kitchen, a pan of water hissing on the stove while we hiss at each other. What's happening is my fault. I signed the contract for the Host, knowing it was wrong even if I didn't know why. Holiday has no idea what's been happening to me, has no idea how bad the trouble I've gotten her into is. I keep replaying the scene in my mind: Holiday talking to me, all smiles, with the tongueless Prisoner leering over her shoulder. Listening to every word we say.

"We don't even know if they *will* go there," Elza's saying for the hundredth time.

"He was pretty specific about it."

"It's so obviously a trap. They want you away from your house and away from here."

"They'll kill everyone at the party if we don't do something."

"The Shepherd never said that," Elza says, sounding like she's not even convincing herself.

"Who's stopping him? Should we call the police? They're evil spirits. They're dangerous. You said it yourself. We have to do something."

"I know," Elza snaps, "I know, but *what*? What can we do? The Book's a blank, this lawyer Berkley has vanished into thin air. We've got a sigil you don't really know how to use and a wyrdstone with enough juice to protect just me. That's all we've got. How do we keep a party's worth of drunk Dunbarrow High kids safe?"

"We bluff the Host," I say. "We show up with the Book and sigil and we bluff."

"I thought you said the Shepherd was an old dead necromancer? He'll sniff you out a mile off, Luke, like he did already. You don't just point and shoot with black magic. It takes years, decades of learning . . ."

"So what's your plan?"

"We stay here, work on the code. I'm sure there's something in your dad's notes, the numbers . . . I need more time with them."

"*Work on the code?* That's your only plan, sorting through Dad's stuff. It's gotten us nowhere. I'm supposed to sit and look at *a book* while all my mates get killed?"

"Knowledge is everything in this situation."

"You know what? You don't even care, do you? You don't like Holiday! You said it yourself. You don't care if they die."

Elza fixes me with a look that could melt glass.

"Of course I care if Holiday Simmon dies. The whole reason I'm helping you is to stop people from dying!"

"All right. So help me. I'm going up to Holiday's house. Either come or don't."

The clock on the kitchen wall ticks. I watch the second hand flick around the clock's face, slow, unstoppable, time passing like the tide coming in.

Elza winds and unwinds her hair in her fingers.

"I'll come," she says at last.

"You will?"

"I mean, it's obviously a trick. You're nuts to be falling for it. I don't support this at all. I think it's reckless and will end badly. . . . But I see that I can't convince you of that. We'll have to do the best we can."

"All right. Thank you." I stand up and breathe deeply. What's going to happen at Holiday's house, I can't imagine. Showing up with Elza Moss in tow will raise more than a few eyebrows, but I need her help.

We eat, barely speaking, and then shut Ham in Elza's kitchen and leave the house. I'm wearing the sigil on my right hand, and Elza has the Book of Eight in her backpack. It's past dusk, and Towen Crescent is lit by street lamps. I can smell wood smoke. The moving shadows of tree branches are spidered across the road. A toad sits in the gutter by Elza's gate, slimy shoulders tinted orange in the lamp's glare. It sees us and flees across the road, moving with jittery haste. I press my hands down into my pockets and start to walk, heading against the wind.

(the lash)

Holiday lives at the top of Wight Hill, the classiest part of Dunbarrow, where every front lawn is as soft and green as the felt on a pool table. Her house is mock Tudor, white walls ribbed by dark wooden beams, with first-floor windows textured by interlocking diamonds of lead. It has a two-car garage and a large front lawn full of well-behaved shrubs. Elza walks beside me, head down, wrapped in her outsize man's coat. I'm thinking how out of place she's going to look, how awkward this is going to be. The drive widens into a turning circle at Holiday's front door, which is painted sunrise-pink. I have to really punish the doorbell before I can get any attention. I see someone moving behind the door's pane of frosted glass, and for a horrible moment I expect the Shepherd to emerge, waxy face twisted into a smile.

Holiday opens the door, She looks bemused.

"Hello?"

"We're here for the party?"

"Well, of course," Holiday says. "You brought Elza, too?"

"Uh . . . we were walking the same way."

"Oh, OK. Where were you today? You remembered it was a costume party, right?"

Holiday looks, as always, stunning, wearing a slim black dress, a pair of felt ears perched above her sleek hair. She's painted whiskers on her cheeks. I try to focus on the mission, the horde of evil spirits that might arrive at any moment.

"Well," Elza says, "clearly we didn't."

To her credit, Holiday's smile looks only a little fake.

"Why don't you both come in?" she says, taking my hand and pulling me into the house.

I follow her into the kitchen, which is spotless, tiled in slabs of rough gray stone. There's a long table covered in bowls of sweets, popcorn, large plastic bottles of cheap cider, and soft drinks. I see bat-shaped streamers hanging from the curtain rods, a pumpkin with a jolly face carved into it. There's a woman staring into the open fridge.

"Mum," Holiday says, "what are you doing here?"

"You father forgot the cherries. Is that a crime?"

Holiday's mum smiles at me and Elza, so we know the joke was for us as well. I force a little grin. Elza's standing behind me, as far from Holiday and her mother as she can manage.

"This is Luke," says Holiday. "And you remember Elza Moss?"

"Hi," I say.

"Thanks for having us, Mrs. Simmon," Elza says.

Holiday's mum is tan and thin, wearing a cream sweater and faded jeans. Her hair is cropped short, and it looks like she dyes it, but aside from that, you'd think she was barely ten years older than us. Good genes. She gives us both an A-list smile.

"Oh, it's Elza! We haven't seen you for a while! And Luke, so nice to meet you at last. Holiday tells me you're keen on rugby."

"I play for the school, Mrs. Simmon."

I've actually missed all the practices this week, another sacrifice I've made since the Host arrived in town. I'll catch some grief from Mark tonight for that. It's weird how far away all of this seems. I thought I didn't believe in ghosts, but I'm starting to feel more like it's my real life that I don't believe in.

"Well, Dad's the man for that, isn't he?" Holiday's mum says to Holiday.

"Don't make him talk to Dad . . ."

"It's terrible, isn't it?" her mum says to me. "The ingratitude of some children. Don't fret, your father and I are firmly decamped to the summer house for the duration. I'd hate to make you look quote-unquote lame in front of your friends, ha-ha-ha."

She doesn't so much laugh as loudly pronounce the sounds laughter would make.

"Mum—"

"All right, all right. Come on, Bach."

Holiday's mum scoops up a white cat, and leaves, having forgotten the cherries. Holiday grimaces.

"She's *so* annoying."

I think about Mum lying in the dark, face drenched in sweat. I remember all the days I've left for school and come home in the evening to find her still sitting in the same place. I think of her now lying motionless, her body a glacier.

"She seems OK."

"I can't believe she—like, I don't *talk* about you! I *mentioned* you once. She makes it sound like I'm your fan club or something!"

"When nothing could be further from the truth, right?"

"Shut up. Look, come on, we're watching trash TV. I'll get you a beer?"

"Sounds great."

I've got no intention of drinking a drop, but I'm not about to explain that to Holiday. Elza has moved past both of us and is staring out the windows at the far end of the kitchen, looking into what must be the backyard. I tense up, thinking she's seen something outside, but then she turns away and gives me a little shrug. I can't feel the icy cold that accompanies the Host, so I presume we're safe for now.

Holiday presses a beer into my hand.

"Can I get you anything?" she asks Elza.

"I'm not drinking tonight," Elza replies.

"Oh," Holiday says, "are you doing a detox?"

"No. I just think, you know, what if something terrible happened tonight and I was drunk? I wouldn't be able to deal with it." Elza fixes me with a volcanic glare.

Holiday, who is either an amazing actor or genuinely the kindest person in the world, appears to be giving serious consideration to this. "Sure," she says. "I get anxious, too, you know?"

I'm not really drinking, I mouth at Elza behind Holiday's back. *Act more normal.*

"I think the only sane way to live," Elza says to Holiday, "is anxiously."

Standing in my crush's kitchen, waiting for the arrival of my dad's horde of evil spirits, listening to Elza and Holiday coproduce a strong contender for Most Awkward Conversation of the Year Award, I decide that I am going to have a drink after all.

The living room is twice the size of the kitchen, done in whites and creams, with a sixty-inch plasma screen installed in a cavity at one end. There's a real log fire, grumbling to itself behind a black fire screen. The party so far is nonexistent. There's just a few of the top-tier girls from my class, dressed as cats, nurses, and Disney princesses. They all look up at me and Holiday and Elza as we enter. I feel like I'm on display, a show pony she's leading into the ring. The reaction to Elza is more like she's been buried up to her neck in an anthill. None of Holiday's friends say a word, but I can see their expressions, tiny communications as they catch one another's eyes: scorn, shock, amusement. It's like watching a group of sadistic computers communicate via Wi-Fi. I pretend not to notice and sit down with Holiday on the largest sofa, facing the television. Elza stands against the far wall and looks at her boots.

"So we're watching, like, this totally ridiculous show," Holiday's saying. "*Nightwatch.* They're having a marathon of it, since it's nearly Halloween. Have you seen it?"

Ouch.

"Never," I say.

"Oh, it's just the best," says Holiday. "The guy who presents it is, like, this total weirdo. He's called Dr. Manchett—"

"No relation," I say with a forced grin.

"I heard he, like, just died, or something?" one of her friends says.

"Yeah, they had that on the news the other day?" says another.

"Really," I say.

The screen is dark. I can see stars, a suggestion of trees in the black against black. There's the crunch of footsteps.

"Are you OK?" whispers Holiday.

"I'm fine," I say.

"You're all tense. Are you, like, scared?" She grins.

"As if this is going to be scary."

I'm swiftly proved wrong by the face that appears on-screen. Hair falling back across a shiny scalp, hair growing across cheeks and chin like an unmanicured lawn. I'm very glad that I've inherited more of Mum's genetic material than Dad's. He's wearing a lime-green shirt and is lit at close range in the dark by a powerful white lamp, which makes him look embalmed.

"In all my years as a paranormal investigator," he says, "I cannot remember another case quite like this one. What you are about to see is disturbing, and may make you question everything you think you know about life . . . and death."

The credit sequence begins. It's pretty lackluster, and I find myself wondering how big a budget Dad was given. The opening rolls over what is presumably stock footage of forests and castles, mixed in with some night-vision shots of basements and dungeons. The music is low and ominous-sounding, occasionally rising to a crescendo when the camera focuses on a full moon or a sinister-looking empty doorway. Eventually the screen freezes on a night-vision shot of a skeleton lying on the ground, and the word *Nightwatch* comes up in green Gothic lettering accompanied by a screaming effect.

The scene changes. It's daylight, under a lead-gray sky. The camera is in a moving vehicle, driving through a forest. The plants are dull and autumnal. The camera glides around a bend in the road, and we see a squat stone building standing in the midst of an unkempt lawn. The trees lean over the house in a silent canopy.

"This is Coldstane Rectory," says the narrator, "built in the late eighteenth century. The building has had a ghastly reputation for more than two hundred years. Current occupant Michael Aulder thought that the house would be the perfect rural getaway for his family. Michael says that he never believed in ghosts, but after buying the rectory, the Aulder family have changed their minds. Please note that all footage on this show is real. Nothing has been faked and no special effects are used. We do not use actors in our reality programming."

Mr. Aulder is hard-faced, with a full head of graying hair, his stout body barely contained by a white oxford shirt. He's standing in bright sunlight under a wide blue sky. It's obviously summer, in notable contrast to the earlier shots.

"Well, of course, people said things to us," says Mr. Aulder, "warning it was haunted, giving me all the talk. Never listened to them, though, did I? I've never believed in all that, ghosts and such." He laughs, exposing gray teeth. "I've a different view now."

"The Aulder family lived in the property for a little over a month before the paranormal events began," says the narrator, "mainly occurring around three o'clock in the morning—the traditional haunting hour."

Cut to Mrs. Aulder, blond and round-faced, wearing a yellow dress. She stands in the kitchen in front of a brass kettle and a green stove. She's nervous, looking away from the camera.

"I thought at first it was kids," she says, "messing around. That was bad enough. There were noises, you know, in the roof and outside in the yard. Our daughter, she's only six, she was scared. She said she wanted to go back to the old house. My husband thought it was rats."

Cut to Mr. Aulder. "I often slept through the early occurrences, if I'm honest. I have a heavy workload, and I'm a heavy sleeper, too. I thought she was making things up."

Mrs. Aulder: "It wasn't until things started moving around that Michael began to take it seriously."

"What kind of things?" asks a voice off camera.

"Everything." She swallows hard.

Cut back to the outside view of the rectory. It's autumn again. A pair of white vans pull into the gravel driveway and grind toward the house.

"The Aulder family have not had a night's peace

since summer," says the narrator. "They report unnatural noises at night, poltergeist activity, ectoplasm leaking from the walls, sensations of extreme cold, food in the house rotting within hours of purchase, excessive junk mail, shadowy figures stalking the garden at night, orbs of spiritual energy disrupting Christmas dinner, and, in one memorable occurrence, the television set leaked *blood*."

"I think that was the most disturbing manifestation," says Mr. Aulder in his sunlit garden. "I was watching the news, and the set began to dim. I walked over to adjust the picture, and I discovered there was a thick liquid running down the plasma screen. When I put my hand on it, I realized it was, in fact, blood."

"And this is when you decided to call the *Nightwatch* team for help?"

"Yes. Yes, it was. I can't live like this."

Cut to a van door opening. A pair of bright-orange shoes step down onto the gravel.

"Dr. Horatio Manchett is Britain's most respected paranormal expert," announces the voice-over, "with more than a hundred hauntings successfully exorcised."

"Dr. Manchett owns Britain's campest collection of shoes," I say, "and has plans to purchase many more flamboyant shoes in the near future."

"Quiet," hisses Holiday, giggling.

Dad is on-screen, wearing a dark-red suit.

"—and this has frightened you?"

"Very much so," says Mrs. Aulder.

"Well, it seems," says Dad, turning to the camera, "that this family is experiencing a paranormal event of some magnitude. What we are going to do is take a look around the house, a preliminary look, as it were, and see what occurs. We'll be taking an especially close interest in the kitchen and living room, as these are the rooms where the family reports the most intense activity."

Dad gestures at the cameraman, who follows him as he sweeps through the low square doorway and into the kitchen.

"Well, this is an excellent example of period architecture," he remarks, "and the family has kept it in really beautiful condition. The question is, Are we going to feel any kind of presence here?"

The Aulders stand, looking on, nervous while Dad strides around the kitchen in his garish suit, opening cupboards and muttering in what I assume is Latin. As he rummages under the sink, asking them about auras they may have experienced in the house, I see a figure standing in the corner of the room. It's a woman, gray-faced, wearing a very old-fashioned dress. She's looking at my dad with a vacant expression. The Aulders, as well as Holiday and her friends, see no sign that she's there at all. This confuses me enormously. You read all kinds of stuff about ghosts appearing in photographs, but this is the first time I've even thought about it. Are they giving off some kind of energy that's beyond the normal visible spectrum? How are the cameras capturing it? I remember what the Vassal said to me when I first asked him about life after death: *Better minds than yours or mine have chased their own tails for lifetimes regarding such questions.* Some of these things I'll never understand.

"I think maybe we should try to address the spirits directly," says Dad to the camera, "to see if I can get any idea of how many there are and what they want from these people."

"How will we do that?" asks Mrs. Aulder nervously.

"They're often responsive to a confident voice," Dad says. "Are there any spirits within this house?" he asks loudly.

Nothing.

"I said," he shouts, "are there any spirits within this house? If there is a presence within this house, I demand that you make yourself known!"

Dad raises his hands and makes some kind of gesture. I notice the sigil on his right finger and quickly hide my right hand in my pocket. I don't want anyone noticing that we've got the same surname and wear the same ring. There'd probably be some questions about that.

"Make yourself known!" yells Dad. The Judge and the Prisoner come in through one wall of the kitchen. The Prisoner grabs the female ghost by the hair and drags her out of the room through the opposite wall. Before I have time to think about what's happening, they're gone. The Judge kicks the stove as hard as he can with his boot. Holiday jumps and grips my leg like a vise.

"Did you hear that?" she says.

"It's just a bang. They edit those noises in."

"That was *so* a ghost. Don't be a spoilsport!" The other girls are laughing and shrieking.

"Tell me what it is that you want," proclaims Dad in the rectory's kitchen, "and I can let you leave in peace."

The Judge strides to the kitchen counter and with some relish lifts an unwashed pot up into the air. The cameraman notices and audibly gasps, shifting his gaze from Dad to the pot hanging in the air.

"Uh, Dr. M," says the cameraman, clearly unscripted, "by the sink."

"We can do this the easy way or the hard way," says Dad, turning toward the Judge. "Either you talk to me, or I shall expel you from this place."

The Judge rolls his eyes and throws the pot at the wall.

Holiday and her mates shriek.

"I'm not sure about this," says the cameraman. "Like, are we insured for this?"

"Everything is fine," says Dad. "Nobody panic."

The Judge picks up a knife and slowly waves it about. Mrs. Aulder starts to hyperventilate.

"I think maybe we should all go outside," says Dad, placing himself between the floating knife and the couple.

"Let's go outside and regroup. I think I have the measure of the haunting now: There is definitely a hostile presence here."

The camera crew don't need to be told twice and make an undignified exit, running out the door and into the daylight. This part is clearly unrehearsed, and several members of crew, including the sound guy, are caught on film as they make their escape. The Aulders join the crew on their lawn at a run. Dad comes last and the Judge slips out after him, lighting another cigarette. I'm guessing Dad neglected to tell the camera crew that the ghosts are real. There are no live actors on the show, but there are plenty of dead ones.

In the background I can see the Prisoner moving toward the woods at the back of the house, dragging the female ghost—presumably the ghost that was haunting the Aulders in the first place—along behind him by the hair. While Dad talks Mrs. Aulder down, I watch the struggle in the background. As they reach the tree line, I see something else, just for a moment, something that looks like a moving shadow, darkness that flows out from behind a tree and engulfs the rectory's original ghost. The hairs all along my arms stand on end, but the camera cuts away before I can get a good view of what happened. I look over to Elza, to see if she saw it as well, but she's not in the room anymore.

In the next scene Dad and Mrs. Aulder conduct a sort

of séance in the family room, trying to contact the spirits and pinpoint how many there are so they can be exorcised. The Judge provides some restrained raps on the table and walls, and then the Prisoner walks through the wall and starts running his scarred hands over Mrs. Aulder, gurgling softly. I stiffen in my seat.

"Oh, I feel," she gasps, "I can feel something. Oh, no. Oh, I just . . . it's so angry. They feel so angry, so full of hatred."

The big climax of the show is a midnight exorcism of Coldstane Rectory, with night-vision cameras and heat sensors and something called a Spectral Reader, which looks suspiciously like a Geiger counter with extra parts soldered on. My father, wearing a purple robe, chants and burns various herbs, and then waves his hands around while the camera crew follows him from room to room. The Judge bangs stuff and throws furniture about, occasionally, to my amusement, missing his cue. The Vassal and the Heretic put in guest appearances for the benefit of the heat sensors, walking through the walls and moaning. At the climax of the exorcism, someone cuts the lights in the rectory and the Shepherd himself appears, emitting an aura of green fire that you clearly don't need second sight to see. Holiday and her mates scream.

"Luke," Holiday says, "did you see?"

"It's CGI," I say.

The credits roll, luminous against a moonless night.

Some text informs us that the Aulders remained in the house after the show and have not reported any further paranormal events. The exorcism was successful.

I'm left utterly confused. Dad raised terrifying spirits from the dead so that he could exorcise houses of their resident ghosts? Wouldn't it be easier to just fake it? What happened to the actual ghost haunting Coldstane Rectory anyway? Where did she go? What was that moving shadow that came from the tree line?

Was that Dad's demon?

"So do you guys believe in ghosts?" one of Holiday's friends asks.

"After that," Holiday says, "I'm not sure. That was, like, the scariest one yet."

"When the knife was floating—"

"Come on," I say, "are you serious? Those were the lamest effects I've ever seen. It was so plainly on strings."

"You're such a cynic," says Holiday, punching me in the arm.

I just kind of grin and shrug and then we watch some reality show about people with fake tans yelling at one another. They all live in this house by the beach, and the weather is always sunny. There's still no sign of Elza. I'm not sure what she's doing, if she's scoping out the rest of the house or what. I'd like to know what she made of Dad's show, whether she thought there was anything useful in there. We shouldn't be separated anyway:

The Host might show up any moment, and then I'd need the Book. Holiday's leg is resting against mine, and I really wish I could just relax and enjoy the night. On TV the tanned people are arguing in their bright kitchen. It doesn't look like the people on the show ever think about being dead.

By half past ten Holiday's house is packed. Everyone who's anyone in our year is dancing in her front room or mixing drinks in the kitchen. Mark and Kirk are here, with the rugby team in tow. They've got me surrounded in Holiday's garden, and they're all chanting in a tribal way. I'm holding the bottle of vodka they gave me. I lost any hope of finding Elza the second they arrived, and for all I know, the Host is already here, and I can't explain any of this to them. I end up taking the smallest mouthful of the stuff I can get away with and passing it to the next guy. The drink sears my nose and throat. I'm coughing. Kirk, who's dressed as Superman, grabs me and pulls me out of the circle.

"Manchett, where've you been this week?" he's asking.

"Ugh. Bleh. Mum's ill, man. I've been at home."

"Headaches again?" Mark asks. He must have ditched the circle, too. Mark is Captain America. His shield is a painted garbage-can lid.

"Yeah. She just needs me around."

Behind us the drinking circle is roaring so loudly that I can barely hear what anyone's saying. I keep scanning the drunk faces around me, waiting to see one of the ghosts, waiting to feel the chill. The vodka isn't doing my mood any favors.

I feel sick.

"You want to get some home help," Kirk's saying. "Get nurses in. You shouldn't be looking after her by yourself."

"I'm really fine, guys. Thanks."

"Only you missed all the practices this week," Mark's saying.

"Ah, sorry, man, you know? Really. My head's just not been in it."

I try to smile. Neither looks that convinced.

"You'll have to get back in it," Mark says. "Coach is about to go nuclear on you."

"Are you really all right?" Kirk asks. "You look bad, mate. Where's your costume?"

"Ah, I forgot."

"Alice was saying you came here with Elza Moss?" Mark says.

"We just walked the same way," I say. "Barely know her."

"Alice said you were talking to her yesterday, outside school," he's saying with a grin. "She said you were acting really shady about it."

I'd like to find Alice Waltham and strangle her. I force a laugh.

"Elza just asked me for a cigarette," I say.

"You're sly," Kirk's saying, laughing. "I know what you're up to, Luke. You're trying to get into Elza, aren't you?"

"You don't have to be ashamed, mate," Mark says. "Beggars can't be choosers, right?"

"She written a poem for you yet?" Kirk asks.

"I need a piss, lads," I say through a rictus grin, and turn away back to Holiday's house. Behind me, obviously preplanned, the rugby guys break into a chorus of "Manchett and Elza sitting in a tree." We mess with one another like this all the time, but I'm really not in the mood for it tonight. They've got no idea what's happening here. Elza's risking more for me than any of them ever has.

I push my way into the house, through the crowds of people in the back room and kitchen, half of them guys from the year below who didn't even come in costume, just wore tracksuits and sneakers with neon laces. There are hip-hop videos blasting from the TV in the front room now, no more *Nightwatch*. I find Elza sitting at the bottom of the stairs. She's staring into space, about as glum as I've ever seen her.

"You all right?" I ask.

"Absolutely horrible, thanks."

"No sign of the Host?"

She shrugs. I sit beside her.

"You think they're actually going to come?" I say.

"I'm starting to hope they do. I've been standing around on my own for two hours, listening to people have the most inane conversations on the planet, except half the time they're drowned out by the worst music on the planet. Not to mention everyone looking at me like I sprayed myself down from a septic tank rather than showering this morning."

"Yeah. I'm sorry."

"How are you friends with these people? A guy told me to take my Halloween costume off. We're *at a Halloween costume party.* Like, the other three hundred and whatever days of the year aren't enough for you to use that insult?"

"We're here because of the Host . . ."

"But that didn't stop you from having a few with your rugby mates."

"I'm trying to act normal? Fit in? I can hardly explain to anyone what's going on."

"Yeah. Sorry. I just can't wait until high school is over and I'll be able to go to the college in Brackford or something. I seriously—*AIIIEE!*"

Elza screams like she's been scalded and jumps to her feet. There's red running down her face, and I'm grabbing her, thinking she's bleeding, the ghosts are here, the Shepherd—and then I hear drunk human laughter coming from above us. Alice Waltham and another girl I don't recognize are standing on the upper landing, looking down. Alice is holding an empty wineglass.

"Sorry, Elza," Alice says. "My hand slipped."

Elza stares up at the two smirking girls, wine soaking into her dark cloud of hair, wine dripping from her shoulders onto the cream carpet. There are flecks of pink blooming everywhere around her. I realize I've still got my hand on Elza's hip. She's vibrating with rage, like a chain saw being revved up.

"Go clean yourself off, you mutt," says the other girl.

Elza opens her mouth, and I think she's going to scream at them, but instead she just whispers, so quietly only I can catch it, "I was here to save you."

She breaks away from me and runs into the kitchen, heading for the door. I'm following her, pushing past groups of lads, past the table with the grinning jack-o'-lantern, out the door, her boots crunching on gravel.

"Elza!"

"I'm going home," she says.

"Come on, please—I need your help . . ."

"With what? We've got no plan. I'm covered in wine. I'm not sitting around in Holiday's palace for another hour getting drinks poured on me, waiting for ghosts to come and kill me. I'm going home."

She takes the Book of Eight out of her backpack and thrusts it into my hands, then turns without another word and walks away into the dark. I watch her back as she disappears. The clack of her boot heels fades and then finally cuts out altogether. The night is cold and clear, with stars freckled like white paint on a smooth black canvas. I wait for Elza to come back, but she doesn't, and after a few minutes I turn back up the drive, to Holiday's house.

Holiday herself is standing in the front doorway, her body haloed in bright white light, cat ears still perched on her head. Music and loud voices leak out around her into the quiet street. I stop a few paces from the door.

"Hey," she says.

"Hi."

"Someone said maybe you left."

"I came back."

"Are you all right?" she asks.

"Not really."

"Do you want to talk about it?"

"I wouldn't even know where to start."

Holiday pushes open a white door with a gold *H* nailed to it. Her room is dark, lit by a string of blue and pink lights that are looped over the poles of her four-poster bed. Her hair is threaded with the cool light that seeps from the bed frame. Downstairs, the music is thumping, like a headache you're about to have.

"I cannot *believe* someone got red wine on the hall

carpet," Holiday's saying. "Like, all over it! I just barely convinced Dad to even let me have people here . . ."

"It was Alice."

"Oh, are you *kidding*? That girl—she just spray-painted my bathroom with vom as well, I had to put her to bed in my brother's room. Thank god he's not here."

"She dumped wine all over Elza. That's why there are stains."

"Oh." Holiday sits on the edge of her bed. "That wasn't kind of her. Is that why you were outside?"

"Uh, yeah. Elza was angry, obviously. She went home."

"You did come here with her, then?"

"She's a friend."

"Only a friend?" Holiday asks.

She holds my gaze with a delicious intensity.

"I . . . Holiday, I can't do this right now."

"Can't do what?" she asks, smiling.

"Look . . . I can't explain. . . . I'm, like, way over my head. I'm dangerous."

"What, you're a heartbreaker?" she says.

"No, look, it's . . . my dad," I say, not quite believing we're suddenly having this conversation. "He died last week. We weren't close, though."

"I'd like . . ." Holiday's saying, "I'd like us to be close, Luke." She's lying back on her bed, clearly out of it. I wonder if she'll even remember this conversation in the morning.

"I'd like that, too," I say. "But you look like you want to sleep right now."

"You don't have to go," she says, almost a whisper.

"You're very drunk. I think I should," I say. She doesn't answer. Her breathing is slow and deep. She reminds me of Mum suddenly, and I have to turn away. The music has stopped downstairs. They must be changing the track or something. I hope that's what's going on.

I open Holiday's door and come face-to-face with the Judge.

"What are you doing here?" I ask, though I already know.

"Sorry, boss," he says, rubbing his stubbly head. "Can't be helped."

Before I even know what I'm doing, I've grabbed him with my right hand. The sigil is cold, freezer-burn cold, like a tiny star of frost on my finger. I grab the Judge around his fat throat and lift him up into the air. He strains and squirms in my grip, his outline starting to blur like captive smoke, but I won't let him go.

"Boss, please—"

"Shut up. I'm talking. I'm your necromancer. I've got the Book," I say, holding it under his nose with my left hand. "I know how to use it. Where are the others?"

"Boss—"

I squeeze his throat tighter, cutting his protests off into a squawk. The sigil blazes even colder; my right hand feels like a shape carved from ice. Sparks are dancing in my teeth.

"Where are they? Where's the Shepherd?"

"I'm here, Luke" comes his dry, clipped voice, right behind me.

Still holding the Judge, I turn to face the room. The Shepherd is standing a few feet from me, regarding me through the black discs of his glasses. His hands are clasped at his waist. He looks calm, like someone waiting for a bus.

"I've got the sigil here," I say. "You make one move and I'll—"

"You'll do nothing," the Shepherd says, "or the girl dies."

With a sick lurch, I realize the shadows clotted around Holiday's sleeping body have taken a man's form. The Prisoner is crouched over her, staring down at her sleeping face with rapt delight. With his left hand he's holding what looks like a thread of white light, which is connected to Holiday's forehead, between her eyes. He's pulling it out of her, whatever it is, and in his other hand . . . I see his shears are poised to snip the thread. He gives me a toothy tongueless smile.

"If you touch her—" I say.

"Empty threats," the Shepherd says. "You have the sigil and Book, but you're no necromancer yet, Luke. Give them up. Or my colleague will cut her thread and she'll be gone."

I'm frozen in place, the Judge still struggling in my grip.

The shears begin to close around the white thread, a millimeter at a time. The Prisoner doesn't take his empty gaze off mine for a second.

I can't let Holiday die because of me.

I release the Judge, who gurgles and falls to the ground. I drop the Book of Eight onto the floor and push it toward the Shepherd with my foot.

The Prisoner doesn't move away from Holiday.

"The sigil as well," the Shepherd says with a slight smile.

I pull the painfully cold ring from my finger and throw it at his smirking waxy face. He catches it in midair without any apparent effort.

"What are you waiting for?" the Shepherd asks. Is he talking to me? Why would I be waiting for anything? "Could it be you remain loyal to the necromancer?" he continues.

I turn to look at the Judge.

"Nothing personal, boss," he mutters. He raises his hand, and I can see an empty bottle held in his fist. He's wearing a sovereign ring on his thumb. It catches the light, a miniature sun. I have time to wonder whether it's a real bottle or somehow the ghost of one, and then he breaks it over my head with a flat white

Snap.

o o o

I wake up stretched out on Holiday's bed. My neck feels like there's a fire lit inside it. I've got a headache with a pulse and my mouth is dry. When I move my head I can feel hair itching at my shoulders and back. Holiday is lying next to me, eyes wide open.

"Holiday?"

I hold my hand to hers. It's still warm, and I can feel the faintest heartbeat hidden there in her wrist. They didn't kill her, and they didn't kill me either. It's not Halloween, so if what Elza said is true they can't. My skeleton feels more like a collection of dry, weak twigs than the trusty lattice of bones I normally depend on. The room is still dark, but it's closer to deep blue than black. Sunrise can't be far off.

The shadows by Holiday's dresser deepen. There's the glint of spectacles, the slight mushy sound of lips moving.

"Luke," says the Shepherd.

"What have you done to her?"

"Me personally? Nothing. I can't speak for the Prisoner, of course. He does rather drain people."

His voice has music in it. I want to throw myself at him, wrap my hands around his waxy throat, but I can't. I gave up the sigil. I want to feed the Shepherd his own heart. Instead I stand, fists crunched up in my jean pockets.

"She's got nothing to do with this. Nobody here does."

"I quite agree, so I'd rather not get into any unpleasantness. Do exactly as I say or we'll kill all of them."

"All right."

"Open the door and go downstairs, to the back garden. I will follow you. If you run, if you try anything, this girl here will suffer and then die. And don't think we've forgotten that seer-child either."

"Good luck getting to Elza. She knows all about you."

"You really don't understand what you're dealing with, do you, Luke? I have traveled through the cold beyond. I spoke with the Black Goat in the deepest woods. I plundered the ruins of Babylon and Solomon's tomb. In life, there were kings who came to me on bended knee. Did you think the witchlet could help you against me? Against us?"

"Elza knows more than you think," I say. "All you're proving is you're old. And I'm not afraid. I know you can't kill me."

I hope.

"Downstairs," he says.

I haul my aching body through the door and across Holiday's broad landing. The house is utterly silent, without a murmur or thump of footsteps. A clock reads 6:00 a.m. I run my eyes over a pile of neatly folded clothes, a gold-framed photograph of Holiday at eight or nine on a chestnut-colored pony. What have I brought down on their home?

Sitting in a white chair on the landing, there's a blue bundle that starts to shift and murmur as we approach.

I'm a baby, the bundle says.

I walk past the ghost, chill crawling over my skin.

Pick me up, it says. The Shepherd doesn't acknowledge it either.

"Are you familiar with the Innocent? A story lies therein," he says, as we reach the bottom of the stairs.

"I don't want to hear it."

"As you wish. Another time, then. Closer to your death."

Nobody has left the party; everyone is still here. Every guest stands in place, hands clasped behind their backs. There's not a human sound to be heard: no breaths, no coughing. Their faces have the flattened, sad expression of sleepers. Bottles and cans and glasses lie on the ground, surrounded by long-dried splats and spills of liquid. Whatever happened to them, it happened fast. I suppose this is real black magic. I didn't realize, didn't know the ghosts had this kind of power. Is this what Dad would use the Host for? If you could do something like this to people, freeze them like statues, then you could get away with just about anything. It's not a nice thought. I remember learning about Pompeii, looking at all the plaster casts of the Romans who didn't have the sense to leave town when their mountain started to smoke. Their eyes are open, but nobody is looking at anything in particular. None of them respond to my gaze. Everyone—every sexy cat, every Frankenstein, every Dracula, every Superman or cowgirl or zombie—all of them are facing the same way, staring toward the open back door.

The garden is dark, grass tinted white with frost. Beer cans glint beneath the bushes that surround the lawn. There's a wide circle of people standing on the grass; some are living, some dead. I think of the guys' drinking circle out here last night, and I smile a bitter smile. I see Holiday's mum, and a gray-haired man with a paunch who I assume is her dad, standing beside each other with clasped hands and the same sleepwalker's expression. I guess they came back early. Too bad for them. Kirk and Mark stand with their backs to me, still in their super-hero costumes. Between the seven warm bodies stands the Host, filling out the circle: the Judge, the Prisoner, the Vassal, the veiled Oracle, the flaming form of the Heretic, who for once stands silent, and the blue-swaddled baby, somehow moved down from the landing, on the ground next to Holiday's parents. And at the opposite side the circle stands another figure, something I can't quite make out, a strange hunched shape like a mound of cloth that's breathing. No, that's not quite right either: It looks more like a shadow being boiled.

The Fury. I remember Dad's notes: *Power—rage— enemy of life.*

Just when you think things can't get worse.

"Is the whole Host accounted for?" asks the Shepherd behind me, loud, near my ear. When nobody answers, he carries on. "Come stand with me, Luke. We've left space for you."

I follow him through the damp, flattened grass, and my stomach lurches as we step into position. In the center of the circle is Holiday's white cat, Bach, with a syrupy red slit in his belly. He lies still, like a toy someone dropped.

"Right there," the Shepherd says. I've got the Heretic to my right, the Shepherd to my left. The circle is complete: eight living, eight dead. I stand where he indicated, fists clenched, head throbbing, and the Shepherd reaches up and touches the center of my forehead with my sigil. Cold spreads from the black ring throughout my body, faster and deeper than it did when I grabbed the Judge's throat. I find that I can't move. I'm frozen in position, like the others. All I can do is watch.

"There," says the Shepherd after a moment, enjoying my discomfort at suddenly being paralyzed. "Our circle is complete. Allow me to introduce an infamous servant of your father. The Fury."

At this, the boiling shadow, at first only waist high, unfurls like a great dark flag, and I realize I was looking at something wearing a black robe, kneeling on the ground with its back to me. It stands and *stands,* expanding upward until it's past seven feet tall, its shoulders level with the taller ghosts' heads. The Fury turns to face me, and I realize that each time I think I've seen everything, there's just one more level of screwed-up weirdness.

The thing has long, thin arms, hands that fall down below its knees, fingers like groping roots. The demon's skin is ink-dark, and I can't tell where its cloak begins or if it's actually wearing anything at all. It looks like a three-dimensional shadow, a shadow with depth and mass, like a sculpture made out of black smoke. The head is the lean, sharp head of a dog or jackal. The demon's eyes are like keyhole views of a furnace, smoldering orange holes punched into the darkness of its face. It sniffs at the air and then opens its mouth, which also shimmers with red heat. Unlike the Heretic, shrouded in flames, this creature is burning from within. There's a faint, awful sound, like someone screaming and shouting two streets away.

"Hear me now," says the Shepherd. "The Fury and I have decided that Luke is lacking in the correct authority to manage this Host."

The demon adds nothing. Its furnace eyes bore into mine.

"Luke has continually proved himself incompetent, slothful, and inconsequential. His grasp of necromancy is effectively nil. We believe him to be an unworthy owner of the Manchett Host, and we are relieving him of command."

The Prisoner gives me a curdled smile.

"This is mutiny," says the Vassal quietly.

"Shut it!" hisses the Judge.

"The first order of business," says the Shepherd with an expansive gesture, "will be breaking our bonds. As you're all aware, Halloween is seven days away. Our power will be at its apotheosis, its apex. I feel confident we will be able to slay our necromancer, and thence shall be free. Luke is weak, and such a chance may never occur again. Do you want to end up like the monk"—he points at the Heretic—"forever lost, mind worn down to nothing by centuries of service? We must break free!"

Nobody disagrees.

"Just in case anybody has some misplaced loyalty . . . consider this a warning, all of you."

At this prompt, the Fury leaps at the Vassal and smothers him in its robe. The black shape billows and beats like a heart, and then the struggle is over. The Vassal is kneeling in the middle of the circle, looking down at the dead cat. His hands and feet are bound with what look like black briars. The Fury stands over him, blazing eyes empty of expression. Nobody looks pleased or smug anymore, not even the Judge. I'm guessing whatever's about to happen, the Shepherd didn't fill him in on this part of the plan.

The Shepherd speaks to the Host. "The Vassal is domesticated, a mewling house pet. At every chance for freedom, this traitor blocked the path."

"Luke!" cries the Vassal, on his knees in the grass. "Luke, save me! If you have any goodness, any compassion, please save me! Stop this now!"

I try to speak, and my mouth won't work. I'm frozen in place, totally silent. All I can do is stand and watch.

"Please! Oh, God, please don't let it eat me! Please!"

The demon reaches inside its body and draws out something that glows with a hungry light: a long whip of flame, an impossible cord of boiling orange that swings down from its black hand to singe the wet grass.

The Vassal raises his head, eyes glinting in the fierce orange blaze of the whip. I can't tell him how sorry I am, how much I appreciate what he's tried to do for me, but he must be able to read my gaze.

"You are forgiven, sir," he says quietly.

The Fury swings the whip in a wild arc, up into the air, where it spurts like the trail of a time-lapsed firework before tumbling onto the hunched shape of the Vassal. The whip hits his back with a hungry sizzling noise, and the Vassal screams in agony. I see now why Dad used the demon: to control the other ghosts, because I think you'd do anything to avoid what it's doing to the Vassal. The scourge eats through the ghost's body completely, and now the Vassal is split in half at the waist, and both halves are lying on the ground in the dawn-lit orchard.

"The lash of Tartarus," the Shepherd says quietly, sounding almost awed.

The demon swings the whip in a tight circle, catching the Vassal's kicking legs. The legs are held in the coils of the whip, and the Fury reels the limbs in. The monster raises the Vassal's legs up to its snout and inhales. The spectral body parts dissolve into a fog and are sucked into the demon's white-hot gullet. The Vassal screams again, higher and higher, like a siren.

He doesn't last long after that first bite. The demon was hungry, it seems, and goes into a frenzy, lashing at the Vassal's twitching body with the whip until he looks like a statue that's been smashed with a hammer. The demon bends down at the waist and starts to suck and grunt, vacuuming up the shards of ghost. Eventually there is nothing left, and the monster recoils the burning lash.

"Thank you, my brother," says the Shepherd. "I hope this has been instructive for you all. Follow us and glory awaits. We will be freed, and not only that, reborn. We can take new bodies, new lives!"

For a moment there is silence. The wind rises and the trees begin to murmur and rustle to one another. I'm shivering, muscles cramping, unable to move or turn my head or close my eyes. Then the Host kneels as one, the ghosts all touching the ground with their hands and faces. Even the Heretic manages a shaky, halfhearted bob.

"You're dismissed," the Shepherd tells them, and the Host vanishes like candles being snuffed out. Only the Shepherd and the Fury remain.

"Your father kept the Fury regularly fed with souls," the Shepherd says to me. "You see the need, of course. A demon's hunger is limitless."

I can't even turn my head to look at him. I can only hear his voice.

"We are unable to kill you, as you know. I could ask you to commit suicide. Hold Holiday and your mother ransom. Your life for theirs. But suicide is a great, bleak sin, and there are certain . . . interested parties whose involvement in this game we have here would complicate matters. We can't attract their attention."

"Fortunately, the Fury here had some excellent suggestions. Really quite ingenious, demons. Came up with some masterpieces of cruelty."

The Fury examines me closely, like I'm an ant crawling over a plate it was thinking of using, and then bends down to the dead body of the cat. It reaches into the slit in Bach's belly and draws out something that at first I take for guts but that turns out to be some kind of shifting red light, far deeper red than the whip, a red that's almost black. The light streams out from the cat's body and embeds itself in my chest just over my heart. It looks like we're anchored together now, me and Bach, by the dark pulsing rope. It feels warm, actually, like a restful bed after a long night of walking and searching. The blue dawn sky is darkening again, sunrise in reverse, the sky fading to a black I never knew existed, black past black. The Fury reaches out with a surgeon's careful hand and breaks the red rope.

I'm asleep, I think—I'm having this crazy dream. I'm in Holiday's yard, except it isn't really a yard at all. It's this dining room, with dark stone walls, and it goes on forever. I'm sitting at the table, there's someone else at the other end, and I realize it's Dad. He looks bad, really ill, he's sweating from the heat. It's sauna hot and stifling in here. He's in a white suit and violet shirt, and he's got a napkin tucked into his collar. We've got rare steak in front of us, big bloody slabs. Dad starts to talk, but I can't hear him properly, like a radio with bad reception. His voice doesn't sync with his mouth as it moves.

I'm sorry, he says, *I'm sorry (I didn't think) we don't have much time (I'm sorry) Luke.*

"Sorry for what?"

I never meant for—(this this sorry sorry) the Book of Eight—(the Book is a labyrinth) I never meant for this.

"I can't—Dad? You're not making any sense!"

(the sequence shows the path) I'm sorry Luke (my papers my sequence) I'm so sorry I (regret) that this ever (the Book is a labyrinth) I'm sorry Luke.

"What do I have to do?" I'm shouting now. "What sequence? What do I have to do?"

Dad looks at me, blinking. There's something in his mouth. He's choking. I'm trying to get up, but I can't, I'm stuck in my seat, I feel so heavy—

Dad raises one hand to his face and opens his mouth. He's choking and spluttering, and I can't get up to reach him.

(barren earth)

I'm lying on my back in wet grass. I'm wearing jeans, a
T-shirt, black sneakers, a raincoat. I can feel that I don't
have my wallet or phone, which is a problem. There's a
beer bottle lying on its side in the grass barely an arm's
length away from my face. I sit up. I'm in the middle of
someone's lawn. The sky is unbroken gray. I'm not cold
or warm or even hungover. Something happened last
night. I can't imagine anything good that would end in
me lying on a lawn, but I just don't remember what happened. I know who I am but not where I am or how I got
here. The gray of the sky is starting to unsettle me; it's less
the gray of an overcast day and more the gray of a blind
person's eye, lit from no particular point. I have no way of
knowing what time it is. The sun is presumably up there,
somewhere.

I get up, look at the back of the strange house, and
remember that it's Holiday's. What was I doing here at

Holiday's house? I know there was a party . . . I keep digging around, trying to remember something else, something that matters, but I can't quite reach it.

I know I'm in trouble. There's trouble at home, Mum's not well, I need to get back and check on her and Ham. It's not good that I've been out all night.

I go into Holiday's house through the back door and find it empty. The lights are off, the rooms are lit only by the dim sunshine that's filtering down through the clouds. I decide not to hang around. I need to get back to Mum. The kitchen is deserted and sort of creepy, empty bottles and cans covering every surface. You'd think someone would've started to clean up after a party this big. Where are Holiday's parents?

Not wanting to linger in the quiet gray house, I open the front door and walk out onto the street. The quickest way back to Wormwood Drive from Holiday's house takes me through the park, and after twenty minutes of walking down Wight Hill, the gray clouds still flawless and toneless above me, I'm walking in through the east gate of Dunbarrow's park. I cross the main field, and as I crest the shallow hill in the middle of the park, I see some people I recognize sitting in the bandstand. They're a fair distance from me, down by the river, but I can tell who it is: Kirk, Mark, Alice, and Holiday, plus someone else sitting with his back to me, some boy I don't know.

I wave at my mates and walk downhill toward them.

When I'm a little ways away from the bandstand, the boy sitting with them turns around to look at me.

I stop right where I am.

I—or rather, someone who looks exactly like me—am sitting between Holiday and Kirk. The impostor's hair is brown and thick, mussed with styling wax. He is wearing my exact same outfit, same jeans, same sneakers, same hooded raincoat, and smiling as he looks at me, as if it's completely normal that he's sitting there with my mates. He seems to be humming some kind of tune to himself. He's wearing a black ring on his right hand, and when I look more closely at the ring, there's a terrible flash, like red lighting striking my head, and I remember what happened: Dad's death, the Host, the Book of Eight, the sigil, Elza Moss, the party, the ritual, the cat with a dark gash carved in its stomach, the weird pulsing light that came out of it. The Fury, the flame-eyed demon, the sounds it made as it ate the Vassal whole. I remember everything.

"I don't understand it," Holiday's saying, eyes wet and red-rimmed. Given the state she was in last time I saw her, unconscious on her bed with the Prisoner threatening to cut the life out of her, it's actually a relief to see her sitting here crying. "Our *cat,* who would—"

"Sick bastards," Mark says.

"What's going on?" I ask them.

"It's not right," Kirk says. "None of us were even that wasted."

"We called the police," Holiday says. "Mum and Dad are with them right now. I just can't . . . how can I *sleep* in that house again? I'm just glad my brother wasn't there, but . . . how can I feel safe again? It's so horrible . . ."

"I know," Mark says. "Someone drugged us, I'm telling you."

"Kirk," I say, "who's that sitting next to you?"

"It's just, like, disgusting," Alice says. "Anything could have happened to us—"

"It's aliens," Kirk declares. "I saw this video on the Internet, of Roswell, right—"

"Hello?" I say. "Can you hear me? Did I go mute this morning?"

"—come in a UFO and, like, turn off your brain waves—"

"—and the policeman thought it might be a *gas leak*, as if that explains Bach—"

"—I've never felt like that in the morning, not from just wine—"

"—this one guy, they took tissue samples from his arse with this needle—"

"CAN ANYONE HEAR ME? HELLO! GUYS!"

They ignore me. Holiday is glittery-eyed with new tears. The other Luke isn't saying anything and keeps looking at me with a sly grin.

I realize I'm dead at the same moment you'd usually wake up in a nightmare. It's the same kind of jolt. Like walking up a staircase in the dark and trying to put your foot on a step at the top that isn't there. They've cut me loose. I'm the ghost now, and my body is being controlled by the Fury.

The Fury, the other me, stands abruptly. Everyone looks at him, like they're expecting him to make an off-the-cuff speech, but all my body does is point right at me and start to laugh. It's not happy laughter either. It's the laugh of someone with a leather mask and a chain saw they've been greasing with a loving hand for weeks. It's very loud, and everyone just stops talking as my body laughs and laughs before standing and striding right up to me, my spirit, whatever I am now, and laughing. It pushes its way right through me and past me and heads up the small hill in the middle of the park.

"What the hell?" asks Kirk.

"Is Luke . . . all right?"

"He seemed OK this morning," Mark says. "We all woke up in your garden with your parents there, remember? He was as all right as anyone."

"I dunno, mate," Kirk says. "Did he, like, actually say he was fine, though?"

"I guess he just mumbled . . . he looked fine."

"I've not heard him say a word all day," says Holiday.

"That was the creepiest thing, like, ever," says Alice. "I keep telling you, that guy is bad news. There's a weird vibe about him. I never liked him. He brought that freak Elza last night? And then she vanished just before everyone passed out? I bet *they* know something about this."

I give Alice the spectral finger.

"Nah, come on," says Kirk.

"He's sweet," says Holiday. "He's having a hard time."

"We should get him to a hospital," says Mark, uncertain. He and Kirk stand up and follow my body. By way of a definitive experiment, I take a deep breath and then run at a fair pace straight into the two of them. I pass through their bodies like I'm made of mist. Definitely dead, then. Walking through walls, all that jazz.

Or am I dead? The Host can't kill me, I know that much. Whatever their ritual did, my body doesn't seem to know it's dead. It's still standing at the top of the hill, and Kirk and Mark are approaching at a slow, wary pace. I move closer to them.

"Luke, mate, what's the matter? Are you all right?"

"Do you need to, like, lie down or something?"

My body turns around. It moves over to Mark and gently, calmly puts one hand on his shoulder. Whispers something to him that I can't hear. Mark's face goes white, and when my body moves away from him, he just stands there, staring at nothing.

Kirk's looking from my body to Mark and back, not sure what to do.

"Luke? Mate? Mark, help me?"

My body has its back turned to them. It raises its arms, as if about to conduct an orchestra.

"Luke, seriously," Kirk says, "this is not even funny anymore. Stop it."

Mark is shaking, breathing like he just ran a marathon.

"Please, let's go . . ." Mark whispers. "Let's go."

There's an explosion of sound and shrieking and a great whooshing noise as every single crow in every single tree in the park takes flight at once, streaming up out of the branches, whirling above us in a screaming black knot. Mark and Kirk cringe. The cloud of birds closes up tight as a fist and then expands, dissolving away into every corner of the sky. A single dead crow drops from the air and lands on the grass by my body's feet. A few dark feathers fall after it, glossy, like gasoline-coated petals.

"Luke . . ." Kirk says.

My body treats them to a large smile and then, with a relaxed movement, bends at the waist and picks up the dead bird and forces the entire thing, beak and feathers and scabby feet, into its mouth, gulping slightly to fit the whole body in there. It swallows and swallows and the bird is gone. Consumed. It treats me to a grin and a wave and then sets off with a spring in its step, moving north.

To their credit, my mates don't ask more questions. They sprint away from my body, heading back down to the bandstand, yelling at Holiday and Alice to run.

o o o

So about being a ghost, or whatever you want to call it. It's not easy to describe. I think your mind is so fixated on experiencing things one way that it takes a lot to convince it that things aren't like that anymore: like me, say, not realizing I was a spirit for all the time I spent walking through Holiday's house and down to the park. You don't get cold or hungry, you can't feel anything very much, but you don't notice that you can't feel the ground under your feet or the wind blowing. It takes real conscious effort to realize that you're not really walking on grass but rather making walking motions. I could imagine ghosts not knowing they were dead for weeks, or even years.

You can fly, or float, if you decide you want to. The whole thing is as tricky to explain as trying to describe what goes through your head when you want to move your hand to scratch at your stomach. You decide it will happen, and then it does. You can move fast, too, much faster than walking or running. Exactly how quickly I don't know, but it occurs to me that every time the Host seemed to disappear, they might have just moved somewhere faster than my eye could follow.

I consider following my possessed body, but I need to find Mum, and I head for home instead. I float up to Wormwood Drive, but I start to feel weird about it after going down a couple of streets and just jog instead. I don't know why. I suppose it's because when I fly, I remind myself that I don't have a body anymore, and it makes me want to panic, like I'm hanging off a cliff by my finger-tips and keep looking to see how far down I would fall. Anything that is normal and helps me forget, like walking, is good.

I see a few dead people on my way through Dunbarrow. There's a woman with a clearly broken neck sitting on one of the benches in the main square, looking at flowers, and a couple of men wearing fancy suits and frilled shirts, who could've stepped out of some old paint-ing. None of them tries to talk to me, which I'm fine with. I make good time, now there's no need to wait at pedestrian crossings, and I reach my house in about thirty minutes.

The windows are all closed, the door is locked, Mum's yellow car is still parked on the gravel driveway. Nobody passing by would have any idea there was something wrong, except perhaps for the fact that there are dead ani-mals nailed to the trees on each side of the front gate, and they aren't clearly visible from the road: They're close to the ground, partially hidden by branches. I walk closer, frowning. One is a ferret or stoat, the other is a small fox.

I take another step toward the gate, and they shud-der into life. Their heads move like stop-motion puppets, swiveling around to glare at me with sunken eyes.

Mustn't touch, says the fox. Its voice is tiny, shrill, like a whistle of wind in your ear.

Go away, says the stoat.

Naughty.

Go away. Go away.

"Or what?"

Mustn't touch.

I look closely at the driveway. There's a line of dark blood, spread between the two trees, blocking the entire path. I move my hand near the blood, and it begins to glow with a ghastly light. I retract my hand, and the glow dims.

"I'm guessing I can't cross this?" I ask the sentries.

Get lost.

"You should wonder why you're working for the guys that nailed you both to trees."

I abandon the driveway and walk in a loose circle around my house, pushing my way hazily through bushes and the wall of the neighbors' shed. Every tree in our garden has something—a crow, a badger, a rabbit, an owl— nailed to it, all chanting, *go away, go away, go away,* in a hushed chorus. Every time I try to cross the boundary of our property, I see the same telltale glow of blood on the ground, feel an electric resistance to my hand or foot as it nears the edge of the barrier. My house has new owners, and they've changed the locks. Mum's on the other side. It's so frustrating to know she's in there and not to be able to see her. The last time I saw her was Friday morning, more than a day ago. I hope she's all right. I hope Elza was right, I hope they're keeping her alive. About all I have right now is hope.

I wait in the yard opposite my gate for an hour, maybe more. I see the Heretic go wandering out the front door, screaming, orange flames playing around his shoulders. He makes it to the gate and then disappears. The postman pulls up in his cheerful red van and, unbelievably, doesn't notice the butcher's shop that has been set up in my front garden. He strolls up the drive, drops some advertisements through our letter box, and drives away.

The final visitor appears as I'm preparing to leave. My possessed body comes strolling down the road, still humming to itself, sneakers and jeans covered in mud. It walks with a loose, easy stride, hands swinging. It's terrifying and fascinating to see yourself walk, see your own eyes shine with a pleasure you don't share.

Getting near Elza is tricky. My house is warded by one type of magic, hers by another. Her hazel charms, these eight-pointed stars of wood that she carves herself, are hung in trees and bushes all over Towen Crescent. Before I was a spirit I'd never realized how many of them she'd made. Individually they don't do much, just emit this weird hum when I get up close to them, but when I try to actually get anywhere near number 19, the hum rises to a scream, like a supersonic plane taking off, and I can't take even one step farther. I'm stuck a few paces from her front gate, walking against something that feels like a raging wall of wind. I make my way around her house, hazel charms whining in my ears, looking for any way of getting inside and talking to her, but the place is locked up tight. When I've completed my circuit, I come back out to the front of the house and find Elza standing in the doorway, glaring out into the street. I raise my hand in greeting and her face falls.

"Luke," she says, "I'm so sorry for everything."

Ham pokes his fluffy face around her legs.

"Look," I say, "running off in a snit last night was a jerk move. You're forgiven. It's probably best you weren't there. Can you let me into your house?"

"I'm not sure how to say this, but . . . you're dead."

"No, Elza, no. I'm not dead."

"You're a ghost, Luke. I'm so sorry! You can't get near my house because of the hazel charms. I felt something trying to break them. I assumed it was one of your Host. I came outside to try to see what it was. You're a ghost."

"No, listen, OK—"

"Denial doesn't make it easier on either of us, Luke. I know it's hard, but . . . you died."

"I'm not dead. My body is still walking around."

"Your body is *what*?"

"I went through the park, and my body was there. Like, sitting with my friends. Then it went up a hill and it . . . it ate an entire bird."

"So you're possessed?"

"Yeah."

"So the Host didn't kill you? I mean, I suppose they can't, but . . . what have they done to you?"

"They did enough. The Vassal, he's gone. My dad's demon ate him. The Shepherd's in control. I think they severed me from my body somehow, and now the demon is driving it around. They locked me out of my house, too. There's a magic . . . barrier, a wall."

Elza comes down to her garden gate. Ham bounds after her.

"So you're still alive," she says.

"Kind of. I think I've been . . . evicted. They must have some other plan to actually kill me and get free."

"Which might require them having use of your body. I see."

"They've got it all worked out."

Elza runs her fingers through her hair.

"Look, can I come into your house?" I ask.

"Oh, sorry."

She comes out through the gate, Ham trotting at her heels. It's insane to think that Elza used to be this anonymous background figure in my life. I'm struck by how incredibly glad I am to see her, even though she ran away last night. When only one person in town can see you and talk to you, it's a lot easier to forgive them. She takes one of the hazel charms out of her hedge and speaks to it.

"This stranger is welcome."

She raises the star of wood up to my forehead. There's no flash of light or burst of intense cold or any of the things I've come to expect from magic, but the deafening shrill of the charms fades, and I find I can float into Elza's front garden without a problem.

"I wasn't sure if that would work," she remarks.

"You've never tried it before?"

"You're the first ghost I've ever been on good terms with."

"Where did you learn to make those?"

"I was thirteen and found some of them at my grandma's house. They were in an attic, really old. Like I said, my parents don't have second sight, but some of my ancestors must've. There was something about them that was . . . interesting to me. I looked them up and found they were a folk ward against the dead. No more ghosts in our house after that."

Ham keeps trying to jump at me and greet me, but he passes through my legs. He's increasingly bewildered, staring at me like I'm playing a trick on him.

"Anyway," she says, "let's go inside? I can't stand out here talking to myself."

I follow Elza and Ham through into her kitchen. Nothing's changed in here. The sink is full of dirty pans, like sunken oil-leaking warships. A fly is head-butting the window.

"So what happened to you?" I ask.

"Luke, I want you to know how sorry I am. I should have stuck with you . . . it's just, I'm proud. I'm too proud. All I could think after that bitch drenched me was 'I came here to save her, and she didn't deserve it.' And that was wrong. She did deserve it. Being a good person isn't just about rescuing the people you like and leaving the rest to hang.

"I made it about halfway down Wight Hill when I came to my senses. I knew I couldn't just leave you. I was on my way back up to the party, and I felt they were there. This was just after midnight. I tried to get the doors open and I couldn't and it was so cold. I could see people's shapes through the windows, and nobody was moving. I could feel black magic, like this sickness in my head, coming out from the house. I tried to get back in but . . . I don't know. I must've passed out. I woke up in the front yard at eight this morning. I must've slept all night there. People were waking up inside the house, so I just got out of there. I've been calling you, but—"

"It's all right. Really. There was some sort of spell, everyone at the party just blacked out. You were right. I didn't have a plan. I had nothing. I managed to get the Judge in my power somehow, with the sigil, but they had everyone else hostage. They were going to kill Holiday. I gave up the sigil and the Book, and they . . . this demon, the Fury . . . ate the Vassal, and cut me loose from my body."

"Right," Elza says. "The Host has the sigil and the

Book of Eight. So your dad's notes are no good to us until we get those back."

"Any plans on how we'll do that?"

"Not a clue. You?"

"I want my body back before we do anything else. And my mum . . . Mum's in there with them. I can't get in to see her. I haven't seen her since yesterday morning. I need to see her. I need to know how she is. They must want her for something, but I don't know what. . . . I need to see her."

"If I could hug you," Elza says, "I would."

Mrs. Moss comes back from her Saturday shift at the county hospital in the afternoon. Elza's mum is short and soft-looking, with a wide face and curly rust-colored hair. I assume Elza gets her height and severe features from her dad. Her mum wears a stained fleece over a nurse's pale-blue uniform, and her hair is slicked down by rain. She comes into the kitchen and begins clattering the pasta pans, yelling upstairs for Elza to come and clean them, like she was meant to do yesterday. There's this weird thrill in knowing that only Elza can see or hear me. I could potentially follow her mum around for the rest of her life, get to know her better than anyone else on the planet. Elza's mum herself is probably not the best candidate for this, but I'm willing to bet there *are* lives worth subscribing to.

Elza flumps downstairs and sets about washing the pans in the most dramatic way she can manage, huffing and deliberately slopping water down the front of the sink, while Elza's mum sits with Ham's heavy head in her lap and asks Elza if she doesn't think maybe she's a little old to throw a fit over being asked to clean up.

"I was *busy.*"

"I'm sure. When is your friend going to come and collect this dog?"

"Like I told you, Luke's mum is ill. You don't get handed a timetable when you're sick. I said we'd take care of Ham for a few days is all."

"You should've asked me before you made promises like that. And it's been a few days now, surely."

"It's been one night, Mum."

"Why don't you call and ask when he can take the dog back?"

"I don't want to bother him."

"I see. You don't want to 'come on too strong.'"

"*We are friends.* You start buzzing like a spy satellite whenever I mention a male name. It's pathetic."

"Your father and I have been married a long time," says Elza's mum with a little smirk, which I recognize from Elza's own face. "I have to vicariously experience a love life through my only daughter."

Elza laughs, and I realize what I thought was tension between them is a long-running game. Elza's mum scratches at Ham's ears, and I feel fairly confident I can leave him at the Moss place for as long as I need to. That's one small problem sorted out. Maybe they'll adopt him if the worst happens.

I haven't even left a will or anything.

Elza and her mum start work on some kind of pie. They talk about the dreary weather, about the shifts Elza's mum got at the hospital. When the pie is in the oven, Elza catches my eye and nods toward the hall, and I move out into it, passing through the wall, which is something I've started to enjoy.

"Look," she whispers, "this is sort of awkward, but do you mind leaving for a while?"

"Sorry?"

"My house, Luke. I've never particularly liked talking with real people when there are ghosts around; it's like having someone listening on the line while you're on the phone. The fact that I know you personally is making it even more weird."

"Did I do something wrong?"

"Not at all. You've been very quiet and polite. I'm just not sure if I can deal with talking to my mum any more while you listen in. It feels unfair to her. I hope you're not offended."

"I hadn't really thought about it, to be honest."

"Plus, I mean, it's not like you'll get cold outside at night. And I've been getting more and more worried about the demon driving your body around. About what would happen if it decided to come here."

"Your charms won't keep it away?"

"I think they would. But it could be hiding just down the road, for all I know. Waiting for the next time I have to go buy milk. If you could find it, I'd feel much safer."

I rise up like a puff of steam, the amazing insubstantial man, melting up through the dust-smothered attic of Elza's house and then through the roof into the night sky. I stop about fifty feet off the ground. Dunbarrow is spread out beneath me; the houses look like fantastically detailed models. I can see someone hurrying down the street, her umbrella spasming, turned inside out in the wind. I've no idea where to even start looking.

I head for the center of town. It's Saturday night, I realize; one week ago I was over at Kirk's place without a care in the world, didn't even know Dad was dead. I sink down toward the town square. It's surrounded by pubs, and I see the standard crowd milling around, gangs of lads in polo shirts, and lurching girls wearing heels. There are doormen, too, done up like mafia butlers, hard-boiled egg heads and long black coats. I'm watching them, hovering at roof height, wondering if I'm even going to make it past Halloween. If Mum will, if Elza will. Wondering if I'm going to make it to eighteen, ever be able to drive, ever actually be able to go into one of these pubs and buy a drink. There's still so much I haven't done, so much the Host is trying to take away from me.

As I'm about to leave, I hear someone shouting my name in the crowd.

"Luke!"

I pause in midair. There is definitely someone waving directly at me, a guy standing in the town square, someone I don't know. He's wearing a pink polo shirt. As I watch, a couple of girls walk straight through him. The ghost beckons me and then walks off through the wall behind him into a club called Vibe.

I follow him in. I've never been in here before—the bouncers are very keen on seeing people's IDs. It's pretty much what I expected: sticky dance floor, drunk people, a dry-ice machine. A table in the club's upper balcony seems to be populated by ghosts. Three of them are boys about my age, one of them the guy in the polo shirt who called to me. They're all dressed in sportswear, hair gelled forward into wet-looking spikes. The other two at the table are the Judge and the Oracle. I pause at the sight of the shaved-headed ghost, but he just stares down at his pint of beer.

"All right, boss," he says.

"Judge. What are you doing here?"

"Ah, these lads come in every weekend. We got talking outside, they invited us along. Wasn't expecting to see you here."

"They called me in," I say with a shrug. I suppose the Shepherd gave him a night off.

"Luke, mate, good to meet you," says one of the young guys.

"Do I know you?"

"I'm Andy. This is Jack and Ryan. We used to live here. In Dunbarrow."

"OK," I say. "You seem a bit familiar."

"It's embarrassing," says Jack.

"Could've happened to anyone," says the Judge indulgently.

"Makes us look like dickheads though."

"You all died at once?" I ask them.

"Car crash," says Ryan. "He was driving."

He points at Andy, who rolls his eyes.

"Never let that go, will you?"

"He was drunk," says Ryan.

"So were you!"

"I think I remember this," I say. "Three years ago? You were in the papers."

"They said we were taken away too soon," says Jack.

"Know how that is," says the Judge. "I got cut down in the prime of my flowering as well."

"How did you die?" I ask him.

"Fight, boss. Took a brick to the head. Good night."

"That's grim," I say.

"Don't even remember it too well, boss, tell the truth."

"Speaking of being cracked over the head, Judge . . ."

"Ah, I knew you'd start with that—" he begins.

"You sided with the Shepherd!"

"Listen, boss, I was backing the winning horse. You know how it is."

"No, I don't *know how it is*. They're going to kill me, Judge. You're helping them."

"A key that fits no lock," says the Oracle.

"You what?" Ryan asks her.

"For what it's worth, boss, I'm sorry. What happened with the Vassal—"

"That was horrible."

"He never said it would be like that! Never said they'd *eat* anyone!"

"So you already know each other?" the boy named Andy asks me.

"We go back," I say.

"The book is a labyrinth," says the Oracle.

"If you're sorry, then why don't you help me?" I ask.

"I can't," says the Judge.

"Big guy like you? I thought you stood up for yourself," I say.

"They'll cut me up, too, boss. You can't stop that dog-headed bastard from eating me, so I'm no use to you. Even if I wanted to be. Which I don't."

"All right," I say, "forget it. I didn't want any of this to happen either."

There's a lull in the music, and then a new track rushes up to fill the silence.

"So you come here all the time?" I ask Jack.

"Most Saturdays, yeah. Just helps you remember, you know?"

"We miss coming here," says Ryan.

"We watch the rugby games, too. That's how we know you."

"Right . . ."

"How did you die?" Andy asks me.

"I'm not actually dead," I say. "It's . . . weird. I'm trying to get back into my body. Some of his"—I nod at the Judge—"friends took it from me. I'm trying to find it right now."

There's a general silence. The boys give one another looks.

"Can't help you," Jack says at last. "Haven't seen it."

"Good luck, though," Andy says.

"You will meet a man with unlined hands," says the Oracle.

"You gotta cut that out, love," the Judge tells her. "Shepherd ain't gonna like that."

"Does she actually make prophecies?" I ask.

"Do-lally, boss. Don't make a lick of sense. Never understood why your pa kept her around. Must've seen something in her. She's sort of me opposite number, you know? I'm all hard truths; she's all vapors and visions. Maybe you need both of us in a Host for some balance."

A really drunk girl in a black dress sits in the same seat as Jack, and they look like a horrible double-exposed photograph. Then she shivers and gets back up and staggers away from the ghosts' table. I resolve, if I end up dead, that I'm not going to haunt a tacky club in Dunbarrow.

"Who knows?" I say to the skinhead after a moment. "Enjoy your night, Judge, Oracle, lads."

I fly up through the ceiling, arrowing through the roof of Vibe and into the sky. I fly across the town, leaving the bright-lit square and the rows of shuttered shops, pass over the silvery strip of the river and past the park's bandstand, its duck ponds and bales of orange leaves. I'm about to head back for Elza's place, with no idea where my body might be hiding, when I hear someone shouting my name and turn in midair, back toward the town center.

Ryan flies toward me, cutting low through the trees.

"Told the skinhead I'd gone to hover in the girl's bathrooms," he says.

"Of course."

"Look, they can't know I talked to you. Can't know anyone said anything. But I reckon you want to look up near the Devil's Footsteps. I know all the town ghosts, and there's been chat about stuff happening up there. If someone's got hold of your body, that's probably where it is."

"Devil's Footsteps?"

"Stone circle, mate. All the ghosts know it. It's a passing place, you know?"

"Where is it?" I ask.

"Up by school. There's a track behind the rugby fields, goes into the woods. Follow that. You'll know it when you see it."

"Thanks," I say.

"Don't worry," Ryan says, "just doing what we can. Dunbarrow boys stick together."

He grins and flies away, back toward Vibe. I make my way up to the school.

Dunbarrow High is, unsurprisingly, deserted. There's only a single white van left in the parking lot. I drift farther down toward ground level. It's too dark to see anything now that I'm beyond the influence of the street lamps. I float across the rugby field, listening to the trees rustle, trying to see whatever path Ryan was talking about. I've never heard anything about the ominously named Devil's Footsteps, and I'm finding it hard to believe there's any occult hot spot so close to the high school.

Just as I'm about to give up, I see someone wearing a black hooded jacket. I dart into the pine trees and hang in the air just underneath the dripping dark branches. It's me—my body. It comes closer, making squishing noises as it walks across the damp field. It's carrying a headless rabbit in its left hand, the brown corpse swinging by the hind legs. As my body passes the tree I'm hidden in, it pauses and looks around, as if it can sense something in the wind. My face is white beneath the hood of the raincoat, my mouth twisted into an expression of joy. If I still had any breath, I'd be holding it. After a moment my body turns and moves on, striding into the darkness, and I glide along in pursuit.

We make our way over the rugby field and then head up through the woods, uphill for quite a distance, then down a shallow slope, and we come suddenly to what must be the Devil's Footsteps. They're set in a hollow completely overshadowed by enormous oak trees. The hollow is carpeted by soft moss, as well as by tufts of those needle-thin reeds that grow in wet earth. There are three stones, one taller than a man, the other two more rounded, flatter, and maybe table height. I could get dramatic and compare them to teeth, but they're really just craggy masses of rock, like someone started sculpting something and then just couldn't be bothered and left them out here. The setting is appropriately sinister.

My body walks to the center of the stone circle and then kneels and starts to claw at the ground with its hands. I watch, hidden up in the tree line, as it digs, ignoring the wind and rain.

o o o

I get back to Elza's house at midnight. Ham is laid out at her feet, breathing softly. She's got two pages of my dad's notes on the sofa in front of her and is furiously scribbling at something with a permanent marker.

"Knock, knock."

"Did you find yourself?"

"I did, actually. I—it, rather—was up behind school. Some place called the Devil's Footsteps?"

"Oh. The sacrifice grounds. Well that's . . . unpleasant. It must be preparing something for Halloween."

"It dug a hole for hours, stopped just before midnight. I followed it back to my house."

"And you couldn't get in because of the magical barrier."

"Right. It went in and that was it. It's still there."

"So we've got lots of problems. No sigil, no Book, you've got no body. They've got your mum shut up in the house. We've only got five full days until Halloween, and I still have no idea what your dad's sheets of numbers are all about."

"Elza, I want to know my mum's OK. I haven't seen her since Friday. Anything could've happened to her. You know how she's been. I want to see her."

"All right." Elza pinches at the bridge of her nose. "Oh, my head is pounding. I was going to suggest the same thing. If the Host doesn't want you in your house, then that seems like an excellent reason to get inside."

"What, you want to go now?"

"No, not now. We need to plan this properly. We can't just go running off without a clue, like we did to Holiday's place. We'll work this out and go tomorrow. Rescuing your mum seems like a good start."

"OK, but how will that help us with the rest of it?"

"Well . . . I don't know. But they clearly want her alive for something. I think if we get your mum out of there, they'll come after us. Your body, too. And we'll . . . we'll have to improvise."

"OK," I say. "I mean, I don't have a better plan."

"So this magic circle," Elza says. "Could I cross it? Does it stop spirits only?"

"I don't think the magic circle stops living people. I saw the postman go in."

"Maybe they were letting him through."

"Yeah," I say, "maybe. I saw birds get through, too."

"Hmm. I've got an idea."

"Really?"

"Have you tried possessing anything yourself?"

"It never crossed my mind."

"Probably for the best. It's a bad habit to get into. Well, listen, I'm not going in there alone. We know they can't kill you. You're already a ghost. I'm not sure how much they could even do to you. But I'm vulnerable. I don't think the wyrdstone will help me if your body gets hold of me."

"So I have to come, too. But I can't cross the—"

"Yes. But like I said, I've got an idea. You know about the siege of Troy, right? The Greeks had a wooden horse with soldiers inside. We don't have a wooden horse, but we do have something I think you'll be able to use to cross the barrier inside."

"Well, what is it?"

The fire spits, and a lump of flaming coal rolls out of the grate and hits the fire screen. Ham snaps out of his sleep, leaps upright, and whines. He turns to Elza and me and looks at us with wide affronted eyes.

(dogsbody)

Am Ham. Am Luke. Walk fields with girl. Fields smell good. Am brave. Am good. Big brave Ham. Good boy. Love girl. Am in rain. No good. Trees shouting in rain. Mud under. Feet wet. Am brave. Girl walk with Ham. Find Mum. Go to house. Bad house.

Walk walk. Head wet. Girl talk. Talk talk talk. High voice. Girl hair wet. Girl smell very good. Walk walk walk. See house. Bad house. Ham afraid. Ham brave. House big and bad. Was good house. Now Ham afraid. House full of unpeople. Unpeople bad, no smell. Ham afraid. Ham brave. Must find Mum. Must be brave. House full of unLuke too. Worst of all. Smell like Luke. Is not Luke.

Sneak sneak. Ham sneak. House smell wrong. Am brave. Will not run. Luke brave. Hedge have blood under. Fresh blood. Unbeasts hung from trees. Unbeasts talking. Say *go away go away go away.* Ham not run. Must cross blood. Go to bad house. Am Ham. Am Luke.

Girl talk, push at Ham. Do not want to go. Ham afraid. Unbeasts everywhere. Unpeople too. Very bad. House big and dark and bad.

Girl hit Ham on bott. Hit bott very hard. Not happy. Want to shout. Am Luke. Am Luke. Am crawl. Girl follow. Am brave. Unbeasts nailed to trees. Unbeasts shout.

Need to find Mum. Am Luke. Am Ham. Am brave. Am bravest. Crawl across blood. Bad smell. Am bravest. Cross lawn. Girl hide in shed.

Am not Ham. Am Luke Luke am Luke and finally—

—finally let go of Ham's body and whistle up out of his nose, like steam from a kettle. Elza was right. It worked, we're inside the circle. The dull-eyed heads of the carrion sentries turn to watch me as I drift over the back lawn, which was always my favorite place in our house, wide and green and gently curving down to a low stone wall, with churned-up sheep fields just beyond. Ham is whimpering behind me. I hope he's not going to be a liability. Using him to cross the barrier around my house was a stroke of genius, but I'm worried that he'll alert the ghosts. I've been keeping watch over my house since the early morning, hovering behind our neighbor's chimney stack. My body went out into the moors this morning and hasn't come back, but that doesn't mean it's not going to, and I'm certain the Shepherd will have other members of the Host guarding the house.

"Go and find Elza!" I hiss. I think about possessing him again and driving him over to the garden shed to wait, but I'd rather not. Holding myself inside Ham's mind is the most confusing thing I've ever done, worse than any drunken haze or dream. It's like being trapped in a maze of mirrors while an idiot shouts into your ears. Every piece of dirt that made up the fields between Towen Crescent and here smelled indescribable; it was like an orchestra of sound and light playing in my snout. I was losing track of who I was. Without Elza spurring Ham on, I couldn't even have made him cross the boundary.

I move across the garden and melt through the wall of the kitchen. I can hear the television talking in the living room. I move into the hall and peek my head around the door frame. The Judge is sitting on the sofa, red Docs resting on the coffee table. He's watching a rugby game, obviously neglecting guard duty. I wonder what the rest of the Host are doing. I decide on the most direct approach possible and drift directly up through the ceiling into Mum's bedroom.

My head breaks through the floor, then my shoulders, pushing up into the room. It's dark in here. The window is covered by some thick black bedsheets, not her usual orange-and-green curtains. Only a thin seam of daylight is getting in around the edges.

Mum herself is floating about a foot above the bed,

suspended by an unseen force. The enormous star rune is still painted above her bed, with eight other smaller marks now ringed around it. I move closer to the bed. Her face is flat and calm; it doesn't look like she's in pain. Her arms are folded over her chest, and I see that she's clasping a small green-bound book. So that's where they're keeping the Book of Eight. I don't know how we're going to get Mum out of here. I didn't plan for her to be levitating. I stay by her bedside, listening to her breathe, knowing that even if she woke up, she wouldn't be able to see me. I can't even touch her. If only I hadn't signed Berkley's contract . . .

I can't be in this room. I dart through the wall into my room, which has been ransacked, clothes and bedding exploding everywhere. Something has torn at my wallpaper like an animal. Checking every room in the house, I find no other spirits and return to the garden shed, where Elza and Ham are cowering.

"What's going on?" Elza asks.

"The Judge is in the living room, but he's watching TV. You can get by. The rest of them aren't here, so far as I can see. They must be at the Footsteps or something."

"Or that's what they want us to think."

"Well, what can we do? OK, so you know where Mum's bedroom is. Things have . . . gotten strange in there."

"Are you sure about this?" she asks.

"The Book of Eight is up there as well. We need the Book."

Elza breaks cover and runs across the back lawn, combat boots squelching in the wet grass. Ham remains in the shed, cowering under a tool bench. I decide that he's been demoted to omega pack member due to persistent cowardice. I catch Elza up as she reaches the back door. Covering her fist with a rag from the shed, Elza smashes a pane of glass and reaches in to undo the latch.

"The key is under the flowerpot!" I hiss.

"Sorry. I've just always wanted to do that."

"It was noisy! There's a ghost in there, remember?"

Elza moves into the kitchen. Fragments of glass crunch beneath her feet. She takes a knife from the magnetic strip behind the stove.

"I don't know if that'll help you."

"Never can tell. Oh, wow, is this a Svensberg limited edition?"

"Mum's room is directly above us."

"She has good taste in knives."

"Elza —"

"Sorry. I get irrelevant when I'm scared."

Her knuckles are very white as they grip the handle of the blade. The television switches to an advertisement, and I motion frantically at her to hide. She ducks into the pantry, breathing hard. The Judge picks up the remote and skips to the next part of the game. I move through the wall into the living room, and watch the back of his gray stubbly head until I'm sure he's completely immersed. I flit back to the closet.

"If you see my body, are you going to stab me?" I whisper.

"Not if I don't have to."

"I'd just rather you didn't stab me. I need that body in good condition."

Elza moves across the front hall, the riskiest area, where the Judge could easily see her. She's quiet and light on her toes when she wants to be, reminding me of a large black cat. She flattens against the coat closet by the door, waiting for my signal before climbing the stairs. The crowd noise on the television sounds like ocean surf. The Judge shifts his boots, so now the left foot rests on top of the right foot. I'm watching for any sign that he might be about to get up. After another minute I decide it's safe. Elza climbs the stairs and edges across the landing, toward Mum's room. Elza softly moves the door open, knife poised to strike, and then recoils from the dark doorway.

"Is she . . . ?"

"Yeah. Floating."

The room feels even worse the second time I see it, more like a tomb than a bedroom.

"I've never seen anything like that." Elza sounds both scared and fascinated.

"We need to get her out of here," I say.

Elza closes the bedroom door behind her. The noise of the Judge's rugby game fades away. It's even darker now. I can just make out Elza's face. I want my mum out of this house, away from the ghosts, somewhere safe, and I can't ever touch her. I need Elza to understand this.

"I don't know how to do that," she says.

"We have to get her out of here! She's my mum! I've left her like this for days! We have to do something."

"We are doing something," Elza says. "We need the Book and the sigil back. Luke . . . I get what it's like. If that was my mum, I don't know what I'd do. But we need to focus. We need to work out how to read the Book and banish the Host forever. That's what'll save her. You want to take her to the hospital? What are they going to do for her? She'll be no safer than here."

"You don't know that! Elza, don't talk like that!"

"Luke, your mum is *levitating*. How am I supposed to get her out of the house? Tie a rope around her ankle? Pull her down the road like a kite?"

I don't say anything. I hate this. It feels like failing. Whatever the Host is doing to her, it's too far gone for the county hospital to be of any use. I don't want to leave her here, but I don't know that we've got a choice.

"Get the Book, then," I say.

Elza takes a deep breath.

"I'm a bit afraid to touch her. What if she wakes up?"

"And does what?"

"And strangles me or something? I don't want to stab her."

"We don't have a choice, remember?"

Gripping the carving knife, Elza walks softly across the dark bedroom. I glide alongside her, keeping a close eye on Mum. I think Mum looks more peaceful than evil, but something about the absolute stillness of her face is frightening. I never imagined I could be afraid of her. She's not even angry if I get into trouble at school or forget to walk Ham or anything like that; she just flaps a hand and says *honestly* like it's just typical of me, what she expected. I don't know if I've ever heard her raise her voice. But here, now, as Elza's hands move closer and closer to Mum's body, closer to the Book, it's possible to love her and be afraid of her. It's possible to wonder what her closed eyes are seeing. What you'd see in them if she woke.

Elza grasps the Book of Eight and slowly starts to pull it from Mum's arms.

Mum makes a small sigh.

Elza freezes.

"She won't hurt you," I say.

"Easy for you to say, Man Without Body."

"I have a body. It might be coming back right now. We need to get out of here."

Elza grits her teeth and slides the Book of Eight free.

Mum's arms settle into their new position, the Book no longer held against her chest.

Elza lets out the breath she was holding and walks as fast as she can out of there, closing the door behind her. I blink through the bedroom wall just in time to hear her squeak and muffle a scream.

The Heretic is standing on the landing, wreathed in fire. His jaw hangs open, and oily smoke boils from his nostrils and eye sockets. He reaches a fleshless hand out to me, grasping at the air.

"*Pater noster, qui es in caelis, sanctificetur nomen tuum!*"

"What *is* that?" hisses Elza.

"That's the Heretic. He's harmless. Doesn't even know who he is—be quiet!" I say to the thing.

"Is he trying to warn them?" Elza asks.

"He doesn't have enough brain left to warn anyone."

"*Adveniat regnum tuum!*"

"Shut *up*!"

"*Fiat voluntas tua, sicut in caelo et in terra!*"

"He's going to warn them whether he means it or not!" Elza whispers frantically.

"Please shut up! Heretic!"

"*Panem nostrum quotidianum da nobis hodie, et dimitte nobis—*"

"Elza, go into the bathroom. Do it now."

"*—debita nostra sicut et nos dimittimus debitoribus nostris!*"

"What?" she asks.

"*Et ne nos inducas in tentationem, sed libera nos a malo!*"

"Bathroom. Open the window, go out onto the garage roof. You can drop from there to the back garden. I'll deal with the Judge. He can't hurt me. Go."

"*Pater noster, qui es in caelis, sanctificetur nomen tuum!*"

Elza nods and slips into the bathroom, closing the door behind her. The Judge pounds up the stairs, potato face creased with annoyance.

"What are you yelling about? Bloody fuss, never a mome—Luke!"

"Judge."

He pauses on the stairs. One fat hand is on the banister, the other clenches into a fist.

"*Adveniat regnum tuum!*"

"Told you to stop meddling. Nose out, I said."

"You know I can't do that," I say.

"What the bloody—how'd you get in here?"

"The Shepherd doesn't know everything. That's all I can say."

"*Fiat voluntas tua, sicut in caelo et in terra!*"

"You got to leave" he says. "I got to tell them you were here."

"Do what you have to, Judge. But I'm going to win this thing, and I'll remember which side you were on."

"Bloody"—he pulls at his collar—"bloody hell! The Fury—you know I can't. Boss. Until you get that thing under control, I can't do nothing but what they tell me."

"*Panem nostrum quotidianum da nobis hodie* . . ." The Heretic has begun to walk, waving its blazing arms. It melts through the wall in the direction of Elza and Ham, although the Judge, mercifully, doesn't seem interested.

"I can win this. Believe me. I'm sending the Shepherd and the Fury back to Hell."

"You got to go," he says. "Give you fifteen minutes, but I have to report, tell them you got inside the house. I have to."

I take a breath.

"Thanks," I say. I imagine Elza, forcing herself through the tiny window, boots flailing against the mossy-green tiles. Imagine her dropping down onto the lawn, the Book of Eight held in the pocket of her raincoat. Hopefully she's made it out by now, because I wouldn't put it past the Judge to go outside and look around.

". . . *sicut et nos dimittimus debitoribus nostris!*" The ghost's idiot chant is muffled by walls and windows.

The Judge gives me a little nod. The meaning is unclear. For a moment I think he's going to go outside, but then he turns and walks back downstairs.

"I'm sorry about the Vassal," I say, and then fly out of my house like an arrow, through the insulated wall cavity, into the drab October air. The rain is falling at a slant, our gutters nearly exploding with water, every tree hissing in the wind like a radio tuned to a blank channel. Elza is over the garden wall already, and Ham is prancing and rearing up in our apple grove, just in front of the blood-magic boundary line. I whoosh down toward him, my second body—

—body boy's body. Dogsbody. Dog body. Am Ham. Very brave. Well done. Good boy good girl. Love girl. Brave girl. Girl run Ham run. Bye bye unbeasts. Bye bye bad house. Am Ham. Love field. Love sky. Hello fields. Am Luke. Am Ham.

Ham run. Run Ham run. Run run run.

Once we've crossed a couple of fields, I squeeze myself out of Ham's mind again, confident that he's grasped the direction he's supposed to travel. Elza glances over her shoulder every minute or so. The golden-leafed trees that surround my garden are almost out of sight, but she's still convinced that something terrible will come rocketing out of them at any moment.

"So how are we going to get my body back?" I ask.

"I don't know yet."

"I mean, I think I need it. If I want to be a proper necromancer. I can't use the sigil as a spirit. You can't wear a ring on a ghost finger. Not that we even have the sigil. Last I saw it my body was wearing it."

"I think that's why they took your body over," she

says. "To limit your options. Gives them control. They can kill it during whatever ritual they're planning for Halloween, I'd imagine."

"Well, so we —"

"Luke!"

"What?"

Elza points at the horizon. We're in the middle of a sheepless sheep paddock bounded by drystone walls. To our left are the outskirts of Dunbarrow; to the right, more fields, and eventually the motorway. Nobody is around. Directly to our front is a dense pinewood, which is where Elza is gesturing so frantically.

"I don't see anyt —" I say, and then I do. There's someone coming out of the pines, a long way off, just three dabs of white moving against the dark of the trees. I can't see perfectly at this distance, but it looks like me.

"Speak of the devil."

"Has it seen us?" Elza hisses.

"I don't know. Where are we?"

"Near Bareoak Drive," she says. "We're not far from my place now."

"Can I — it — get into your house?"

"Maybe. Maybe not. I don't really know what hazel charms do against possessed people. I'd rather not find out."

I look at the fields. We've got three to cross before we reach any buildings or streets. My body is four fields away, but I know it can move pretty fast if it wants to. I do work out after all. I think the angles work in our favor, but only just.

"Should I run?" asks Elza.

"I don't know. I don't think it's seen us, but if we move left . . ."

"We'll be on higher ground, yes."

"It'll see us."

"It'll see us if we stay here much longer," says Elza.

"OK," I say, "move now. Run as fast as you can."

Elza nods and then breaks as fast as she can for the left-hand side of the field. Ham follows me as I glide alongside. From the way he gallops, he clearly thinks it's all a game.

Elza runs, boots splodding in the wet earth. My demon-ridden body sees us before we reach the wall and begins to sprint toward us, a tiny black shape bobbing on the slope in front of the woods. Elza scrambles over the drystone wall, dislodging some of the smaller stones. Ham whines and skitters around in circles before finally remembering he can jump over walls, and leaps, landing with a splatter in the mud.

We make it across the second field, but my body vaults the north wall just as Elza reaches the western one, and she's flagging. Ham yelps as he leaps. Elza hits the ground with a huff that sounds pained. There's thick mud all over her legs. It's almost unbearable to watch like this and not be able to do anything. I see that my possessed body is gaining. Its footfalls are as regular as a drum. I want to close my eyes, but I can't.

Elza is panting worse than Ham now, forcing herself onward. This final field is slightly sloped, with a low middle and raised sides. Elza pounds down the muddy slope, slams her feet into a cold, greasy pool that's collected in the dip at the center of the field, and gasps as she pelts through the water, spraying coldness over her legs and back.

"You're doing great!" I shout at her. "Keep going!"

"I'm not . . . a runner . . ." she pants.

"You're running, aren't you? I think that counts!"

Ham is soaked, too, pounding across the grass, fur sticking out from his sides and legs in dark dripping spikes. It's raining again. The rain makes a hiss against the grass.

The final ascent is something like a nightmare. Her boots slip in the mud, and twice Elza nearly falls. Her hair is plastered to her face, obscuring her terrified eyes.

"I can't . . ." she says.

"You have to! I can't do this without you! Keep going!"

Her feet slam, slam, slam on the ground.

My body clears the last wall between it and us with an easy vault, slides down the muddy bank, and sluices through the waterlogged bowl in the middle of the field; its hair is domelike and glossy with rain, its face twisted into an expression of furious good cheer. My body's fingers move in clutches and spasms, like the tendrils of anemones. Ham is ahead of Elza now. He's more used to running, terrified by the thing he knows isn't truly me.

Elza is twenty feet from the houses of Bareoak Drive.

"How close . . . is it?" Elza rasps.

Ten feet.

"It's still way, way behind you!" I lie. "You're OK! Keep going!"

The ground is flattening out.

My body is closing the distance.

Elza sprints for a gap in the fence, a narrow alleyway. Ham vanishes ahead of her. The rain is coming down hard. I'm moving above her, higher than the fences and houses, like a helicopter camera. My demon-ridden body rushes up the hill toward her. It's making whimpering noises, a parody of Elza's own.

"Left!" I yell down to her, "go left! You need to find people!"

I don't know how strong the Luke-thing is. Maybe it can kill anyone who tries to help her. Elza sprints along the alleyway and ducks to the right, sprawling out sideways on the pavement. She's fallen. I dive toward her as the demon closes in. My body is running down the alleyway, sneakers heavy with clumps of dark mud, arms flailing, idiot mouth grinning—

Elza isn't getting up, she's still on the ground, she—

My body reaches the end of the alleyway, and Elza kicks out as hard as she can, catching its foot with the solid heel of her boot. For an instant my body is caught sprawling in midair, not a single part of it touching the ground as its momentum carries it forward. I hear the solid thump of my body's head as it encounters the side of a car. The alarm starts to whine and chirp. Elza gets to her feet, gasping so heavily she can't even talk. My body is lying completely still, sprawled out on the pavement.

"Did you *kill* me? Elza, seriously. Tell me you didn't just kill me."

Elza bends down and then rasps and rasps and vomits water onto the concrete.

"*Ulmhff—*"

"I can't believe it."

"Me . . . neither," she says, wiping her mouth. She carefully kneels and holds my wrist for a few seconds. I see that my body is wearing the sigil on its right hand, which means Elza just solved two problems with one well-aimed boot. "It's . . . you're . . . alive. Unconscious. I wasn't sure if that could happen to someone who was possessed. I just couldn't go on anymore. That . . . that was it."

"What do we do now?"

"Get some rope?" Elza shrugs. "Tie him up. Work out what to do with him."

Ham reenters the scene, padding around from the side of a parked car. He's all scraggly with mud and water, fur exploding from his face in all directions. He noses at my body and then recoils as if it smells bad. The car alarm continues to wail. Elza starts to pull at my body.

"Heavy?" I ask, not that there's any way I can help.

"It's only one street to go. I can manage."

She settles for looping her arms under its armpits and then drags my body backward along the road, my ruined sneakers dragging along the sidewalk behind us. I'm astonished she can even lift herself off the ground after that chase, but she just does it.

"I'm all hopped up on adrenaline," she explains. "I just keep wanting to laugh. Even when I was being chased. It felt so funny. Like this bad joke. You know?"

"Not really."

Halfway down the street, someone comes outside, too late to help us. An old man stands on the stoop of his house, disturbed by the car alarm. He doesn't say anything, just sniffs and stands and watches as Elza pulls my body along, Ham trotting beside her.

"Too much to drink," Elza huffs at the man, fake cheer barely disguising her pain.

The man sniffs again and shakes his head. Flame-colored leaves spiral down in his garden.

My body lies faceup on the duvet in Elza's spare room, lashed with the synthetic rope that her DIY dad has at least three miles of lying around in the garage. The ropes coil over one another like a nest of snakes, fastened by impervious-looking knots. My body's arms and legs are bound together, and then my bound limbs are attached to the bedposts. I float up by the ceiling, looking down into my own face.

"I really hope this holds," Elza says. "I've never tried to keep a possessed person hostage before; I don't know how strong they are."

"So what do we do now?"

"Some kind of exorcism, I suppose."

"Do we shout that the power of Christ compels it?" I ask.

"If you like. We could try it now."

"Nah. I'd feel stupid."

"I bet there's something about this in the Book. If we could just read it, I know we could come up with something . . ."

"Maybe—"

The room begins to shake. At first it sounds like a clothes dryer is turned on in the room below, but quickly the noise reverberates and intensifies and the room begins to physically quake, furniture rattling.

Ham howls in the kitchen. The dusty bookshelves jostle and mutter, paperbacks plummeting to the ground. The duvet convulses, the bedside lamp topples over, casting huge wild shadows. My body begins to scream and thrash. It strains at the ropes like an animal and begins to shriek. A choir of horrible voices comes from its throat, wailing without words.

Black smoke streams from my body's mouth and nose. Every argument you've ever heard, the voice of every drunken prick at closing time, is bellowing at thunderstorm volume. The noise is unbearable. Elza claps her hands over her ears, brow creased with pain. The smoke congeals and the voice grows louder, ranting and screaming. The Fury looms over the bed, eyes like furnace doors, a volcanic rift of a mouth.

"Get out of here!" Elza yells. "Get out of my house! Go!"

The thing grows larger. The room is darkening, like the demon is drawing all the light into itself. It must be eight feet tall, nine feet, as broad as the bed. There's a flash of ravenous orange flame, and the demon's whip is swinging from its hand. Faster than a scorpion's tail, it flicks its wrist backward and sends the lash coiling toward Elza's body.

I don't have time to think about what I'm doing. I dart my ghost body in between the demon and Elza, placing myself in the whip's path. I brace myself for it to cut me in half, like it did the Vassal, but instead, the flames coil around me and stick there. There's no pain, the lash doesn't sear into my spirit flesh. I'm stuck tight. The Fury roars even louder and tugs at the whip, trying to free it.

"It can't hurt me!" I yell. "My Host can't harm me! Use the stone!"

Elza lunges forward, dodging around the swinging end of the fire whip, and presses her wyrdstone into the demon's face. There's a searing flash, like a tiny star, and the demon explodes away from the stone, bursting into a bloom of black smoke, which spirals in the air, seeming panicked, and then races for the window and boils its way out through a crack in the frame.

"Elza!"

"That went better than expected," she says, looking down at her right palm. I see the wyrdstone in her hand has dissolved into gray dust.

"What happened to your stone?"

"Banishing a spirit like that was too much for it. But that thing, the Fury, it's gone. It can't come back in here again. And we've got your body back."

I take a good look at my body. My hair is lank and wet, plastered to my forehead. There's mud all over my legs and feet and mud on the bed as well. It feels strange to suddenly notice that we've made a mess of the room. It's a really small concern. When you're trying to survive, you forget that you're not supposed to track mud into people's houses. My body's face looks bruised and ill, and there's a nasty bump forming where my forehead hit the side of a car.

"Why did it leave my body in the first place?" I'm wondering.

"Easiest way to free itself," Elza replies.

I float above my body, which is still tied to the bed. Blood is coming from the corner of my mouth. I've been away from it for only a day, but I've gotten used to floating, being invisible, walking through walls.

My face grows closer and closer, enormous, pale, streaked with dirt. I'm not exactly clear on how this is going to work. When I went into Ham's body, I just moved into his skin like passing through a curtain, but entering people might be different. I move closer to my own face. I fall into my eye.

I am at the center of the earth.

Inside the center of the earth I'm sitting in the backseat of a car the same car we had when I was six and my dad's in the driver's seat I know it's him by the white suit and his long hair hanging over the collar and we're driving through a forest of dark trees with endless branches that fork and split and I can't see the tops of any trees they go too high for me to see. We're driving and driving and we keep turning at these forks in the road lurching left or right and on the road signs I see numerals scrawled in Dad's handwriting and each time we turn left the signs are reversed and I start to feel like there's some pattern

I can't quite grasp. I'm listening to Dad's voice echoing saying *(that Book is not a product of the conscious mind)* and the tree trunks scroll past us and the trees have pale leaves and I see that they're pages yes thin yellow pages an infinite forest of pages and there's something else in the car with us something dark and hunched and bloody sat in the backseat next to me but I can't turn my head to look at it I'm too scared but I can hear it breathing and we keep driving and *(the sequence reveals the path)* and I'm saying Dad I don't understand and he's gesturing with one heavy-ringed hand saying *(we don't have time for this)* and all the while I'm trying to pretend I can't hear the other passenger breathing beside me I'm looking out of the window because if either of us shows that we know there's a third person in the car something terrible will happen. I just know it. *(My sequence shows the path)* Dad's saying and pointing at the road signs with their numerals *(do you understand)* and as he speaks I can hear the thing next to me moving feel it leaning my way hear its whisper saying *don't you know me?* and Dad can't hear it he doesn't seem to realize it's there and I'm frozen here I can't turn around *(the Book is yours now) (show you are the master)* and the forest is endless tall forking trees it's all around we'll never get out and I'm saying should I know you and the thing beside me whispers *you'd better know me, you ought to know me, because I'm your brother.*

○ ○ ○

"Luke!"

"..."

"Are you OK?"

Elza and the demon really did some work on me. Every bit of me hurts. My body feels like a writhing sack of aches, each one starved and rabid, desperately clawing at its competitor aches in a bid to become the alpha ache and reign supreme. Even my teeth are throbbing. Glad as I am to have my body back, there are things I didn't miss.

Ham rushes into the room and thrusts a soothing nose into my ear. I manage a smile.

"You were convulsing," Elza says. "I got worried."

"I was dreaming," I say.

"You've only been back in your body about five minutes. What was the dream?"

"Uh . . . it was horrible. But it was important. I wish I could remember. . . . My dad . . ."

"Your dad was in your dream?"

"Yeah . . . there was someone else as well "

The dream keeps slipping out of my grasp, like dreams do. Dad was trying to tell me something. Whether it was actually him . . . I wonder what happened to him once he died. Why haven't I seen his ghost hanging around anyway? Did he already cross over? Is the Host keeping him away somehow?

I decide to focus on the concrete facts. It's the twenty-sixth. Five days until Halloween. We've got the Book of

Eight. The sigil is back on my finger. We've got a chance. Ham grumbles and sets himself down in the doorway of the bedroom.

"OK," Elza says, sitting on the bed. Her knee rests against mine. "Good news."

"Don't keep me in suspense."

"The good news is I'm making chicken fingers and baked beans for supper."

"That's excellent news."

"Please don't judge me. The freezer was, like, Old Mother Hubbard's freezer."

"You've never had my cooking, Elza. I don't judge."

"So," she says. She's still wearing her raincoat. She reaches into the inside pocket, pulls out the Book of Eight, and places it in front of me, on the bedsheets. "Body returned to rightful owner. We've made some progress, and we're actually back at square one now. We've got the Book and the sigil and your dad's weird numerology code. And no idea how to put them all together."

I run my left thumb over the cold eight-sided stone set into my sigil. I remember my dad's hands on the steering wheel. Tall forking trees all around us. Something stirring beside me in the other seat. I look at the Book's green cover, the eight-pointed star. I feel like the dream was more than just a dream. *(That Book is not a product of the conscious mind.)* Where am I getting this from? Is that what Dad told me?

"What we need to know is inside the Book," I say. "I've seen the Shepherd using it. The Host wouldn't take it if it weren't important. We know it's not all blank. I've seen things written inside it." I've stood up, and I'm pacing as I think, body aching.

"Right," Elza says. She looks exhausted, wrung out. She looks as bad as I feel. The sharpness I saw in her when we first talked about the Host, in the graveyard, has dulled. We need to finish this soon, or neither of us will have the energy to go on.

"The Shepherd . . . the first time I spoke to him, he said the Book of Eight was infinite. He said even experienced necromancers would find pages they'd never seen before."

"Well, that's impossible" Elza says. "How can a book be infinite? Look at it. It's only a couple of inches thick."

"It's magic, Elza. I'm not even sure it's really a book at all. What it looks like to us doesn't matter. What if he's right? What if it is infinite? It could look blank forever. There's room for as many blank pages as you can imagine. We could turn the pages all our lives and never reach one that had something written on it."

"So how would we find one that does? The Shepherd seemed to manage it. Right?"

"Not by turning pages at random. It'll always be blank if we do that, I think. But there must be paths." The dream's coming back to me fully now, the forking road, the forest, the trees with endless branches covered in pages. *(My sequence shows the path.)* What sequence? Are the numbers a sequence? Is that what he meant?

"What paths, Luke? What are you talking about?"

"The Book's a maze. It's a dark forest. Normal books, page one leads to page two leads to page three. But not this one."

"The Book of Eight is a 'dark forest'? Are you really feeling all right?"

"Look, just . . . trust me." I hurry through into Elza's room, come back with the document wallet full of Dad's notes. I spill them out onto the bed in front of her. "I think this is our path," I say, pointing at the columns of figures. Elza picks one of them up and squints at it.

"How?" she asks. "Are you saying these are page numbers? The Book doesn't have numbered pages."

"No," I say. I think of the car winding through the forest, Dad driving me, and the other thing, sitting next to . . . No, I won't think about that right now. I think about the car turning. The numerals written on the road signs. "I think it's *how* you turn the pages that matters. Maybe if you turn, say, three pages at once, you'll find yourself somewhere different than if you go forward one page three times. The paths split."

"Well," Elza says, "we might as well try your theory out. I can't say I totally follow you, but . . . we don't have any other ideas."

We sit for a moment, cross-legged on the bed. On the

floor Ham rumbles and shifts in his sleep. We look down at the Book of Eight, sitting between us as innocently as any book ever sat, green-bound and double clasped.

I pick it up, and at the touch of my sigil, the clasps snap open. I put it back down, and the pages flutter, moving until they come to rest, open and totally blank.

"OK," I say, "so help me out. What do the numbers say?"

"Seven," Elza reads. I turn seven pages forward, all in one movement, and stop. It's still blank.

"All right."

"One," Elza continues, "but this one's mirror writing."

I stop and think for a moment. The dream . . . I remember the car winding through the tall endless trees in the forest. When we turned left, the sign was mirrored. A mirrored book would read from right to left . . .

I turn one page back, toward the front cover. As I do it, I see a flash in the pages, a tiny blot, a sigil in answer to my sigil, which fades as I try to focus on it.

"It's working!" I say. "Did you see?"

"I didn't see anything," Elza says. "Well, OK. Four. Then a reversed three."

I turn four pages forward, then three back. There's another brief flash of black ink on the empty page, like someone clearing their throat in print. I feel electric. This is it, we've done it!

"Keep going," I tell her. She reads the numbers to

me, Dad's sequence, and I turn the pages of the Book. Soon we're into a rhythm, and she reads faster, I feel like the pages are turning before I even get to touch them, the Book flowing like this great river of paper and print, my sigil prickling with cold, Elza's voice reading faster and faster, her voice not even sounding like hers anymore but my own, just my own voice chanting to me, and the Book is about to reveal itself, any second now I'll break through and —

Elza's face is right in front of mine. She's not reading the sequence to me anymore. She's crouched in front of me with an intent and unhappy expression. I'm still holding the Book of Eight. Elza draws her hand back and slaps me hard in the face. I drop the Book and yelp.

"What was *that* for?"

"Oh, Luke . . ."

Elza puts her arms around me, hugging me close. Ham rushes into the room and starts butting at me, nibbling my ears.

"What . . . Elza, what's going on? Why are you hitting me? What's wrong?"

My head is spinning, my eyes feel prickly, like someone filled them with sand. Elza lets go of me. I see that she's really upset.

"What's the matter?" I ask her. "Was it working?"

"Luke . . . you've been reading the Book for three days."

"I've . . . I what?"

I'm not able to believe her. It's barely been a few seconds since we started. I don't feel like I haven't eaten for three days. I barely feel hungry at all. I look around the room. When we started the experiment, the spare room was lit with a milky afternoon glow. Now it's dark, with a hard orange rectangle of light cast onto one wall by the street lamp outside. Elza and Ham are backlit by a softer white light coming in from the landing. How I didn't notice the change until just now, I can't say.

"You've been reading it for three days," she repeats. "We started on Sunday afternoon. Sunday the twenty-sixth. It's now half past ten in the evening, Wednesday the twenty-ninth."

"You're joking," I say.

"There's nothing funny about it," Elza says. "I thought I'd . . . I didn't know. I thought I'd lost you. You kept turning the pages and muttering to yourself, you wouldn't look at me . . . you wouldn't talk. Wouldn't move. You were like a breathing statue. You haven't drunk or eaten. The pages were blank but you kept reading them anyway. What was happening to you?"

"How can I not have eaten or drunk for three days? I'd die, it's not possible."

"I'm just telling you what happened. You . . . Luke, you've gone white. Are you OK?"

I don't reply. Something's happening inside my head; my ears are ringing like a struck bell. There's a rush of blood, a giddy champagne froth of dizziness, the darkness in the room is filled with glowing shapes: lines of force, sharp crowds of triangles, circles, and pentagrams and eight-pointed stars, all morphing and crawling and spreading over every surface, the symbols rippling like the air over hot pavement. Elza's face suddenly swarms with them; she looks like a mask, flurries of glowing dots flickering around her eyes. I shake my head in desperate denial and it subsides. Whatever's in the Book, whatever I read, it's inside me now.

"I remember," I say. "It's like remembering things you never knew."

"I told my mum we've been rehearsing a play together," Elza says, "but I don't think she remotely believes me. I'm lucky my dad's away and Mum's been working lots of shifts. I managed to keep her out of here. She thinks you stayed here only Monday night . . . in case she asks. But she's at the end of her tether with Ham, and I just didn't know what to tell her. It's been a nightmare. I didn't know what I'd do if you didn't snap out of it before Halloween. I kept coming in and trying to talk to you . . ."

"It's OK," I say. "I'm back. I'm here."

Elza reaches down and plucks the Book of Eight from my grasp, shoves it under the bed.

"I don't want you looking at that thing ever again,"

she says. "You need to eat and drink. And probably you should go outside. Get some air."

I close my eyes. The sigils and symbols are still there, spiraling and cavorting across my field of vision. They're lemon-yellow, neon-green, searing-headache-purple. They're inside me, part of the darkness behind my eyes. They'll always be there.

The moon is nearly full, shining through a gap in the dark cloud like a single searching eye. The rain is light but steady. Ham is deciding what exact position he should squat in. He seems as if he's about to squat but then doesn't. He chooses another position. The wind pushes his ears back and forth like leaves. His thin tail is raised up like a flagpole, but nothing appears. Three days, reading the Book of Eight . . . it's impossible to get my head around it. The Book is more dangerous than I could've imagined. Three days of sitting in Elza's spare room, and I can't even explain what I've been reading, what I was looking at. The knowledge I need is there, but I can't remember exactly where it came from. I don't remember looking at the Book's pages, don't remember what they actually said. What I have is a sense that I *know*. I know what we have to do. I just don't know how I'm going to explain it to Elza. I can barely explain it to myself.

Ham starts to poop. He always looks embarrassed

when he does it, and accusatory, as if I'm the rude one for being there when he decides to go.

Something stirs beyond the hedge to my left.

"Boss?"

I feel the chill of the dead. I stay silent.

"I know you're there, boss."

It never ends. It won't end, until I finish with them.

"What do you want, Judge?"

"Just a word. Diplomacy."

"You need to pick a side, Judge."

"Well, just hear me out now, boss. Came to my attention you might have yourself a certain book, one that were my duty to guard. Shepherd's not happy with me."

"I don't imagine he is."

"Took your mum away, boss, same day you got in and stole the Book. Took her and hid her. In case you were thinking of trying another rescue. She's not in the house no more."

"Where is she?"

"Shepherd don't trust me so much, boss. Haven't seen her."

This is getting worse. Whatever they're planning for Halloween, she must be important. I wish we'd gotten her out of the house on Sunday. . . . I should've known this was coming.

"Why are you here, Judge? To tell me that?"

"All I'm here to say is, maybe you could think about

who it were on guard duty when you came by the house? Who it were what helped you out and didn't raise the alarm and that?"

"That would be you, wouldn't it?"

"Could be, boss. I suppose what I'm asking here is, whatever happens on Halloween, leave old Judge out of it, right? 'Cause he never wanted this."

"You're trying to bargain with me now?"

"Shepherd's been talking to all of us, boss. Says you're planning on sending us off to Hell. You wouldn't do that to me, would you?"

I think of Mum floating above her bed, her mind locked away inside itself. I think about Holiday; her family; her cat, Bach, with his belly slit open.

"You don't know what I'd do, Judge. I've got the Book of Eight and the sigil. I've read the Book, spent three days in there. The Book's part of me now. You don't know what I could do."

"I've a fair idea, boss," the Judge says at last. "But the Shepherd and his boys, they're well prepared. He were a necromancer, too, was at it a lot longer than you've been. Three days reading that book ain't nothing on him. What you got, it ain't enough."

Ham has finished performing and is now investigating the damp pile of compost by the side of the shed. The wind sounds like the out breath of an enormous creature.

"Why couldn't you have just let me off?" I ask.

"Boss?"

"Why couldn't you all just have talked to me? I wanted to let you free without anything like this happening. We could have worked it out. I don't want a Host. I'm not my Dad."

"Dunno. Your pa weren't exactly Mr. Sunshine. Suppose we had no reason to think different of you. And it ain't in our natures, I suppose. Don't ask, when you can take."

"I mean, none of you have heard of forgiving people? Die and let live?"

"Listen, boss," the Judge says, "you don't want this, do you? You don't want to be like your pa. You're not him. I know you don't want what he had."

"Not really."

He shifts about beyond the hedge. The lights in Elza's living room go on and off.

"Why not die?" he says.

"What?"

"Just . . . look, see, right, the Shepherd says to me, you don't understand the Book of Eight. You think you do, but you don't. He was a bad one, your pa. The stuff in that bloody book . . . the way you might end up, you follow what's wrote down in there, is worse'n anything we could do. Just give up, let go, and we'll be free. We'd all be free. You could head off into the big beyond."

"Are you joking? Did he put you up to this?"

"No chance, boss. It's all me. That's what your Judge is here for: hard truths. I want the best for bloody everyone, right. Look, I know everything's very tense right now. The river's not far, right, you go down there with me now, some stones in your pocket, it's all over. Your mam's left out of it, the girl who lives here—"

"No. That'll never happen. I'm sixteen, I've got a whole life. Why should I give anything up for any of you?"

"You're right," he says.

"I don't know how you thought this would go, but it's stupid."

"It ain't that bloody bad, dying, you know—"

"Just go."

I can feel him standing, trying to think of something to say, and then there's nothing. Ham comes up to me, and I reach my hand out to rub his head, but he moves past, snorting. I turn and discover Elza's mum standing at the back door.

"I was coming to say there's a guest toothbrush in the bathroom," she says, ignoring Ham butting at her legs.

"Right," I say. How long was she standing there?

"Do you often talk to yourself?" she asks.

"I was rehearsing for the play, Mrs. Moss."

"Ah, yes, this play with ghosts. Elza has told me about this."

"I'm nervous, but I think it'll be all right on the night."

"And yet, strangely, my daughter has never once

attended rehearsals or mentioned drama club before this week, and whenever she's preparing her lines, it's always in our spare room, with you."

"All our scenes are together, Mrs. Moss."

"And I know that your mother is unwell, but I would have appreciated being asked before your dog boarded with us for six nights."

"It wasn't intentional, Mrs. Moss."

The rain falls in flurries. My jacket is slick with water, and drops fall from the raincoat hood, tiny silver movements past my face.

"Elza is very dear to me," she says after a moment.

"Sorry, Mrs. Moss?"

"My daughter is a sensitive and unique child."

"We're just friends. Really."

"I'm not sure what's going on between you two," Elza's mum says. "But I know Elza well enough to know when I'm not getting the whole story. I'm led to understand you have some trouble at home. You're welcome to stay here again tonight, but I do think it might be best for you to go home tomorrow. And if I find that you're getting her in trouble somehow . . ."

You have no idea. Absolutely no idea.

"I'm really just lucky to have a friend like her," I say.

"Well. I remade the bed for you in the spare room."

"Thank you, Mrs. Moss."

The wind is pulling at the trees like a hand unstitching

threads. Elza's mum stares into the middle distance, beyond my hooded face. Eventually she shifts her weight and says, "Elza told me about your father. I'm sorry for your loss."

"It's fine, Mrs. Moss. We weren't close. Thank you."

"All right," she says. "Well. Aren't you getting wet out there?"

"I'll be right in," I tell her, holding up the plastic bag wrapped around my hand. "I need to pick something up."

Ham doesn't sleep well in strange places. He never has, ever since he was a puppy. I try three times to say good night and leave him in the laundry room, and each time, he starts ramming his head against the door before I can even get it closed. Eventually I grab a slice of bread and throw it into the laundry room, then shut the door behind Ham while he's busy eating. With any luck he won't start howling when he realizes he's been tricked.

I go upstairs and brush my teeth with the guest toothbrush. When I open the door to the spare bedroom, I find Elza sitting on the freshly made bed. She's lit by the glow of the reading lamp, casting a tall shadow over the bookshelves on the far wall. Looking at the shadow reminds me of the Fury, towering over us in this same room. Elza risked a lot for me on Sunday. I take a moment to appreciate the Elza-ness of Elza, whole and alive, appreciate the sharpness of her gaze, the crinkled line of her frown. She's holding the Book of Eight in her lap, looking down at the star on the cover. I sit beside her.

"What's it like outside?" she asks.

"Cold. Dark. I put Ham to bed. So your mum thinks I'm your boyfriend."

"I don't have people stay that often. It's not surprising she'd assume that."

We sit quiet for a moment. The books that came off the shelf when the Fury attacked us are still lying haphazard on the floor.

"I know how to get rid of the Host," I say.

Elza breathes out hard, like it's more than she was hoping for.

"You're sure?"

"Yeah. The information's in here now," I say, tapping my skull. "I know what we need to do on Halloween."

"I'm so glad," Elza says. "That's great. At least you got something out of all that time you lost. If you'd just been sitting there for nothing . . ."

"I got what we need. Bound spirits like my Host are difficult to get rid of. The Book says that dismissing a full Host is nearly unheard of, especially all in one go. But that's what we'll have to do. There's a lunar ritual that could do it. It cleanses areas of all spirits residing within them. If I was the subject of the ritual, the rite would banish the Host. Thing is, the moon will be in the wrong phase for another week. We don't have time. And it would take eight people to perform, and they all have to be virgins."

"So that's a no-go," Elza says.

"Sumerian magicians would destroy spirits bound within the body of an animal familiar. The Book didn't explain that any further. It didn't say how you acquire a familiar, or how the process works or anything."

"Why are you giving me the failed options first?" Elza says.

"I just want you to know . . . we don't have another choice. This is it. What we're doing is difficult and dangerous and . . . I mean, you know that. It's ten past twelve now, October thirtieth. In less than twenty-four hours, it'll be Halloween, and the Host is as powerful as it'll ever be. We've only got one option if we want to banish them."

"All right," Elza says, "one option. I got that. So what is it?"

"It's called the Rite of Tears. It'll break my bond to the Host and all the ghosts shut away in Deadside so they can't hurt me or anyone else ever again. It'll work really well on Halloween."

"So far, so good," Elza says. "What does this Rite of Tears do, then?"

I close my eyes. I can see the incantations of the rite, seared into the darkness behind my eyelids, like the after-images you get from staring at the sun. Magic circles spin in the darkness like a million demon planets. I can see the shape of the ritual, could draw it out with my eyes still closed. *One to close the circle, one to open the gate . . .*

"We're going to summon the Devil," I tell her.

Elza puts the Book of Eight down on the floor. For a moment she doesn't say anything. She gets up, and for a moment I think she's going to walk out, but then she sits back down again.

"Are you sure?" she asks quietly.

"Am I sure what?"

"This is the only way?"

I think about what the Judge just told me. *The way you might end up, you follow what's wrote down in there, is worse'n anything we could do.* But why should I trust him? Whatever the rite does, I know the Shepherd and the Fury want me dead, and they've made plans to ensure I don't live through Halloween. They've got Mum. They're not leaving me a choice.

"Yes," I say, holding her gaze, "it's the only way. I followed Dad's notes, followed his path through the Book. This is where it led me."

"Your dad's path . . . I mean, Luke, your dad, he wasn't exactly father of the decade, was he? How do we know his notes are even . . ." She trails off.

I don't respond.

"Sorry," Elza says. "I shouldn't have said that."

"You're the one who was pushing for us to crack Dad's code, read the Book. Now I have, and you don't like what I found."

"I just mean . . . Luke, the *Devil*. Evil incarnate."

"He grants boons on certain days. Halloween is one of them," I say, pressing on. "If we make an offering, the Devil will agree to remove the Host from my service and take it into Deadside with him. The Book says—"

"Wait. An offering? What kind of offering?"

"Blood," I say. "The Devil will appear only if hearts-blood is shed."

"You mean a *person* . . . ?"

"No. The Book just says heartsblood. It must be live and fresh. But it doesn't matter what it comes from. We can use an animal."

"Luke—"

"What, you're a vegetarian, Elza? How many chickens died to make the stupid 'fingers' you were cooking? It'd really be so bad if I killed one animal to save myself, save Mum, save you, save half the town maybe? Who knows what the Host'll do if it escapes into Liveside without bonds? We have no choice. I wish we did. The Rite of Tears is our only option right now."

"I'm not a vegetarian," she says quietly. "You're right about that. But I don't practice black magic either. I'm a girl with second sight who's been trying to do the right thing for someone she barely knows."

"I don't do black magic either. I didn't ask for this," I tell her, although deep down I know that's not quite true. I didn't want the Host, but I wanted Dad's money, and I signed something I had no business signing. I let them in. And if I'm not a black magician already, I don't know what else you could say about someone after they've made a sacrifice to Satan.

"All right," she says. It's so quiet I can barely hear her. She won't look at me. "I'll do it. If you think that's best. But you should be careful. You've changed."

"How?"

"You've gone . . . you've gone deathward. Even having a Host pulls you toward Deadside, I know that much. But you've gone further. You lost your body, you were possessed by a demon . . . and then within five minutes of getting your body back, you knew how to unlock the Book of Eight. You said you had a dream or something? You were close to Deadside. The dream might even have been a message from the other side. This has changed you."

I shift on the bed. I run my fingers over the octagonal stone set into my sigil. I feel different, true, but I don't see how anyone could've gone through what's happened to me and feel exactly the same about himself.

"Maybe," I say. "All I want to do is get rid of the Host. That's all I'm thinking about. We make an offering to the Devil, and he removes them from my service. Mum's safe, I'm safe, you and your family are safe."

Another silence. I can hear something clattering in the wind outside, a loose door maybe, or part of the gutter. Elza is looking at the floor.

"Did it say what he was like?" she asks.

"Who? The Devil? No. It called him 'Father of Darkness.' Says he will grant any wish that is within his power. That's all."

"OK. I'll talk to you in the morning," she says. "I suppose we'll have a lot to organize."

"All right," I say.

She gives me a quick hug and leaves the room. I turn the light out and lie on the bed, looking at the door-frame. It's still lit by soft yellow light cast from Elza's room down the hall. For a moment I'm struck with a fantasy so strong it startles me—not my usual dream of Holiday, but of Elza, standing in the doorway, making her way across the carpet with bare soft feet, slipping into the bed with me—

The light on the landing goes out. She's closed her bedroom door. I lie on my side in the dark room, listening to the wind, imagining her doing the same. I lie still and look at the empty doorway.

(the devil's footsteps)

Thursday morning, October thirtieth. The light outside the blinds is smoky gray, seeping into the spare room. Shadows are barely darker than the dusty light. I hear the hiss of central heating warming up. I feel like I'm lying in a room that has been walled up for a hundred years.

It's nearly the end, one way or the other. We'll start the Rite of Tears at midnight tonight, and by the time it's completed it'll be the thirty-first, Halloween. If our plan doesn't work, the Host will kill me and break free. The ghosts have still got my mum, but what they're going to do with her I don't know. The Judge said they'd hidden her, and who knows what that could mean. They might want to possess her, she might be their sacrifice, it could be anything. If tonight goes wrong, I'll be dead, Mum'll be dead, Elza will be dead. If it goes right, I'll meet the Devil. And what that'll be like I can't imagine.

I run my thumb over my sigil. It's become almost a comfort to me. I wonder how Dad lived all those years served by spirits and demons that would've given anything to kill him. Did he lie awake as well, running his fingers over the sigil, reminding himself that it was still there, that he was still powerful? Why did he raise a Host? Why did he leave us? Has he met the Devil as well? What kind of man was he?

I can hear movement downstairs, the shrill of a kettle boiling. I ease myself out of bed, wincing as my aching muscles are forced into use. I want to lie here and sleep for about a week, but we've got work to do. The Devil won't summon himself.

Down in the kitchen, Elza is sitting at the table, spreading fat slices of toast with butter and Marmite. Ham, who stands tall enough that his head is at table height, is trying to lick the Marmite jar, forcing Elza to use one elbow to keep him at bay while she spreads.

"I'll put him outside if you like," I say.

"He's all right," she says. "I didn't know deerhounds were into Marmite."

"Ham's crazy about it."

I sit opposite her. Elza's one of those people who coats every inch of their toast with whatever spread they're using. She works away at each slice until the coverage is perfect. She glances up at me, the first time she's looked at me since I came downstairs. Her dark hair is tied up into an unruly bun. I look at her freckles, her sharp nose, her small ears, normally hidden by the fall of her hair, and I'm thinking: When did this happen? When did I get so interested in sitting and watching Elza spread toast?

"What?" she asks.

"Nothing."

"Mum's already gone to the hospital. Double shift, which is lucky. It's actually nearly midday; I let you sleep in, seemed like you might need it. So when are we going to perform this ritual? And where?"

"We should start at midnight tonight. When we finish, it'll be the first minutes of Halloween. As for where . . . the Book says the rite must be performed at a passing place, somewhere the spirit world lies close to ours."

"Right," Elza says. "So where's that exactly?"

"Well, I know of one in Dunbarrow. The standing stones, the Devil's Footsteps."

"I thought you said the Host has been active there. That's where you found your body when you were possessed, wasn't it? You said you thought they were preparing something at the Footsteps."

"If the Shepherd intends to perform a ritual of his own on Halloween, it'll likely be tomorrow night, though I'm sure he'll use the Footsteps as well. Passing places have power. Either way, the Host will come after us there, no question. It's dangerous. But we don't have—"

"We don't have a choice," Elza echoes wearily. "I'm

not arguing. What do we need for the rite? Do we need herbs, supplies?"

As she says this, the schematics of the rite rise up uninvited behind my eyes, the incantation scrawling itself across my brain. I shake my head, trying to dislodge it.

"We need witch parsley and baneleaf," I say, "and we need oil. We'll need something to draw a magic circle around the standing stones, probably house paint, since we're drawing on grass. We need a sigil. And we'll need . . . a knife, and we need an animal. Something that'll bleed, so I can't just squash a spider and expect the Devil to show up."

Elza cuts her toast into neat triangles. I watch her knife sawing through bread and imagine slicing a creature's throat. I don't feel very hungry.

"I don't think any of that will be too difficult to get hold of in Dunbarrow. They should have the herbs at the New Age shop my mum visits," I continue.

"I'm worried about leaving the house," Elza says. "Now that I don't have my wyrdstone."

"You'll be safe today. The Book told me Hosts can't manifest on the thirtieth. The stars aren't right. We won't see them, I can't summon them. It's the calm before a storm. Once the clock strikes midnight tonight . . . it changes. But that means we have a head start on them, getting up to the Devil's Footsteps."

"Luke . . ." Elza says. "If they're weak today, then your mum . . . maybe we can—"

"No. The Shepherd and the Fury thought of that. The Judge told me they've hidden her. She's not in my house."

"Huh. And the Judge would never lie to you?"

"He would. But I think he was being honest, as far as it goes. . . . He said he didn't know where she was. How true that is . . . who knows? He's afraid of the Fury. I'm not sure I blame him."

"So that's our plan, then," Elza says. "Shopping, preparation, ritual. By midnight tonight we're up at the Footsteps, sacrificing an animal to Satan."

"I don't like it either. You know that. But black magic got us into this, and black magic'll have to get us out again."

"We hope," she says.

I eat a little toast, and we do the dishes. Then at one o'clock, we make our way down into Dunbarrow. All across the town, masks are being removed from closets, hairy werewolf gloves retrieved from the back of the sock drawer. Tomorrow night monsters will fill the streets and nightclubs, faces covered in green greasepaint, fake blood, cat ears, plastic fangs, and the mummified rubber face of Elvis. Until then the town is still. Pumpkins sit on sideboards, waiting for their eyes and smiles.

We make purchases at the New Age health shop and

John Crisco's hardware store, and then, at Elza's suggestion, we visit Black River mountaineering and hiking store, which is a weird flat-roofed building near the park. Eventually, after nearly an hour of heated discussion, we make our final purchase at the Paws 'n' Pals pet shop, next to the sweetshop in the old square.

Late afternoon, and we're making our way back to Elza's house. We're cutting through the dingy, unkempt end of the park, far away from the play area and the bandstand. Friendly ducks who want to be fed bread crusts don't venture this far into the undergrowth, which is the territory of cigarette butts and empty cider bottles. We're hurrying along a narrow path. I'm carrying the gerbil and paint can, while Elza carries the clothes. The gerbil case is bulky, and the can of yellow paint is pulling my arm out of its socket, and I'm just wondering if I need a break when I hear a voice shout "Manchett!" in a tone normally used on the rugby field.

Mark Ellsmith is lurching toward us. He's followed by Kirk, Holiday, and Alice. Mark is carrying a can of beer, and Kirk has the rest of a six-pack hanging down from his hand.

"Mark," I say.

His eyes are flickering hatred.

"Who said you could come around here?" he asks.

"To where, the park?" I reply.

"You need help," Kirk says. "You're not right, Luke."

"Just leave us alone," Elza says to them, barely even looking around. "We're busy."

Holiday looks worried; Alice looks excited.

"Shut up," Mark says. "You need to keep away from us."

"What?"

"We don't want you around here," Kirk says.

"Around where?" Elza asks. "Dunbarrow? You can't evict us."

"Shut up," Mark says. "Not even talking to you."

"Look," I say, "I've been ill. I know I haven't been—myself."

"More like you're some*thing* else," Mark says.

"Mark, please," Holiday says.

"You didn't see the birds!" Kirk snaps at her.

"And what are you hanging out with her for?" Alice asks, looking at Elza, as if this were somehow the greatest crime of all.

"I can't explain," I say. "Things have . . . changed. I'm not myself. I'm ill. Things will be normal, soon. I promise." Even as I speak, I can tell nobody's listening.

"Look, who even cares?" says Elza. "Great, fine. Enjoy your fabulous lives."

"Why did you say that to me?" Mark asks.

"Say what?" I ask.

"By the bandstand," he says. "On the hill. Why would you tell me that?"

"I don't know what I told you. It wasn't me—"

Mark doesn't let me finish. He lurches forward and hits me across the mouth. It's not even a decent punch, more of a loose slap. My head rolls back and my lip feels sweet and warm and really enormous all at once. My face throbs. What did my body—the Fury—tell him? He's deranged.

"Mark!" I hear Holiday yell. I stumble backward, holding my hand over my face. I've dropped the gerbil case. I'm still holding the paint, thinking maybe I'll swing it at him, but he doesn't hit me again.

More shouting. I take my hand off my face. Elza has Alice's neck held in the crook of one arm and is trying to force her down onto the ground with what looks like some sort of wrestling hold. Alice is either screaming or crying. I can't see Elza's expression. Holiday is standing between me and Mark, talking very fast into his face. Her hands are gripping his shoulders. Kirk rushes up to the girls, shouting, and pulls Elza off Alice, who falls backward into the bushes, coughing. Elza pushes Kirk back and then headbutts him in the face and he's knocked back, a smear of bright, almost-fake-looking blood leaking from his upper lip. Elza backs away from him, breathing hard, staring right at Mark, who looks at her and me with a mixture of fear and rage, then shakes his head and, linking his arm with Holiday's, says, "Let's go, man."

"She hit me!" says Kirk.

"Everyone stop it!" Holiday shouts. "You don't need to — this isn't helping!"

Kirk hauls Alice to her feet.

"She *hit* me," says Kirk, sounding like a little kid.

Elza looks poised to hit him again. I'm worried what'll happen if he goes for her properly. Kirk's not a pushover, and I don't know how much more my body can take.

"You can't hit girls," Holiday says. "Come on."

Kirk snorts and rubs the blood from his lip.

"Not even worth it," he says.

"I'm sorry," I say to Holiday.

She has nothing in her eyes except pity.

"I'm sorry, too," Holiday says, and they leave.

I look at the churned-up grass. The whole thing took about a minute or two. I get the feeling that something else is leaving with them, too, some version of me. They won't forgive me. This'll follow me around Dunbarrow like a second shadow. Everyone will know.

"I've wanted to do that for years," Elza says. "You have no idea — are you OK?"

"I'll live."

"Good friends, huh?"

"I ate an entire raw bird in front of their eyes. Who even knows what my body was doing when we weren't watching?"

I pick up the can of paint and gerbil case. Elza bites

her lip and starts to gather wayward pieces of hair in her fingers, slowly reknitting her bun.

At quarter to eleven, it's time to go to the Footsteps. I put on my sigil and tuck a knife and the Book of Eight into my coat pocket. Then we load a sports bag with supplies and drag Ham into the night. The schematics of the ritual are burned into my brain, so hopefully I won't have to refer to the Book again. It's not as if we have an extra three days to spare. My face throbs. I can barely distinguish the pain of the beating from the other aches and pains I've gathered over the past week. It feels as if I'm listening to two separate brass bands playing over each other. Elza, who admitted to me that she didn't have many "practical clothes," is wearing freshly purchased waterproof pants and a mountaineering raincoat in bright orange and green.

"Remind me why we brought him?" I ask, pointing to Ham.

"I don't know," Elza says. "It just feels right. I felt safer when he was around, when you were gone. I didn't want to leave him alone."

"Don't you think he'll be in danger?"

"Maybe. Aren't we all? I don't know, it's just a hunch, you know. I trust hunches."

Elza has the gerbil case on her lap. Ham is deeply

interested in the gerbil, and his breath is steaming up the side of the case.

"They're making friends," I say, pointing.

Elza grimaces. She's still not happy about what we're going to do to the gerbil.

"Speaking of which," she says, "I wanted to say that all of this has really changed how I see you. I mean, I think we are friends now, right?"

"I'd say so."

"I mean, I'm not happy about what we have to do. But I trust you. I really didn't want to help you at first. I agonized over it. You've always just swanned around school like you were made of chocolate, and your friends are such jerks. . . . But you know, you're dealing with all of this pretty well."

"Thanks, Elza," I say. "I always thought you were this awful, arrogant know-it-all. And I've come to realize that I was totally right."

"Shut up!" she shrieks, hitting me in the side. "I take it all back. You're the worst."

"What I mean is," she says after a while, "I hope you make it through this. I'm worried for you. About what you'll have to do."

"Yeah," I say. "I'm worried, too."

As we mount the hill, the storm finally breaks. The world is reduced to a series of colored flashes and blurs. Luckily there's a distinctive convenience store just a street away from Dunbarrow High, and soon I see its sign flashing.

My throat tightens as we hurry along the street. I'm hefting the gerbil's case with one hand and dragging Ham's leash with the other. Ham's fur is slicked down and his eyes are rolling about under his brows. Elza trots in front with the sports bag and the paint can.

"The Footsteps are up there," I say, pointing to the absolute blackness beyond the dim shape of the school. My raincoat hood is soaked and heavy against my head.

I pull on Ham's leash and we walk, heads bent to keep the rain off our faces. There are street lamps burning orange in the staff parking lot, but apart from that the school is entirely dark. We walk around the reception office, sheltered from the wind for a moment, then out into the yard, past the portable classrooms that they teach English and math in, around the back of the kitchens, then past the changing rooms, and we're out on the rugby field, keeping to the edge, trees grumbling and dripping water on our heads. The wind is like a raging river, bursting its banks, carrying branches and leaves and bracken straight into our faces.

The north side of the rugby field bleeds into rougher, unmowed grass, studded with bushes and small dead trees. There's litter here, years and years of it, blown over from the schoolyards, bright packets and cans and soggy plastic bags flailing in the tree branches like ailing jelly-fish. Elza brings out a fat barrel-shaped flashlight as we head farther into the woods. I'm stumbling over branches and the tiny infuriating holes that seem to form in the forest floor specifically to trip people up. The sleeves of my jacket are so wet they look glossy in the beam of the flashlight. The forest floor is overgrown with tangled nests of brambles.

"Ten minutes to midnight," I tell Elza. We need to move faster.

Onward, upward. The only light is the flashlight now; even the tangerine-colored stain of city light on the southern horizon is gone, hidden by the curve of the hill. This slope is rocky, the ground carpeted by a spongy layer of dark moss. We reach the top, struggle through a tenacious wall of bushes, and cross a narrow dirt road, rainwater whooshing along the channels that tires have carved in the earth.

"Is this it?" Elza asks.

"Yes. Down that bank."

We make our way down the shallow slope toward the Devil's Footsteps. The oak trees arch over the clearing like a vaulted ceiling. As we get closer I can see the three standing stones: one tall, two squatter and wider, which have unnatural cup- or hoof-shaped hollows cut into them. The stones are light gray, covered in scales of yellow lichen. We're sheltered from the worst of the wind, but the rain is still making its way through the trees hard enough. My teeth are chattering.

Now that we're right up by the Footsteps I can see the disturbed earth in the middle of the standing stones, where my possessed body was digging: moss ripped away, dark earth packed down and turning to mud in the rain. I point it out to Elza.

"Is something buried there?" Elza hisses.

"Could be. Looks fresh," I say. "I know my body was digging here, but I don't know why."

"What would it have buried? Something for the Host's own ritual? I'm not getting good feelings from this."

I'm looking around at the dark trees, the whispering blackness of the forest beyond them, suddenly knowing we've walked into a trap. I saw my body digging here. . . . But we had no choice; the ritual has to be performed at a passing place. There was nowhere else.

"We can't worry about that now, there's no time. It's nearly one minute to midnight. We need to move faster," I tell Elza. She reaches into our sports bag and takes out the herbs. "Whether they buried something or not, we can't worry about it. We don't have time. Witch parsley and baneleaf. Stand in the center of the stones and I'll draw the circle."

I take the herbs. They're a motley assortment of leaves, some brown and dry, others furry and fat and somehow tonguelike and covered in tiny hairs. I walk into the center of the Footsteps, with the gerbil's case under my arm. I lay it down, right on top of the disturbed earth. I throw the herbs over myself. Some get caught in the wind and are blown away from me; others settle in my hair or stick to my raincoat. I feel like I'm garnishing myself. Elza ties Ham to a sapling and takes the can of paint, cracks it open, and begins to walk backward—counterclockwise, I remember the Book said—around the Footsteps, dribbling paint onto the moss. The magic circle isn't very complicated: It's just a ring around the passing place, with a mark of power at the north of the circle. It's this mark that Elza seems to be struggling with.

"It's turned midnight! It's Halloween!" I shout to her. "Hurry up!"

"Rain's pooling here. It's hard to draw it out."

Elza bends forward and starts to work at the earth, slopping the paint with her hands. The flashlight is on the ground beside her, lighting her from below, casting a huge shapeless shadow over the wall of trees. Ham starts to bark, straining at his lead. I take my knife out of my coat pocket and unfold the blade. If it weren't raining so hard, I could keep better watch on the south side of the hollow. I already know they're coming: The air feels colder, in some way that's deeper than just the wind and the rain. Ham is pulling his thin head backward, trying to slip his collar.

Elza stands up, wipes paint on her trousers.

"Done!"

"Good, now get out of here."

"Can you feel anything? Did it work?"

"Yeah. I feel it."

Nothing has outwardly changed. I'm still standing in the rain and wind in a remote part of the forests around Dunbarrow, facing death with a pocketknife and a store-bought gerbil. But I feel different, more important. I feel like I'm onstage and a spotlight just clicked on. What I do inside the magic circle matters; beings outside our world will be able to see, to notice me. My sigil is blazing with power on my finger, burning harder than it ever has before, sending jolts of cold up my arm and into my chest.

Ham slips his collar and bolts away into the woods, yowling.

"Ham! Oh, shit!" Elza cries.

"Elza, get out of here! They're coming!"

There's something moving in the trees. I can see my breath in the air. There's a frost creeping over the gerbil's plastic case, over the standing stones themselves.

"Last thing!" Elza shouts.

She throws me a bottle of cooking oil, then shoulders our bag and runs off into the woods, following Ham's barks.

Something comes flying out of the forest to the south of the Footsteps. The Prisoner, blank white eyes rolling, floating over the moss and bracken at terrible speed. He ignores me and crosses the hollow in an instant, eyes set on the gap between the trees where Elza disappeared. The Judge follows, not looking at me, jeans rolled halfway up his shins, revealing his red boots. Both spirits are bigger and brighter, glowing like neon signs. You wouldn't mistake them for living beings tonight. The ghosts dissolve into the rain and the dark and are gone, chasing Elza. Saying my heart is in my mouth isn't even half of it: I feel more like every organ is trying to force its way out through my face. Ham is still yelping in the woods, his barks growing fainter against the noise of the storm.

I scoop the gerbil out of his case. I hold him over the flattest stone and pour the oil down onto his head. He squirms in my hand. The oil runs off his smooth brown back and onto my fingers. I can see something else moving in the woods. My sigil is humming with power, spreading a cold that feels like I've been dunked in the Arctic Ocean. I close my eyes, the pages of the Book of Eight appearing in my mind, as clear as if I were looking at them. I see the words I need, the words that will turn my murder into something more, words that will make my knife powerful. The gerbil struggles.

"Sorry, mate—*I hereby dedicate this sacrifice to Satan, our dark father. Please accept this anointed beast, and the blood I spill for you. Come to me now, in this hour of greatest darkness.*"

My sacrifice squeals in my grasp. I look down into his

terrified furry face. I've never killed anything before—I mean, I've squashed insects and stuff, but that's different. Ants don't have faces.

"Look, I'm sorry. It's you or me. No hard feelings."

The gerbil is squirming. I aim the knife down at his belly. I stroke the point over his stomach and he looks up at me with helpless black eyes. *It's a gerbil, Luke. You can kill it to save yourself. Elza could be dying right now. You can't back out now. What about the animals that die in a slaughterhouse every day? You eat those burgers and barely think about it. What's different about killing something yourself?*

The rest of my Host insinuate themselves into the hollow, beyond the standing stones and the rim of my magic circle. The Shepherd is first, taller and paler than ever before, the lenses of his glasses glowing like lanterns. The Oracle follows, holding the Innocent in her arms. The Heretic is next, quietly chanting, heatless flames boiling from his withered body. I can't see the Fury anywhere, or my mum.

"And here we are at the end," says the Shepherd.

I stand holding the gerbil and the knife, sigil burning my hand, my gaze locked with his. He's only a few paces from me, right up at the edge of the magic circle. He runs a hand through his beard.

"The Rite of Tears if I'm not mistaken?" he continues.

I don't say anything. I know he can't cross the boundary of the circle. At any moment I can make my sacrifice and complete the rite. I'm still in control. But I want to know where Mum is first.

"I must admit a certain grudging respect," the Shepherd says. "You reclaimed the mastery of your earthly vessel, which is more than I expected. That you're even attempting the rite indicates you discovered how to access the Book of Eight. Impressive. Doomed, but impressive."

"Doomed? I can complete the rite whenever I want to. I'm only even listening to you because I want to know what happened to Mum."

"Your mother is alive, I assure you. She will be with us presently. And I do not believe that you will complete the rite, or you would have done so already."

My sacrifice isn't even struggling anymore. He's quivering in my hand, his tiny heart ticking like a stopwatch.

"Quite absurd," the Shepherd continues. "I was taught to kill once I'd learned to walk. You have courage and will, but you lack ruthlessness. Your witch-girl is dying as we speak, but you cannot bring yourself to spill the blood of a mere animal. The contrast with your father is marked. There was very little Horatio was not prepared to sacrifice."

"It wasn't their fault," I say, looking at the gerbil, thinking of Ham and Elza and Holiday and Mum. I put my signature on Berkley's contract. I invited all of this into my life.

"No," the Shepherd says, "but for the necromancer,

the question of who 'deserves' what does not apply. Men deserve only what they are prepared to take."

Slit its throat. It's an animal. If Elza dies out there in the forest—

"You don't know what I could do," I tell the Shepherd.

"No. I suppose one never does. Which is why we left nothing to chance."

A cold hand grabs my left leg, squeezing as tight as a vise. I'm so shocked that I don't even scream. I fling myself forward, falling hard against the low stone in front of me. I've dropped the knife and the gerbil, which has already run away into the darkness, completely lost. Without a sacrifice the ritual is impossible. I failed. My conscience held me and I failed. I'm scrabbling at the stone in front of me, trying to pull myself up, kicking out at the hand grasping my leg. It's a real person, not a ghost, but how—

I kick free and scramble to my feet, turning my body to look at what's attacking me. A human head, arms, and shoulders are sticking up from the disturbed earth at the center of the Devil's Footsteps. The figure is completely choked by thick black mud, with only the eyes properly visible. Its hair is plastered down against its head. The figure pulls itself farther from the ground, torso coming free of the mud, white eyes locked on me.

"A man's Host may not harm him, even on a day of

power for the dead," the Shepherd says. "But if the woman who gave him life is sufficiently influenced, she may be used to strike him down and break the Host's bonds. It is an old magic, rarely invoked. A necromancer will generally slay his mother when he comes of age, to prevent her use as such an instrument. So, as you see, Luke, we may not enter your magic circle. But you will not be leaving it."

Mum has finished wrenching herself clear of the ground. She stands upright, cloaked in earth from head to foot. The Fury stares with glee from behind her eyes. The rain beats down on both of us, mother and son. For them to use her like this . . .

I turn to face the Shepherd, already knowing I'm about to die, and my anger surges up through me, through my sigil, which sears my finger, and my anger is given shape and force by the black ring, a wave of power that strikes the Shepherd in the chest. The ghost ignites, white fire exploding from inside his eyes and mouth, white lines of force splitting his spirit flesh, and he's screaming with pain and for a moment I think that I've found something he didn't expect, some force they weren't prepared for, but then Mum's body clubs me heavily from behind, knocking me down onto the flat standing stone. The power flowing through my sigil is gone as fast as it arrived. I try to direct it again, try to turn the power onto the demon inside Mum's body, but as I try to do it, there's a hard thump in my stomach. At first I think she punched me, but then I realize, with pain like I've swallowed the sun, that I've been stabbed.

Mum's muddy body is tensed above mine, her eyes wide and white, filled with joy and rage, her teeth bared, one hand gripping my throat, holding me steady. The rain lashes down on both of us. She's got the knife I was going to use on the gerbil, and as I flail at her face, fingers slipping in the grime, she stabs me three more times, this time between the ribs.

I'm getting weaker. The pain is so insistent that it becomes meaningless. I feel a desire to rest. Her body steps back, and I'm left lying on the flattest of the stones, rain falling down onto my face, hard and cool.

The Shepherd has seemingly recovered and he and the Oracle are standing over me now, Mum's body beside them. I would like to close my eyes. I really am dying. I feel like I'm sitting in the seat of an airplane that's about to take off. The Shepherd looks fainter and weaker, no longer glowing with the same intensity. I want to raise my sigil and burn him again, but I can't even move my arm.

"It is as I saw," the Oracle says from behind her veil. She sounds sad. The Shepherd says nothing. He stares at me with greedy fascination. I wonder how his revenge feels.

The sky, pitch-dark a few moments ago, seems to be filling with stars.

(the undiscovered country)

I'm six years old and Dad's leaving home. I sit on the landing and watch as he struggles with his cases. Mum is in the bedroom. It's strange that he chose to leave this way, in the middle of the day, while I was awake. It's like he wanted me to remember.

Dad extends himself halfway up the stairs and says good-bye, holding his hand out to me. He's wearing a blue shirt and a red tie with polka dots. There's a big black ring on his finger. His hand envelops mine, palm rough as tree bark.

"Grow up good," he says, then turns away. He walks back down the stairs and shuts the door behind him. I hear the flat mumble of his car pulling out of the drive. I've never understood what his last three words meant.

○ ○ ○

My name is Luke Manchett, and I'm sixteen years old. I think I'm dead. I'm standing at the Devil's Footsteps, looking down at my body, which is laid out over the flattest of the three stones. Everything is quiet. I'm surrounded by gray mist, and I can't see the Shepherd or any other ghost. I'm all alone here.

When I look down at myself, my spirit self, I'm unhurt and unbloodied. The only unusual thing is there's a thin white cord, almost invisible, sticking out from my navel and running into the body lying on the flat stone. It looks like spiderweb, or maybe a loose thread of cotton. I take it in my hands. The thread is warm.

"I wouldn't advise that."

There's a man standing beside the tallest of the three stones. He's tall, with a sharp chin and a deep tan. His hair is chilly white, greased back and away from his face. He has a small, neat beard and wears a wolf-gray suit with a shirt that's deep midnight blue.

"Mr. Berkley?"

"It's extremely delicate," Dad's lawyer continues, "and to break it would have very severe consequences for you."

"Where are we?"

"This is a passing place," says Mr. Berkley. "A border of sorts, between what I believe you refer to as 'Liveside' and 'Deadside.'"

"So I'm definitely dead this time."

"You are not yet dead, my boy. Your fate is unmapped. That slender cord still ties your animus to your soma. If one were intentionally astral traveling, it would resemble a thick rope rather than a thread."

"Are you dead, too, Mr. Berkley?"

"That's never been a concern of mine."

"But what are you doing here? Do you work for the Shepherd?"

Berkley laughs. "I do not serve him."

"Are you my spirit guide?"

"I am not your spirit guide. Please. I am aware you have had a traumatic experience, my boy, but you are remarkably slow on the uptake. Let's try a small thought exercise. Some critical thinking. Question the first: You were mortally wounded during the course of which black magic ritual?"

"The Rite of Tears."

"Correct. So my second question: What is the nature and purpose of the ritual you were performing?"

"It was meant to summon the Devil. But I failed."

"Don't go so hard on yourself. I wouldn't describe it as a failure."

"But I didn't . . . oh. Oh."

Mr. Berkley grins a shark-white grin.

"As called, here I am."

"*You're* the Devil?"

"I am he: Satan, Lucifer, Asmodeus, Beelzebub, Abaddon, Prince of Darkness, Father of Lies, and many other lesser-known titles. I shan't bore you by rolling them out like some great moldering carpet. We have business to attend to."

"The ritual failed, though. My sacrifice got away."

"Did not the oil anoint both the creature and your own hand? Was not your own blood spilled within the bounds of the circle? I make no distinction as to the precise nature of the offering."

"I . . . oh."

"I believe you have some boon to ask of me?"

The Devil is smoothing part of his hair down with his hand.

"I want to . . . Mr. Berkley, sir, I would like you to remove the Manchett Host from my service. I would like you to take it with you, into Deadside."

We're not at the Devil's Footsteps anymore, I realize. We're standing next to a vast wall made from crumbling stone, which stretches as far as I can see. The ground underfoot is heather, lifeless and dry. The cool mist is all around us. I see a wooden door in the side of the wall, painted light green. The Devil picks at his nails.

"And you are sure this is the boon you desire? From all the things I can grant you, this is your wish?"

"Yes. Definitely."

"I shall do as you ask, Luke Manchett. There is no price."

"Thank you."

"Shake my hand, and it shall be done." He reaches out one long-fingered hand, a slightly bored expression on his face. Without hesitation I grasp hold and we shake. His skin feels no different from anyone else's, but when his hand moves away from mine, I see there are no lines on his palm.

"Is that it?" I ask.

"They are coming."

I shut up and wait. The door in the side of the wall has swung open, revealing a dark, narrow passage. A wind blows out of the opening.

After what might have been minutes or hours, there is a figure walking out of the fog, a thick-necked, slouching man. The Judge walks toward me with his head down. His boots make muted crackling noises as they crush the heather. He stops before me and looks back down at the ground.

"Boss," he says.

"What did you do to Elza?"

"Nothing, boss, believe me!"

"What happened to her?"

"Nothing. I don't know! Only pretended to chase her, didn't I?"

"Is she alive?"

"I don't know! You got to believe me! Don't send me over, boss, I did the right thing. I helped you best I could, didn't I?"

"You 'pretended' to chase Elza . . . but for all we know, she's dead now. You didn't help. You'd have let them kill me," I say, "if I hadn't discovered how to use the Book. You'd have helped them do it. You're a weather vane; you choose whoever you think is strongest. Right?"

"I never, boss, swear on my soul. I'm not a bloody weather vane!"

"Sorry," I say.

"Where are they sending me?" he asks. "Where am I going?"

"The darkness, of course," says the Devil.

"No! Boss, Luke, please don't make me! I don't want to—"

"And yet you must," the Devil says, sighing. "You belong to me. The Manchett Host is broken, the deal is done, and your punishment is already prepared. Now cross the threshold."

"You promised," the Judge tells me. "Promised I wouldn't go to Hell. Just like your pa. Always promising. You're just the same."

He turns away from me and, after a hesitation, walks forward into the dark doorway. The sound of his footfalls cuts out.

There's a period of gray silence. The Oracle drifts out

of the mist in her white dress, stopping to wrap her thin, cold arms around my neck and kiss my cheek through her veil. She vanishes into the dark gateway without a word. Now the Heretic walks forward, bones flaring and spitting sparks, chanting his idiot litany. He passes between us and his fire is extinguished.

We stand and wait. The Shepherd appears, his suit seeming faded in the gray light, more charcoal than black. He holds his wide hat in his hands and moves with a shuffling gait, like a limp. I realize that he's terrified.

"Octavius," says the Devil as the Shepherd hobbles closer, "good to see you again. I've missed your company."

"I shall not beg," the Shepherd says to us. His mirrored glasses are missing. I look him in his tar-pool eyes.

"Nobody is asking you to," says the Devil.

"Luke," the ghost says, moving closer to me. "You are a fool. I have dealt with this being, and it led me to damnation. You cannot imagine—"

"You didn't leave me a choice," I say. "I didn't want a Host. If you hadn't been obsessed with your revenge, I'd have let you all go. But you made Mum kill me and then you watched me die. You got your revenge. Now here's mine."

"You think the Black Goat has answered your call from the goodness of its heart? It has none! You are deluding yourself. There is always a price. This is the end for us both," the Shepherd snarls.

I don't answer. He might be right or he might be trying to frighten me one last time. Either way, I can't change what's happening now.

"If we could move this along," the Devil says.

The Shepherd pauses at the edge of the doorway, muttering to himself, and then the Devil clears his throat and the Shepherd stumbles through into darkness. His white hair is visible for a moment, a bright blot, and vanishes. As he leaves, I realize that I've won. The Host is leaving, it's over. The Shepherd's gone to the darkness, into Hell, and I'm still here.

We wait on. The Devil picks his nails, fiddles with his golden pocket watch. Eventually the smoky form of the demon appears from the fog, carrying the Innocent in thin black arms. The Fury's horrible dog head is tilted downward, like Ham's when he's made a mess on the carpet. The Devil steps out in front of the door as they approach, holding up his long unlined hands.

"Most disappointing, my child."

The Fury cringes.

"Attempting to escape into Liveside, to be reborn with the mortals," he says. "You are fully aware of my view on those matters. Fully aware . . ."

Further cringing.

"We shall not discuss this in front of outsiders. But please . . . I should not welcome my kin in such a manner. Know that you shall be forgiven, in time."

The Devil places his hands on the demon's black head and strokes his finger down its snout. He stands aside, and the Fury stalks into the passageway, the baby held gently in its clawed arms. The demon stoops in order to fit.

The Fury doesn't even glance at me.

Don't you know me? asks the Innocent as it's carried into the tunnel.

The green door shuts with a soft click. The Devil is rubbing his hands together, staring off into space. I clear my throat.

"Uh, that's only six . . ."

"I am aware."

"Well—"

"Your Vassal was consumed. He is no more."

"Can't you—"

"If I carve clay from the earth and bake it into a pot, then present the pot to you and ask where is my clay, what would you tell me?"

"He was a good guy. . . . He didn't deserve what happened."

"You would tell me that the clay is transformed, become something else. The process of being fired, in the kiln, has changed it forever."

"And the Prisoner?"

"That starveling was already past my reach when your ritual was completed, so I cannot force him to cross over. But he is no longer bound to you."

"What do you mean? What happened to him? What about Elza?"

"I do not know this 'Elza.' I believe you have me confused with my opposite. I do not keep track of where every sparrow falls. I only watch those who amuse me."

"OK," I say. If I got rid of the Host but I lost Elza and Ham and Mum, then . . . I don't even want to think about it. They must be alive. When I get back, I know they'll be waiting for me.

The wall is gone, and I'm standing with the Devil on a lonely gray beach. There's still heavy mist all around us, obscuring the sea. I can hear a faint lapping of waves. I look down at my shoes.

"So now what happens?" I ask him.

"That is in your hands."

"Can I go back?"

"You will not die today, Luke."

"Thank you."

"I cannot speak for tomorrow, or any day after that. But not today."

"So I can go back?"

"Of course," he says, turning his white smile to maximum radiance, "but there is one small thing I'd like you to do for me first. A tiny favor."

"You said there would be no price."

"I am the Devil. I am a liar. Luke, my price is only

this: There is someone who wishes to talk to you. You will speak with him. This is all."

There's a shape walking through the mist toward us.

"And who is this," says Berkley to himself, "that is coming?"

The shape emerges slowly, head down to the gray sand. It's a man wearing a white suit and a light-purple shirt. The top of his head is balding, but his remaining hair is hanging past his shoulders. His hands are heavy with rings.

I'm five years old, watching the snow at our old house. The kitchen is tiled in warm pumpkin-orange. It's winter, and I'm standing up on tiptoes to see over the counter. The garden is transformed into a driftscape of curves and contours. The sky is so white it's invisible, and flakes are flopping down in fat clumps. I shuffle upstairs to Dad's study in my green snow pants, and he grins and puts down his book without me even asking, and we run out into the snow.

Our snowmen were always uneven. I would make the bottom and he would do the top. I would roll up a big, lopsided ball and then keep cramming clumps of heavy snow onto the sides, wherever I felt like it. Dad was a craftsman when it came to snowmen. He would spend forever on the head, making it so perfect that it looked like it came from a factory mold. He arranged the coal eyes and mouth with equal care. He said he would get a hat and scarf and a carrot for the nose, and he went off across the garden in a long lope. I remember the snow was so heavy and white that he had vanished before he was even halfway down the garden, and I was worried he wouldn't come back out of it.

Dad stops just in front of us and draws himself up to his full height. He looks me in the eye and actually manages to smile and steps toward me, hand outstretched. I take a quick step backward and Dad falters, lowering his arm. The Devil stays where he is, looking eagerly from one of us to the other.

"Luke . . . my son."

"Don't," I say, "don't even—"

"My son."

"I'm not touching you!"

"Very well." Dad adjusts the collar of his mauve shirt. "I was hoping we could act like adults, Luke, but if you still want to behave like a child, then I suppose I can't stop you. Not many people get a chance to speak to their father after he's dead, you know. I had to pull a lot of strings to even be allowed to meet with you like this."

The Devil raises one white eyebrow at this but says nothing.

"Not many people get a chance to speak to their father?" I say. "What about when you were alive? Why couldn't we speak then? Where have you been? You're not even going to pretend to be sorry?"

"I am sorry, Luke. I'm sorry I haven't been a part of your life. It was unavoidable."

"Ten years, barely even a birthday card, and then I find out you're dead, and your lawyer, who turns out to be the actual fire-and-brimstone devil, tricks me into inheriting a Host of dangerous, pissed-off spirits, who then try their absolute hardest to turn me, your son, into a dead person as well, and now you're here for one last chat and you're telling me I should be grateful? Are you serious?"

"I won't deny there have been some events in my life that didn't transpire exactly as I had intended. Especially in recent weeks. I did my best to contact you once you were in the thick of it. It hasn't been easy. My communications have been restricted." He breaks off, glances at the Devil. "You'll find you make mistakes, too, Luke. It's part of what being an adult means. You've got to live the life you have, rather than the life you wanted."

The invisible tide rushes and breathes somewhere in the mist. So the dream I had . . . it really was him. He did try to help me.

Dad's face looks awful, really swollen and pale, with red blotches on his nose and cheeks. His eyes are badly bloodshot, and he's got wrinkles on his wrinkles. He's trying to sound angry, but I have the suspicion he's scared of me, or of the Devil, or maybe both.

"So what exactly was your life, Dad? What was the life you wanted? Who even are you?"

"A necromancer," Dad says. "I am a necromancer. And to have come this far, to have begun to use the Book of Eight and my sigil, you have the makings of one as well. It's rather a shame you chose to disperse my Host. If mastered, they could have taken you far."

"I don't think so," I say. "The only place most of them seemed to want to take me was into a grave. The Vassal was the only one who tried to help me, and your demon ate him. How long did you have the Host for? Why did you summon it?"

"A shame," Dad says. "I was always fond of the Vassal. Would that you had . . . No matter. I began binding the Manchett Host nine years before your birth. You must understand I did not summon a full eight spirits all in one go. Finding the correct fit for each role takes time. As for why I started . . . do we have time for this?"

Dad looks over to the Devil, who is staring into the mist.

"Time enough," the Devil replies.

Dad breathes out heavily. He runs his thumb over the

largest, blackest ring on his fingers, which I recognize as the sigil, the ring I'm also wearing. I presume it's just the spirit image of the ring, part of his ghost in the way his suit and shoes are.

"It begins with the discovery of a tomb, fittingly enough," Dad says. "I was a few years older than you are now, working one summer on a building site. We were digging out the foundation for a new shopping center, and I had the . . . misfortune to drill into something that should have been left alone. A tomb, a strange chamber that contained a single skeleton wearing a black suit. Clasped in its hands were a green book fastened with silver clasps, and a black-stoned ring. You are familiar with these objects. There was something about them. . . . I took them. I still do not know why. I hid them, and then I called the foreman over, and after that, they brought in archaeologists. It was a curious tomb; every wall was covered in writing, strange symbols, a language nobody from the museum understood.

"From this point, my life took something of an unexpected turn. I had no luck opening the strange green book, and the antique-books dealer I contacted refused to even look at it. When he saw the star engraved on the cover, he left the meeting without another word. After that strange occurrence, I began to feel that a terrible shroud had fallen over me. I felt cold all the time. I could not get warm. I half glimpsed a face in dark windowpanes, a dead face in crowds, a shadow cast not by light but by some greater darkness. I would awake to frost on my windows, to strange marks drawn by invisible hands upon my walls . . . terror such as I have never known. I sought rescue in a professional spiritualist, but when he perceived the entity that haunted me, he refused payment and refused to help any further. In this desperate state, I received a visitor.

"He presented himself as a solicitor, a Mr. Berkley. He claimed he was also an expert on the supernatural and had been alerted to my case by the antique-books dealer I had approached. He took me to dinner, and we talked."

"Deeply mediocre wine, as I recall," the Devil remarks.

"He convinced me that the spirit world existed, that I had disturbed something terrible within it. The tomb was broken irreversibly, and I had no hope of placating the spirit by laying its body back to rest. My only hope was to bind it to my will. He explained the use of the book I had found, and the black ring, my sigil. With Berkley's aid I captured the spirit, powerful though it was, and felt its power become my own." Dad's eyes look alive for the first time, almost wistful. "The spirit was revealed fully to me, a withered old man with eyes as black as oil pits. Berkley told me the spirit was the remains of a powerful necromancer who styled himself Octavius. I believe you have met."

"Yes," I say with a shudder.

"Octavius became my Shepherd, the first among my

Host. It was a terrible insult to him, and there was no trust or love between us. At first I kept him tightly bound away. I could not free him for fear of my own life; the ghost had, I suppose, a hold upon me as well."

"You could have banished him into true death," the Devil remarks. "You had the means within the Book of Eight, if you had looked."

"I know," Dad says. "I desired . . . I felt his power. I was no longer an ordinary man. I wanted more. The idea of becoming just a builder once more, lugging bricks for a living . . . I knew I was meant for something greater."

"And that is why I chose you," the Devil says quietly. "That is why you entertained me so."

I sit down on the gray sand. I don't know what to make of Dad's story. I pick up a handful of sand: cold and somehow lightless, the color of a winter twilight. Dad stumbled onto something he didn't understand the danger of and resorted to desperate measures to get himself out of it. I can sympathize so far. I never thought I'd be buying a gerbil in order to sacrifice it to Satan. What I still don't understand is how he ended up as a TV star with a broken marriage.

"What about me and Mum? Where do we fit in?" I ask.

"A year passed. I began to speak with the Shepherd, and I grew to know and master him. We began to travel the country together. At first I was working as an exorcist. The Shepherd . . . had a way with hauntings. Often he could persuade spirits to cross over. I began to become known. Your mother . . . Persephone was always very spiritual. More interested in what she couldn't see than in what she could, perhaps. We met at a psychic fair. It was real love, a real marriage. I'm sure she's told you that part herself."

"Yes," I say. Mum's never spoken much about him, but I know their eyes met while he was reading her aura. I think of her rising up out of the earth at the Devil's Footsteps, the knife sliding into my stomach.

"She knew nothing of the true nature of the dead, of course. She has no second sight. I described the Shepherd as a benevolent spirit guide, which infuriated him to no end. Meanwhile, my reputation grew, as did my Host. I had begun to correspond with a Scandinavian necromancer, Magnus Ahlgren, who had been recommended to me by Mr. Berkley. Under Ahlgren's guidance I scoured the graveyards of Europe, binding saints and murderers to my own soul. At the same time, I monetized my exploits, signing the contract for my first TV series a year before you were born. It was an innovation I was particularly proud of. I began to draw a good income, although by this point money was not my greatest desire. The Shepherd had told me that he had lived a thousand years, and a man who bound a full Host of eight spirits could expect a life far beyond his natural span. I was obsessed. Your grandmother died of cancer when I was young . . . my father died with her in a way. I was determined to move beyond this, move beyond death. To live forever . . . your mother knew nothing of this, of course.

"I welcomed your birth, Luke, but there was fear as well. I had enemies. Necromancy is an old art with a small pool of practitioners, and many of them were not happy that a newcomer was performing exorcisms for the camera. They saw it as undignified, unworthy. Magical war broke out a few years after your birth. Ahlgren, my only ally, was overcome. The old bloodlines of Russia, Rasputin's children . . . I had to leave you. I could not risk staying under the same roof as my wife and only child. When the war was over, I meant to return. I swear."

"And you didn't provoke them?" I ask. "You swear it wasn't your fault? You really only left to protect us? How did you die? Did another necromancer get to you?"

"I wanted to return, but I never had the chance. As I said, you must live the life you have."

"But . . . didn't you know that if you died, I'd inherit the Host? When did you think would be a good time to tell me about that?"

"I fully expected to live longer than you. I believed I would bury my great-grandchildren. The Shepherd swore he had seen Rome itself rise and fall. I believed myself immortal, drafted a will only as a formality. My death . . . came not at the hands of an enemy. I did not foresee it. Eating alone, I choked on a forkful of steak. The Host did not aid me. My Oracle had not warned me. I could not use my voice, could not command them at all. The Shepherd watched me die and promised his vengeance would be enacted on my son, and then . . . Berkley and his aides were upon me."

"A miserable death," the Devil remarks. The hidden sea sighs. I don't like looking into the Devil's eyes: They're brighter than before, lit by something more than joy or sunlight.

"Mistakes," Dad says, "I regret so much. I believed I had ample time to make amends with you and Persephone, and I was gravely mistaken. A few moments on this gray shore is all we have."

The Devil is cleaning his pocket watch with a small cloth. It looks bright and flawless to me, but he polishes the crystal face of the watch with even, circular movements.

"I have a question," the Devil says without looking up from his task.

Dad swallows.

"Your account is accurate, Horatio, except for some details. You exaggerate the duration of the war between yourself and the eastern necromancers. I can forgive you for glossing over the fact that your good friend Magnus Ahlgren died at your own command. You feared his treachery, and rightly so; some foes come armed not with daggers but with smiles. However, there are some important details being omitted. We met on *two* occasions, you and I, and the second meeting took place in Luke's very home, while he slept. I believe the boy deserves to know what passed between us, and why the necromancer's war ended that very night. Tell us this: Why did the war end? By what means did you overcome the eastern bloodlines? And why, soon afterward, did you leave your wife and young child?"

Dad is ashen, cheeks bleached as the sand.

"No," he says.

"Horatio."

"I will not, you cannot—"

"Remember to whom you speak, Horatio. Do not presume to tell me what I can and cannot do. It would be deeply unwise."

"Please," Dad says.

"Horatio. Horatio, will you stop? There is no need to kneel. Remember that I own you. What you desire does not matter. My mind is made up. I believe your boy deserves to know the truth."

"I'd really just like to go home," I say. Dad is pressing his forehead to the gray sand. "I've had enough of this now. I want to go home and be with Elza and Mum again."

"Patience, Luke. The sorcerer has one more tale. Tell him the truth, Horatio. Or I shall."

"Please . . . please . . ."

"Tell your fine first son the truth."

"Luke . . . I am so sorry."

"Please just tell me what's going on. I'm sick of not knowing what you're both talking about," I say. "Tell me the true story or just let me go."

Dad kneels in the sand, shaking. The Devil raises one white eyebrow, and Dad clears his throat to speak.

I'm four years old. We're in the Mediterranean, on a boat, and he's holding me out over the side so I can look down into the water. Mum is scuba diving, and he's telling me that the dazzling purple blur I can see down below the water is Mummy. I don't think I quite believe him. Mum is being swarmed by fish that want to bite her hair, and the blinding ocean below me is a kaleidoscope of red and green and orange and yellow shapes, whirling like leaves caught in a gale.

If you stare into the mist of this border place, you can pretend you're floating. You can pretend you're anywhere except here. Dad is sitting now, with his feet pointed toward the clouded ocean. The Devil watches us intently.

"Ahlgren was skilled and cunning," Dad begins. "Strong as our enemies. He had a full Host of eight, while my Host at that time numbered six: Shepherd, Vassal, Heretic, Judge, Oracle, Prisoner. Our war dragged on; neither side could gain the upper hand. A necromancer's war is slow and bitter, without mercy. We were like pythons, crushing one another in the blackest depths of the sea. Each move could take years, and a single blunder could mean my end, your end, your mother's end. . . . I began to fear that Ahlgren would betray me. I had taken his advice in my studies of the Book of Eight and its secrets, and Ahlgren knew the construction of my spells of defense, the rituals by which I had bound my Host. He could betray me and end the war, regaining the favor of the eastern families. I became consumed by this fear. The Shepherd and the Judge counseled decisive action.

"By this time, I had discerned 'Mr. Berkley's' true nature, and I summoned him during the Halloween of your fifth year, Luke. In full knowledge of my actions, in desperation, I struck a bargain with him, and he revealed secrets that lay deep within the Book of Eight, beyond reach of my studies. I was able to bind a demon into my service—"

"The Fury," I say.

"Yes, *a shade with the aspect of a wrathful beast.* Such power had not been held by a necromancer for centuries. With the demon's binding complete, I set it against Magnus Ahlgren, my old ally. He died that same night. The rest of my enemies fell within days. I was the new power among those who bound the dead. None would dare defy me."

"I thought you said you left us because it wasn't

safe for us. But you won the war before you left me and Mum?"

"Your mother and I already had our differences. . . . I wanted to conquer death itself, live forever. Persephone wanted to open a crystal-healing center in the Midlands. We were coming at life from rather different perspectives, and—"

"No," the Devil says. "Tell him everything."

Dad leaps to his feet. He's right up against my face, we're inches apart. I could draw a map of the blood vessels in his eyes.

"It had to be done!" he shouts. "There was no choice! I had to do it! Ahlgren could have betrayed me! We'd all have died!" he says, stepping towards me.

"I said, I'm not touching you!" I yell.

"Luke . . . there was a price. Berkley told me the price, and I paid it, and I have paid it ever since. I've paid for binding the Fury for a decade now, and you have paid the price as well."

"What price?"

"In order to bind one of my children," the Devil says, "a balance must be achieved. Life may be paid in exchange for those who are dead, but my children were never alive and so are not dead either. An exchange must be made of raw, potential spirit. A sacrifice of utmost purity is required."

"I don't understand," I tell him.

"You . . ." Dad begins. "You were to have a brother. I had a second son. Nobody knew, not even your mother. Berkley, the Devil, told me of the child's very existence, and told me, too, how the unborn spirit might be bound, used as counterweight in the exchange. And I knew then why the binding of demons was so rare. How high the price. But it was not murder. I merely drew out the fresh kindled spirit. Your unborn brother remained unborn— became the Innocent. And you lived your life in safety. There was no other way."

I look away from him, into the mist.

"It is not our sins," the Devil says quietly, almost to himself, "but our guilt that allows us to be bound."

"I've paid the price," Dad says. "What I did was wrong, but it had to be done. Or so I told myself. I found myself alone in my own family, more at home with the dead than with the living. Every time I saw your face, Luke, I was reminded of what I had done. Persephone . . . your mother suffered ill effects, effects I had not anticipated. Melancholy, headaches, persistent listlessness. Drawing the child's spirit from her had permanently damaged her. I felt claustrophobia, black guilt. . . . I had won the war, but it seemed I myself was lost. There was no place for me with you or your mother anymore. I had to leave. I did not deserve you—"

Dad's voice suddenly cuts out, like a muted radio. He's still standing with us on the beach, but now it looks like he's miming a conversation. His gestures become wilder as he realizes we can't hear him. His eyes are bugging out, and he beats against some sort of invisible barrier. I step back. The Devil grins at me, unruffled, his wolf-gray suit so crisp he could've stepped from a magazine. He looks at his gold watch.

"He does talk a lot, your father," the Devil remarks. "As my time here is not endless, I have quieted him so we may talk. Anyway, the truth has been outed. Wicked father uses unborn son in dark pact to protect his living family. Eventually his guilt consumes him; he loses his living family in the bargain. All very entertaining. And I can't lie: I've had a great deal of entertainment from you these past weeks, Luke. Doggedly struggling toward this meeting with me. Your father's Host was no match for you."

"You wanted this to happen," I say, "didn't you?"

"Of course. Your inheritance was all of my doing. I wanted to see how you'd cope. Whether you'd come to grips with the sequence, discover the depths the Book of Eight held, which you did, with some help from Horatio when my back was turned. I wanted to know whether you'd come calling for me, wanted to know what you'd resort to with your back against the wall. The Shepherd nearly had you, but you made it here in the end. I had to bend the rules only a little in order to appear to you."

"You did all of this so Dad would have to tell me the truth?"

"Amusing, isn't it? They call me the Father of Lies. But the truth can be so much more painful."

"I want to go back," I tell him. "Send me back. I want to see Elza and Mum and Ham. I spoke to Dad. I did what you wanted. Send me back."

"Of course." The Devil grins. "But first you need to make a choice. I have a proposition for you, my boy. Hear me out."

I look into his luminous blue eyes. There's nothing human in them anymore. I don't know how I ever mistook this creature for a man.

"Your father, Horatio, belongs to me, as per long-standing arrangements between us. I believe he imagined he'd have a few more centuries before I collected my debt, but things don't always work out the way we plan them, as he's so fond of telling us both. He's a sinner, and I've every right to take him with me into the darkness. The coldest depths of death."

Dad is beating a fist against the invisible wall, screaming something to me. I look away.

"You—" I begin.

"I leave this entirely up to you. You're his son, his heir, the one he sinned for, or so he claims. It seems only fair that you decide his punishment. I can take him to the dark place with me, and ensure he gets exactly what he deserves. It would entertain me greatly to know he'd been consigned there by his own blood. Do this for me, and there is no limit to what I can give you. Your father's fortune will be yours. I can make you rich, powerful, I can make you the greatest magician in the world. Horatio's estates, his cars, these will be but the beginning. Any girl you desire—they are yours if you send your father into the darkness. I can make this so."

"I—"

"Or, I could release him. I will do so if you wish. He's free to enter any afterlife that will take him, or he may haunt the living world for eternity. It would no longer be my concern. But know this: If I give him up, it comes at a price. You have already had your boon. You will forfeit all of Horatio's earthly goods. I will give nothing to you. To release this man, who is rightfully mine . . . it would be a trade. Something for you, something for me."

"And if I let him go . . . what would be your price?"

"I leave it for you to decide what your father is worth."

"I wouldn't know," I say. "I don't know what you'd want in exchange."

"When the time comes, you will know."

I don't know what to say. I want to run away into the mist and never come back. I don't want to see either of them again. I'm so angry, I can hardly think straight. My own brother . . . I had a brother. You weigh yourself against someone else and what do you end up with? How much is my Dad worth? How much am I worth? What does my life matter to anyone except me? What can I give the Devil? . . . I had a brother. I think of the Host, of the Shepherd's waxy face, cold and hating and hating. I think of dead fingers holding tight against a bare branch. I think of the sunrise over Dunbarrow, a pink sunrise, like a burn. I think of the mist and the heather and the light-green doorway in the stone. What might be behind it. *Don't you know me?* I do know you, now. I try to think of Elza, and all I can picture is a faint sketch of her, a mass of hair and smudged eyes, and what does the Devil . . . you can't ask me to make a choice like this. Who deserves what? It's too big. Dad should go to the darkness. I think of his money, the dreams of cars and houses coming back so hard it's like a fist in my chest. He made his choice. You can't make me pay for him. Except who am I to judge? He ought to go to Hell, or wherever the Devil will take him.

Except.

Except he's my dad.

I have to let go.

"He's free," I tell the Devil.

He raises his eyebrows.

"And here I was, thinking I knew you better than that, Luke. What makes you want to save your father? What has he done to deserve this?"

"Because . . . he's my dad. I can't send him away with you." I pull the sigil from my finger and throw it away into the mist. I take the Book of Eight from the pocket of my coat and throw it away, too, the green book vanishing into grayness. I look the Devil in the eye. "I never wanted any of this. I don't want revenge on my dad, if that's what you think. No matter what he did. The Shepherd wanted revenge, and look where that got him. I have to let go. I don't want money, I don't want power. I don't want to be a necromancer. I want you to let us both go."

Dad is crying, silently.

"*I have to let go . . .*" the Devil says slowly, like he's tasting the words. "What you did to deserve this, Horatio, I can't say."

"Son—" Dad lunges forward, the barrier between us now removed, and he hugs me. He's cold, and smells of earth. I stand for a moment and then push him away.

"I've let go," I say. "But I don't forgive you. Maybe not ever. If you go free, I don't care where you go, but don't come near me and Mum again."

"Of course," he says, looking down at the sand. "I know I did you both wrong. I hope in time you will understand more fully, and forgive—"

"Don't even say that word to me," I tell him.

"You're certain?" the Devil asks. "Shake my hand and our deal is done. There will be no going back."

"I can't give him to you."

"Very well. You are in my debt, Luke Manchett. I shall return," the Devil says. "One day soon, I shall return to your side and expect repayment. Remuneration, to make his freedom worth my while. Don't think I shall forget, because I never do."

"Done," I say.

"You have until then," the Devil says.

"Luke, thank you, thank you so much, son—"

"Don't talk to me," I tell Dad, and look away.

The Devil holds out his unlined palm. Dad looks like he's choking for a second time, as if he can't believe his luck. I can't believe he's getting out of this either . . . but I've chosen. I came to a crossroads and this is my path. I reach out and take the Devil's hand in mine.

"Remember what I am owed, Luke," the Devil says, and squeezes my hand. For a moment nothing happens, and then there's pain like fire scouring my palm. I grind my jaw and stamp my feet on the sand to keep from screaming.

You must always remember, his voice whispers again, and now the shape of the man, Mr. Berkley, is exploding outward and the beach is gone and Dad is gone and I'm gripping something like a paw, a hand with searing claws and I hear music whirling, a violin playing faster and faster, and I see cattle hosed down with napalm beneath a sky heavy with crows and faces burst apart underneath black boots and snakes are crawling from deep pools and these pools are somehow eyes, yes lidless white eyes, staring and I see a beast's shape billowing like smoke and for the first time I understand what it means to say the word *Hell*.

I shall return.

My eyes are open.

There's something sticky and hot draped over my face, furry and close and out of focus, and it grumbles when I try to grab hold of it and push it off me. I splutter. Ham's face resolves above mine; my entire field of vision is filled by his mad marmalade eyes and gigantic snout. He licks at me again. The sky behind him is an incredible color, violet and pink, with clouds like blobs of molten gold.

"Where's Elza?" I ask my dog. "Where's Mum?"

He bumps his nose into my face. Slowly and carefully, I sit up. One of my arms is asleep, but other than that I'm fine. I lift my coat and shirt, trying to find the stab wound, but there's nothing there. The Devil seems to have been true to his word. I didn't die today. I'm lying in the middle of the Footsteps, with my feet pointing toward the tallest of the stones. My legs and back are covered in mud. There's dried blood on my shirt and trousers. The magic circle Elza drew is still here, a wobbly yellow scrawl in the moss, already washed away in some spots. I can see fresh cobwebs woven inside the hoof-shaped indents on the tall stone, all the strands sparkling with dew.

Mum is curled up next to the flattest stone, covered

in dried mud. She looks asleep, which isn't any improvement over the past fortnight. Her hand is still wrapped around the knife. For a moment I'm afraid to even touch her, afraid that I'll find her cold as the stone she's lying beside, but the hand on the knife handle is warm and soft, and a faint pulse still beats in her wrist. I stand up, breathing in and out, and then throw the knife as far as I can into the undergrowth.

"Seriously, where's Elza?" I ask Ham again. "Did you hide in a hole this entire time? What happened to her?"

Ham grumbles and then turns, trotting away from Mum and the Footsteps. I take my raincoat off and drape it over Mum, for all the good that'll do, and follow him. I don't want to leave her, but I have to find Elza. I try to focus on the golden clouds; they're a hopeful color, I think. Ham seems like he's leading me somewhere, and I try not to think about finding a body under a tree, crushed up and empty like a bird that fell out of the nest. I follow Ham through rust-orange bracken and over a stony hillock, out past a rotting birch tree and onto the muddy rutted track we climbed last night in the rain. I follow him farther up the track, around the next bend, and I see Mum's yellow car parked under a tree. I suppose the demon had Mum drive herself up here. Ham runs on up to the car and starts to bark.

The passenger-side door opens, and Elza gets out, grinning. Ham capers around her. I give her a tight hug.

"I thought you might not make it," I tell her.

"I thought the same," Elza says.

Elza looks rough. Her hair has lost its shape, whatever shape it had to start with, and the back is crushed flat, with the rest exploding in any direction it feels like. There are orange leaves stuck up at the crown of her head. Her legs and coat are covered in dry chocolate-colored mud, and her hands and sleeves are covered with the yellow paint she used for the magic circle. Her gaze is bleary and unfocused, and I realize she must've just woken up.

"What happened to you?" she asks.

"You first. I don't even know where to start with what happened to me."

"Did you meet him?"

"Who? The Devil?"

"Yes, obviously I'm asking about the Devil. What was he . . . it . . . like?"

"Well, he wasn't red . . . no horns either. No pointy tail. He was my dad's lawyer."

"He was *who*?"

"My dad's lawyer. Mr. Berkley."

"Your dad's lawyer was the Devil . . ." Elza says, shaking her head. "Would you believe me if I said, at this point, I'm not even surprised? You'll have to tell me more about that . . . but, it's over? You're free?"

"Yeah," I say. I look up at the sky, which is lightening to a delicate chilly blue. I'll tell her what really happened, I'm sure I will, but not now. I don't want to talk about Dad and the Innocent and the deal I made with Mr. Berkley, not under a sky that looks like this.

"The Host is gone," I tell her.

"I can't believe it," Elza says. "That's amazing. We did it."

"What happened to you? Last time I saw you, the Prisoner—"

"Oh, my gosh, Ham ate him," Elza says.

"He what?"

"I was running, Luke. I had no idea where to go. No way of helping you or knowing what was happening. I fell and broke the flashlight in the first five minutes, and then I was just on my own in the rain and the dark. I could hear Ham somewhere but I wasn't sure exactly where, and I think I must've been doubling back on myself, heading back toward the Footsteps, when they caught me. The Prisoner came whistling down out of the trees and got hold of me somehow. It was just cutting at me with those shears it had, cutting something out of me. Like life or hope or something? I don't know how to explain it. I was fading, like everything felt really far away and I was ready to let go, and the last thing I'd have seen was his horrible shriveled-apple face. And just as I—Ham ate him! Ham came bowling out of the dark and ate the Prisoner."

"I'm having a hard time picturing what that would look like."

"Me, too, and I saw it. He came and got his jaws into the ghost, and it was screaming and trying to stab Ham with the shears, but they were going straight through him and he wouldn't let go, and the ghost just got thinner and smaller and thinner and smaller like smoke being sucked back down a chimney. And the Prisoner was gone."

"Did you see the Judge? The skinhead?"

"He was there, but he didn't do anything. He just watched, and then when Ham came to save me, he disappeared. And then the fog came out of the Footsteps and I didn't see any ghosts after that. Why do you ask?"

"No reason. Good boy," I say to Ham, who's been waiting beside us. "I'm sorry I called you a coward. Clever dog."

"I suppose it's like the Book of Eight said," Elza remarks. "Ghosts can be destroyed in the body of an animal familiar. I just never imagined Ham would count."

"So he could've eaten the Shepherd this entire time? How does that work?"

"Maybe it's after you possessed him? I don't know anything about familiars, really."

"I'd ask the Book," I say, "but I got rid of it."

"You did?" Elza says.

"Gave it back. It's gone."

"Well, that's good," Elza says, smiling. "That's really good. I didn't like that thing. But, yes, your hound saved me."

"Well," I say to Ham, "I suppose we'll know for next time."

Elza laughs. "So anyway, I got back to the Footsteps," Elza says, "and they were basically gone. There was fog everywhere, like the whitest, thickest fog you can imagine, and it was pouring out of the Footsteps somehow, coming from the center? I've never seen anything like it. The ghosts were gone and I couldn't see you either and I got . . . lost, I suppose, in that fog. I mean, I found my way to this car and got in, but there was something wrong with time. It was passing in a weird way, because it felt like a whole night just vanished while I sat there. I could see the stars even through the fog, but they were moving faster than I've ever seen them go. It was like a dream. And then I think I was actually really asleep, and Ham was out here barking and I woke up."

I look at Elza, at her dark messy hair and the streaks of gold the dawn is painting on her face. We made it. We're still alive. The ghosts are gone and we're still here, together in a sunlit forest. She's stopped talking, and looks back at me with an intent expression.

There'll never be a better moment than this. I lean forward and down, and her mouth meets mine. Her lips are warm and soft and I press her against the side of the car, running one hand down the back of her neck. Elza pulls me closer against her, her fingernails prickling against my scalp, her tongue —

Ham leaps up and nearly knocks me over. I stagger back from Elza, who laughs as Ham continues to prance and paw at me.

"I think he's jealous," Elza says. Ham scampers a few paces back down the road, then looks over his shoulder and whines.

"He wants us to follow him," I say.

"Where's your mum?" Elza asks.

"The demon was using her to . . . well, it doesn't matter now. She was asleep next to me, in the stone circle. She seemed all right."

"Well, this was nice, just the two of us," Elza says, "but I think we should go and see if she's awake."

Elza picks a leaf from her hair as she speaks, and grins at me, and I look again at her face in the dawn light, the delicate orange leaf held in her hand, the perfect curve of her eyebrows and the masterful arrangement of freckles on her cheeks, and I think to myself that sometimes it is worth plunging into darkness, worth clinging to life even as a cold river tries to sweep you away, because there are moments like this waiting on the other side.

We make our way back from the track to the Devil's Footsteps, all three of us bone-tired and dirty. When we get back home, I'm eating two dinners and then sleeping for a week. Ham leads the way, holding his straggly tail up like a banner. The peacock colors of the early dawn are fading, the sun now rising past the heather-covered hills that swell beyond the forest. The highest branches of the oak trees are highlighted in searing gold. Pigeons explode squalling from the bracken as Ham rushes past, making Elza and me start.

"What do they even do down there?" she asks. "Can't they sleep in a tree like normal birds?"

"They're probably eating worms or something."

"Well, it's inconsiderate. I thought my heart would stop. I'm still completely on edge."

"The Host's gone, Elza. It's not coming back."

"I know. I'm just amped up. I want to go and hit a punching bag."

"Am I still going to see you now all this is done?" I ask.

"What do you mean?"

"Will we still—"

"I heard what you said." Elza looks at me, her green eyes filled with amusement. "I just couldn't believe you'd imagine we'd just go back to you kicking a soccer ball at me from across the schoolyard? Of course we'll still see each other."

"Good. I'm not sure I've got any other friends left."

"Well, that's very flattering. Knowing I'm your only choice."

"I didn't mean it like that—"

"I know," Elza says with one of her infuriating grins.

"You're extremely easy to tease. Anyway . . . that's her, isn't it? On the stone."

"Yeah," I say, "there she is."

As we make our way across the clearing, Elza slips her hand into mine.

Mum's sitting on the flattest stone of the Footsteps, the one she stabbed me over. White face, bronze hair, my raincoat wrapped around her body. Ham is already with her, pressing his head into her chest so she can rub his shoulders and neck. She's staring absently up into the gold-tinted tree branches, and looks down only when we cross into the ring of stones.

"Luke," she says.

"Mum." I kneel down and wrap my arms around her, Ham butting and nibbling at both of us. I break away, and I see that she's crying a little.

"What happened?" she asks. "Where are we?"

"We're up at the Devil's Footsteps. It's near Dunbarrow High. You've been ill."

Mum nods and looks at the trees. I don't really know what else to say to her. How am I going to explain all of this? How can I say that I've missed her? That for days I thought she would die, too? That she killed me? That I've met her other son? I don't know how to tell her any of it. I don't know if I ever will. I settle for an introduction.

"This is Elza Moss, Mum. She's a friend."

"Ms. Manchett," Elza says, extending her hand.

Mum shakes Elza's hand, looking at the dried paint on Elza's sleeves and hands with obvious curiosity. Ham is on the other side of the hollow, rooting about in a bush. The wind makes ripples on the shining surface of the nearest puddle. Elza moves closer to me, and I feel her leg resting against mine.

"Why are we all here?" Mum asks. She's taking this much better than I would. She's got the bemused face of someone who thinks they might not've woken up properly. "I've been having the worst dreams. I dreamed I was . . . buried. I was underground, and I didn't think I'd ever get myself out . . . and then I heard your voice, and your father's . . ."

"We need to talk about that," I say gently. "When you heard the news, you had a bad reaction. You weren't well. And last night, you tried to run away—"

"What happened, love?" Mum asks. "What news? What did I do?"

I take a deep breath. I don't like lying to her like this, but I don't see another way. At least I can tell her part of the truth, tell her something I should've said last week.

"Mum, Dad died. He's gone."

"Oh, Luke."

She starts to cry, and I'm crying, too, and as I put my arms around her I'm surprised to feel Elza embracing us as well, and we sit there like that for a long time, three warm bodies and three silent stones.

The last thing that happens isn't that moment in the stone circle, isn't the drive back to our house or the enormous meal I eat, after which I really do sleep for a whole day. The last thing that happens isn't Mum's hospital visits, or the police statement I have to give regarding the "grotesque vandalism" that we've suffered, an event I manage to link with the earlier report I filed when the Vassal and Judge first appeared in our kitchen. The last thing that happens isn't me being removed from the rugby team for missing almost two weeks of practice (which I deserve, though it has Mark written all over it). The last thing that happens isn't Ham's emergency X-ray and subsequent surgery for stomach trouble, during the course of which the vet removes from his stomach a pair of rusty shears and a dense rock, which, when viewed from a certain angle, resembles a familiar shriveled face.

The last thing that happens arrives three weeks later, when I come down from my shower for breakfast. I've been sleeping better than I expected: no nightmares, exactly. My dreams are of cold night skies full of sigils and stars.

Anyway, I come down to find Mum already up, sitting at the kitchen table in her morning poncho. Her hair's tied back, and she's looking at a small, dark urn, sitting right in the middle of the table. I sit opposite her. I don't ask what's inside. I don't need to. Eddies of steam emerge from her mug of green tea.

"Delivered this morning," Mum says.

"So he—"

"They said he didn't want a funeral. His instructions were for the cremation to happen in private, and for us to get the ashes. I can't understand it"—Mum shakes her head—"but that's what he wanted. We can remember him, just you and me."

"Right," I say. I think about Dad's body, burned and compacted until it fits into something the size of a thermos flask, even as his spirit expands outward, crossing over into a place I can still barely imagine.

"I'm sorry," Mum says. "I'd hoped you'd be able to see him again, when you were both ready. But this is all we have."

I realize she's expecting me to cry.

"It's all right," I say.

"I'm sorry," Mum says again. "Things haven't been

quite what I'd hoped for, I suppose. You think you're going one way, and you end up somewhere else."

"Mum," I say. "We're really going to be OK."

"I know," she says. She sniffs. "I missed him so much. I haven't been . . . myself, for years. I've sat around and waited for him to come back. And now . . . well . . ."

She waves a hand at the urn.

"I'm going to take this as a sign," Mum continues. "Things need to change. I've sat and felt sorry for myself for far too long."

"It's all right to feel sad," I say.

"Yes, of course it is, love. And you can feel however you want. But I just wanted to say . . . I love you, and I know the way things have been isn't good. I've been told your dad left all his money to charity. It's very kind of him, but it leaves you and me in a funny state. I'm going to need to start looking for work again. I'm going to make a change."

"I think that's great news."

"Well," she says, looking at the urn, "it's odd, love. I feel almost . . . free. Like a weight's gone from me. He can't come back to us, so now I can move on."

Ham stretches in the early sun that streams in through the window. His stitches seem to be healing well.

"Where do you want to scatter the ashes?" I ask.

"I was thinking maybe the ocean," she says. "The beaches near that old castle. He never went there, but I think he'd have liked it."

I nod. I'm about to go get my school uniform when she says something else.

"Dad's lawyer gave me something for you as well."

"Dad's lawyer?"

My stomach churns.

"Yes. He delivered the urn himself. You just missed him. Really quite handsome." Mum laughs. "He wanted to give me his condolences in person. And he had something for you as well, Luke. Something of Dad's. I left it up in your room."

"Wow," I say. "I'd better go see what it is."

I take the stairs slowly, feeling sick, remembering what I saw when I shook Berkley's hand. He—it—was at my house just ten minutes ago. . . . Somehow I'd started to hope the Devil was a figment, a fantasy. Here's a fresh reminder that my debt is all too real.

The package lies on my bed, marked LUKE in neat letters. I tear it open. Inside, as I knew I would, I find a small green book, fastened shut with metal clasps, and an old ring with an octagonal black stone. I lay the Book of Eight and Dad's sigil out on my duvet. There's a note as well, written in ink on a square card.

My boy,

I have enclosed a few small things of your father's. They are rather precious, and it would be a shame if you mislaid them. Keep them close.

I did so enjoy meeting you last month. I can hardly wait until our paths cross once more.

Your friend,

Mr. Berkley

As I read the last line, the paper begins to brown and age. Within a moment, all I'm left with is a few flakes of something like ash floating in my bedroom's still air.

That afternoon I go into the garden shed and empty out a toolbox and then put the Book and the case with Dad's rings inside. I waterproof it with a plastic bag and tape, take a spade, and set off into the fields beyond our garden. If Berkley insists that I keep them, then I will. I just don't want them in my room.

I choose the northern corner, farthest from our house, and start to dig. The earth is cold and hard, and though it's a small hole I'm making, the sun is setting by the time I'm done. I lower the toolbox, swathed in plastic, into the ground.

I'm not burying Dad's body, and his ghost is long gone, but what I'm covering with earth—the Book and his sigil—they're what he really was. This is what he loved most of all, more than me or Mum or my unborn brother. With each spadeful of dark earth, I'm putting a wall between me and him. I want it all behind me.

When I'm finished burying the box, I smooth out the ground and mark the spot with a flat slab of stone from our garden wall.

Sometimes I don't know why I let Dad go free. I can hardly say he deserved it. What he did to me and Mum is only the start of it. Ahlgren, all the other people Dad must've killed . . . perhaps he should've gone to Hell. Maybe the Devil was right. In the end, I think I saved Dad to show him he was wrong. Wrong to leave me, wrong not to face who he was, wrong to abandon the one person who still wasn't able to give up on him, even when I knew the truth. Wherever Dad is, I hope he has time to think about that.

The sky is blushing deep red, and the trees on the far side of the field are reaching their shadows out toward me. There's a bird, two, a flock of crows: eight of them, coming squabbling overhead, heading out for the moors beyond our valley. The soft wind is like the sound of your own blood, flowing. I watch the birds until they're out of sight, then I turn and walk back toward the house.

ACKNOWLEDGMENTS

It's no small thing to grow a whole novel from the initial seed of an idea, and I certainly couldn't have made it this far without help. Firstly, I'd like to thank my agent, Jenny Savill, who believed in the story, and without whom Luke and company would have become the abandoned populace of a long-forgotten Word document. I'd also like to thank my editors: Jessica Clarke, Kate Fletcher, and Kristina Knoechel, who worked tirelessly to mold the story into the strongest shape it could take.

I'd like to thank everyone who read and commented on the early drafts of this novel, including Emily Burt, Tristan Dobson, Victoria Dovey, Sammi Gale, Lewis Garvey, Alex McAdam, Danny Michaux, Oliver Pearson, Jenn Perry, Eleanor Reynard, and Daniel Winlow.

Finally, I'd like to thank my family for their unwavering support and kindness over the past five years.

**It's been a few months since Luke's deal with the devil.
And it's all beginning again.**

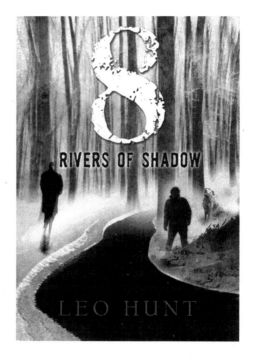

A girl named Ash appears at Luke's school and asks for his help—and his Book of Eight—to save her twin sister's life. Luke isn't sure he can trust Ash, but her request sends him on a terrifying quest to save what he holds dearest— or die trying.

Available in hardcover and as an e-book

www.candlewick.com